THE
PRINCE
WHO TURNED
INTO A ROOSTER

Other Books by Tzvi Rabinowicz

The Will and Testament of the Biala Rabbi

A Guide to Hasidism

The Jewish Literary Treasures of England and America

The Legacy of Polish Jewry

The World of Hasidism

Treasures of Judaica

Hasidism and the State of Israel

Hasidism: The Movement and Its Masters

A Guide to Life

Hasidic Rebbes

A World Apart—History of Hasidism in England

THE PRINCE WHO TURNED INTO A ROOSTER

One Hundred Tales from Hasidic Tradition

Tzvi Rabinowicz

JASON ARONSON INC.
Northvale, New Jersey
London

7/95

This book was set in 14 pt. Bem by Lind Graphics of Upper Saddle River, New Jersey, and printed by Haddon Craftsmen in Scranton, Pennsylvania.

Library of Congress Cataloging-in-Publication Data

Rabinowicz, Tzvi, 1919–
    The prince who turned into a rooster : one hundred tales from
Hasidic tradition / by Tzvi Rabinowicz.
        p. cm.
    ISBN 0-87668-685-4
    1. Parables, Hasidic. 2. Hasidim—Legends. I. Title.
BM532.R33   1994
296.1′9—dc20   93-31396

Manufactured in the United States of America. Jason Aronson Inc. offers books and cassettes. For information and catalog write to Jason Aronson Inc., 230 Livingston Street, Northvale, New Jersey 07647.

To my grandchildren
Saul, Sara, Lisa, Dina, Adina, and Rachel

Contents

Introduction

It was in the mid-eighteenth century that Eastern Europe gave birth to Hasidism, the greatest revivalist movement in Jewish history. Hasidism was not a new form of Judaism but a revival of Judaism. It focused on simple and sublime principles that the prophets had preached in biblical times—the joy of living, the love of God and of man, service to God, prayer with devotion, humility, and the curbing of temper.

The founder of the movement was Rabbi Israel Baal Shem Tov, who was born in 1700 in Okopy on the borders of Volhynia and Podolia. His parents died when he was very young. But although he had neither father nor mother, sister nor brother, the child never felt lonely. All around him he could sense the presence of God. In every blade of grass, in every flower, in every tree and every hill, he saw the reflection of the glory of God.

Israel began to study the sacred writings of *Kabbalah*, which concerns the mysteries of heaven and earth, life and death. Once he had tasted the goodly fruit, Israel was filled with a yearning to share these joys with the world. He felt passionately that the ordinary man—the farmer, the baker, the stallkeeper in the marketplace—was as precious to God as the learned scholar.

For many years Israel lived withdrawn from the world. He found a retreat in the Carpathian Mountains, where he dwelt with his wife, Hannah, devoting himself to study and meditation. It was a period of preparation.

Then came the gradual revelation. Israel first became known as a wonder-worker. He healed the sick and cast out demons. There were at that time many such healers, called *Baalei Shem* ("Masters of the Name"), but Israel alone was known as Baal Shem Tov, the "Master of the Good Name." People flocked to him from far and wide. He became a famous leader and founded a great movement, Hasidism.

Ordinary men and women were at once drawn to him. He spoke a language they could understand. Often he spoke in allegories, and each story was a lesson and an inspiration. He taught his followers that the essence of prayer was sincerity. He taught them to express themselves freely in prayer and to open their hearts to their Heavenly Father. His followers felt at home in their Father's house, and little synagogues (known as *stieblech*) became lively places where the worshipers prayed as they danced and danced as they prayed in fervent ecstasy. Song and dance were important means of self-expression.

Rabbi Israel died in Medziborz in Podolia, not far from Brody, in 1760. He left many followers, and his devoted disciples spread his word throughout Jewry. By the beginning of the nineteenth century, Hasidism had much expanded, and by the time of the Second World War there were two million *hasidim* in Eastern Europe. In the Second World War the great hasidic centers were utterly destroyed by Nazi brutality. Poland became the graveyard of European and hasidic Jewry. The hasidic centers became piles of rubble, the physical symbol of their almost total destruction. It is miraculous that out of the ashes, phoenix-like, Hasidism is once again flourishing. Today, it adds vitality, color, and character to Jewish life in New York, Jerusalem, Bnei Berak, and London.

In the period of its existence, the movement has produced many great teachers. The *tzaddikim* founded many dynasties in which the teachings and the traditions were handed down from father to son. The hasidic teacher or the *rebbe*, as he was called, was counselor, friend, and father to his followers. *Hasidim* came to him for advice on all manner of problems: an illness in the family, financial difficulties, trouble with the local squire, harassment from a business competitor, or a suitable match for a marriageable child. In each case he gave careful and considered advice; he comforted and encouraged. He strengthened the faith of his followers, a faith that could move mountains and make miracles an everyday affair.

Among the spiritual giants of the movement was Rabbi Levi Yitzhak of Berdichev (1740–1809), the great advocate of the House of Israel. For the sake of his beloved people he would plead with God Himself and would plead his case with heartrending eloquence. Another bright star in the dazzling hasidic galaxy was Rabbi Nahman of Bratzlav (1772–1810), a most gifted storyteller, a spinner of fantastic tales filled with magic and meaning. It was his opinion that "hasidic tales purify the mind and arouse the heart with longing for God."

Hasidic literature is a vast storehouse of wisdom, law, and legend. Many of the hasidic rabbis did not give learned discourses. Instead, they often told stories that held their hearers spellbound. They appealed to the heart as well as to the mind, and they felt that to reach the less educated it was necessary to explain matters by the use of a story. Hence, to speak of Hasidism is to tell a story that glows like sunshine in the darkness. Myths, legends, fables, and tales swiftly came into existence. The air was literally buzzing with miraculous, wondrous tales of tormented souls and evil spirits.

Storytelling is the oldest of human arts. Before people could read or write, they told one another stories. Customs and manners change, but stories survive the passage of time. The tales of the Bible have called forth the admiration of mankind throughout the ages and still possess eternal freshness. One-third of the Talmud is replete with picturesque legends, allegories, visions of the ideal world of the future, anecdotes, and stories. The compilation of *Ein Yaakov*, the nonlegal sections of the Talmud by Rabbi Jacob Ibn Habiv in the fifteenth century, became one of the most popular Jewish books. The post-talmudic literature, too, is a veritable treasure house of Jewish legendary material. "If you wish to know the Almighty," counsel our sages, "study the *Aggadah*."

The tales of the *hasidim* have a regenerative power and were also a powerful medium of popularizing the movement. Hasidic tales gained a tremendous hold on the popular imagination of Eastern European Jewry. Around no other figure in Jewish history, ancient or modern, have evolved so many legends as on the founder of Hasidism. Ever since the publication, in 1815, of the *Shivhe Ha-Besht*, the book in praise of the Besht, interest in the legends of Hasidism has grown enormously. Many other hasidic legendary biographies were published in the nineteenth and twentieth centuries. Philosophers, writers, and theologians have found in the legends a rich source of inspiration, for the movement is more than a collection of fine ideas and principles. It is a way of life, a civilization, and a culture that transcends the barriers of time and place.

This book is a sequel to my *Hasidic Story Book*, published in 1984. The original hasidic stories have been modified and adapted for young readers. I would like to express my special appreciation for his sustained support to Arthur Kurzweil, to whom this book owes its origin. I also wish to acknowledge with gratitude the help of Janet Warner, Production Editor at Jason Aronson Inc., for her valuable suggestions. My special thanks to my son, David, for his comments and suggestions. As always my greatest debt is to my wife, Bella, for her constant encouragement and support.

1

The Slave and the Princess

Eliezer and his wife, Sarah, lived in Okopy, a little village in Podolia. They were good, God-fearing people, and they were highly respected by all the villagers. Eliezer set aside regular times for study and meditation. He was always the first to enter the synagogue and the last to leave it. His wife would help the poor and the needy. A stranger was always sure of finding a warm welcome in their home. They were poor themselves but they loved to share with others, to lend a helping hand to people in want. Every Friday night Eliezer would bring home a guest for the holy Sabbath, and Sarah would give the newcomer a royal welcome. Eliezer and Sarah were contented with their lot. They did not wish for wealth. There was only one thing they wanted—a son. And for many years the childless couple prayed that God might grant their hearts' desire.

Suddenly, without any warning, panic fell upon the community of Okopy. The peaceful countryside was invaded by the fierce Tartars. Like locusts they swept the country. The robbers feared neither God nor man. They plundered and murdered, sparing no one. They had no respect for the aged, no pity for the little children. Wherever they passed, they left a trail of blood. The defenseless Jews, scattered in remote villages in Podolia, were easy prey for the murderers. The voice of lamentation and the cry of distress were heard in Jewish homes. The robbers were greedy. They released only rich victims who could pay ransom in silver, gold, and precious stones. But as Eliezer was so poor, they carried him off to sell him as a slave on the open market.

Many customers came into the market to examine the human merchandise. The king's vizier was among them. He saw Eliezer, who, though a slave, stood as stately as a prince, and bought him for his own household. The vizier was a mild and tolerant man. He was greatly impressed by Eliezer and grew to like him and to trust him. The new slave worked conscientiously and zealously. But he did not forget his religion. He worshiped God with even greater devotion and observed the Torah in every detail. The vizier was content. He found Eliezer a reliable servant, an efficient secretary, and a wise counselor. He was fascinated, too, by Eliezer's strange and unseen God. He loved to listen when Eliezer raised his eloquent voice in song and prayer to the Great Unseen Deity.

Often, Eliezer thought about Sarah, his wife. The unhappy woman was all alone in Okopy struggling to earn her daily bread. In all their years of marriage they had never before been separated. Eliezer knew how much she depended on him and how helpless she would be without him. He yearned, too, to be back among his fellow Jews. The thought of escaping often entered his mind. He devised many schemes and prepared many plans. There was only one armed guard at his door, but escape for Eliezer meant death for the guard, and that was unthinkable. Kindly Eliezer had no wish to buy his freedom at the cost of another's life. The thought of killing or even hurting a fellow mortal was so hateful to him that Eliezer resigned himself to slavery forever.

At that time, the king was fighting a bitter struggle against one of his enemies. Eventually, he succeeded in crushing the revolt, but the chief rebel escaped into a fortified city. The king then attacked the city of refuge. He launched assault after assault, but all onslaughts were successfully beaten back, and the royal army suffered many casualties. The fortifications were elaborate and the defenders were brave. They fought recklessly, preferring death to surrender. For six months, the king and his army besieged the rebel city without success. They could neither cut off the supplies to the city nor break the spirit of the fighters. As winter approached, the king grew desperate, dreading the effect of frost and snow upon his soldiers. Frantically, he summoned a council of war and appealed to his generals for advice. But they, too, were baffled and could offer no solution. "I am surrounded by fools!" cried the furious sovereign. Bitterly, he reproached his vizier. "Of what use are advisers who fail their master in the hour of need?"

The vizier took the king's reproof to heart, and his grief weighed heavily upon him. Eliezer was quick to observe the change in his master. "Tell me, my Lord, what is it that troubles you? You have been so good to me. You have permitted me to serve my God and to live according to our holy law. I would, therefore, like to help you. My God is the God of Gods and the King of Kings, the Creator of heaven and earth. He is Wisdom. He is Understanding. Confide in me and God may help me to help you."

The vizier told Eliezer the story of the rebel city and the king's despair and of the failure of his advisers. "If only you could devise a plan whereby the king could capture the city," said the chief minister. "But it is almost impossible. Everything has been tried, and nothing has succeeded."

"My Lord," replied Eliezer, "take me to your king. My God is also the God of battle. He will surely listen to the prayers of his servant."

New hope sprang up in the heart of the vizier. He quickly went to the king. "Your Majesty," he began, "I have a slave whose counsel is wise and whose judgment is sound. He worships a most powerful God. No one has ever seen this God. But my servant speaks with Him. And this God listens to the prayers of Eliezer." The words of the vizier brought fresh courage to the anxious king, who was willing to see anyone and to try anything. Eliezer was summoned to his presence, and his dignity and assurance impressed the whole court. Eliezer was given complete command of the king's armed forces.

Eliezer lost no time. Thoroughly, he explored the approaches to the well-guarded city. The walls were very high and thick. The defenders were many, and they stood on watch day and night. But Eliezer discovered an old disused underground shaft that led into the city itself, and this seemed to be the answer to his earnest prayers. It was a very narrow shaft. There was just enough room for one man to creep through. Eliezer volunteered to take the lead. He stole through the long, dark tunnel, closely followed by a handful of chosen soldiers. Quietly, they entered the city. No one saw them. No one heard them. The rebels were taken unaware and were too surprised to fight back. By dawn, the city was captured and the defenders overwhelmed.

The king was filled with great joy. He showered many honors upon Eliezer. With the full approval of his council and his people, he appointed the one-time slave his chief counselor and offered in marriage his daughter, the fair young Eleanor. The princess admired the courage and resourcefulness of her bridegroom, the man who had succeeded where everyone else had failed. But she noticed that amid all the banquets and bouquets Eliezer was steeped in sorrow.

As the young princess sat with her betrothed one evening, she spoke to him gravely and affectionately. "Soon we shall be married," she said. "Surely we should not have any secrets from each other. Tell me, O my beloved, what troubles you. There is a sadness upon your brow."

Then Eliezer opened his heart to her. "Honored princess," he replied, "I can never marry you." The princess grew pale, paler than the water lilies. She had refused many suitors. The princes of Persia had sought her hand and fought over her favors. She, the fairest maiden in all the land, had rejected them all.

"Have I not found favor in your eyes?" she asked anxiously.

"Beautiful princess, you are a pearl among women, a flower among maidens," Eliezer said with tenderness and true feeling. "I am already married. For the last three years I have been a slave in a strange country.

I have been torn away from my beloved wife, and I dearly long to go back to her."

The princess was not only beautiful, she was also very kindhearted. Eliezer's words moved her to pity, and with great nobility she responded to the tragic tale. She gave him gold and silver and helped him to escape from the palace. But the secret could not be kept for long. When the king found out, he was furious. He could not bear the thought of losing his valuable counselor and sent his soldiers in pursuit. Eliezer lost his silver and gold and barely escaped capture. After many hardships, he arrived in Okopy, where he was warmly welcomed by his loving wife and by the whole community.

—— **2** ——

The Prophet Elijah

Eliezer and Sarah lived very happily. One thing, however, was missing from their lives—they had no children.

One Sabbath, a stranger appeared in the village. He carried a walking stick, the use of which is forbidden on the Sabbath. As the villagers were all very pious, they resented the stranger's insensitive behavior and did not even greet him. They could not tolerate his open violation of the Sabbath, and some of them were ready to drive him out of the village.

However, to everyone's surprise, Eliezer welcomed the stranger and invited him to spend the Sabbath in his home. Eliezer and Sarah treated the man kindly and with respect and did their best to make him feel at home. At no time did Eliezer criticize the stranger for breaking the Sabbath laws.

When the Sabbath ended, the man, having gotten ready to leave, announced to his hosts, "I am not what I appear to be. I am none other than the Prophet Elijah, sent from heaven to test you and to find out whether you would shame a sinner in public. You have passed the test. You never put me to shame or criticized me for transgressing the Sabbath laws. As a reward for your kindness and consideration, you will be blessed with a son."

A child was born to the old couple, and they called the boy Israel. The soul of Israel was pure and holy. Before Adam had committed his grievous sin in the Garden of Eden, a few souls had escaped and taken shelter under the heavenly throne. One of these great spirits was Israel, the son of Eliezer, who later became known as Rabbi Israel Baal Shem Tov, the kindly Master of the Good Name.

3

The Miracle-Worker

Rabbi Adam was a great scholar who knew the holy mysteries of the Torah, for he owned unique writings that held the keys to the secrets of heaven and earth. Day and night he studied these wonderful works. He had grown wise and powerful. At his will, he summoned angels, and he could even bring the Prophet Elijah to his presence. The power to do this had come to him through the mysterious writings that were his most precious possession.

But his wisdom had brought him no wealth. He and his wife, Rebecca, and their only son, Yehiel, lived in a humble hovel of a cottage. They were so poor that they could not even afford to buy bread. In the winter the roof leaked, and they had no money to mend it. They lived a life of poverty and deprivation, for Rabbi Adam hated to ask favors or to accept gifts. He never complained. He was too deeply absorbed in heavenly matters to worry over earthly problems. With Rebecca it was quite a different story. She respected her husband highly. She knew he was a saint and a holy man. But the years of painful poverty had embittered her, and she never missed an opportunity to reproach her husband on this score.

"Adam," she would say, "how long will you sit over your books? Look at me! Since our wedding day, these twenty-two years ago, I have not bought myself a single dress. I am even ashamed to go to the synagogue on the Sabbath. All my friends dress themselves in fine garments in honor of the holy Sabbath, and I wear the same wretched rags full of patches and holes. What is the use of all your studies if they cannot bring us a little ease? Is it not time that you thought of me? Go earn some money!" Day by day she reproached him. Rabbi Adam answered not a word. He well knew how easily he could obtain riches. But for himself he preferred a life of poverty.

One day, unexpectedly, the rabbi gave way. He could not bear to see his wife's tears and to look upon her distress. "If it is fine clothes you want, you shall have them. Costly robes, as many as you desire."

Rebecca's eyes lit up. "Can I really?" she asked in wonderment. "Give me the money, and I will buy them."

"No need for money," replied the rabbi. "Just go into the next room."

Rebecca quickly obeyed. She stepped into the next room and stopped in amazement. There on the table lay elegant garments of silk and satin, rich with lace and embroidery. She threw off her torn rags, robed herself in the new finery, and walked proudly to the synagogue. How the people stared and whispered!

"She must have found a treasure." "She must have come into a fortune." "She must have borrowed them."

The following Sabbath, Rebecca was seen wearing different garments, even more beautiful and even more expensive. Then it was rumored that this was all due to the mighty magic of Rabbi Adam, and the entire town began to look on him with different eyes. They began to realize his extraordinary powers, and from all sides people flocked to him. He healed the sick in mind and body. He performed miracles. He even created the first artificial man, the *Golem*.

The reputation of the wonder-worker spread through the land. Even the Gentiles regarded him as a holy man, and the local squire became anxious to meet his famous tenant. Rabbi Adam was summoned to the manor, and he made a deep impression on the squire. The two men became close friends. The squire found Adam a man of great wisdom and consulted him on almost every problem. This grieved the squire's manager, Stephen. He hated Jews, especially Rabbi Adam. Stephen was a cruel master. He had no mercy on any Jew who could not pay his rent on time and would pitilessly throw the poor man into the dungeon. The friendship of the squire and Rabbi Adam angered him. He feared that his influence would be undermined and that Rabbi Adam would eventually usurp his position.

Stephen began to scheme. In order to win over his master, he invited him to a banquet and spent a good part of his savings to buy the costliest wines and the finest foods. The squire was very pleased indeed. "My lord," whispered Stephen, "you regard Adam as your friend!"

"Indeed he is," agreed the squire. "He is the wisest of counselors, a true man of God."

"If he is as fond of you as you are of him," hinted the schemer, "why does he never return your hospitality? He visits you almost every day, but has he ever invited you and your retinue to his home?"

There was truth in this, and the squire took the manager's words to heart.

The next day, Rabbi Adam once again visited the manor. "Rabbi Adam, I have known you for a long time," began the squire. "I would dearly like to visit you."

"My Lord," replied Rabbi Adam. "Your wish is my command. I shall be greatly honored if you and all your friends will come to me in seven days' time. I shall be only too happy to offer you hospitality."

Stephen was overjoyed. He well knew the miserable hovel in which Rabbi Adam lived. He knew how hard the rabbi struggled for his daily bread. Stephen rejoiced at the prospect of putting Rabbi Adam to shame, and for him the seven days dragged by like seven years. Every day Stephen passed by the cottage and saw Rabbi Adam studying the ancient books, while Rebecca busied herself with housewifely chores. There was not a single sign of preparation for the feast, and Stephen was puzzled but pleased. His plan could not fail.

At last the day arrived. In the morning, Stephen, riding to the manor, once again passed by Rabbi Adam's home. The hut looked as wretched as ever, and the rabbi was bent over his books as if utterly unaware that the squire and his retinue would be arriving within the hour.

The fatal moment arrived. The squire, with Stephen and all his friends, set out for Rabbi Adam's home. The journey was a short one. But at the end of the journey there was a shock in store for Stephen. The cottage had disappeared, and in its place stood a fabulous palace. The visitors entered and were warmly welcomed by Rabbi Adam and his wife, Rebecca. The tables were laid as if for a royal banquet. Servants in rich livery stood attentively at each chair, and Rabbi Adam and his wife were excellent hosts. "Eat and drink and be merry!" they urged their distinguished guests. "Everything you see is here for your enjoyment. Use it by all means, but please do not take anything away."

The squire was proud and happy. His friend had not failed him. Never had he enjoyed such fine food or drunk such good wine. He particularly admired the golden dishes and the silver vessels. The goblets were exquisitely fashioned, made by fine craftsmen. The squire could not resist temptation. He took two goblets and slipped them into his pocket. Then, with gratitude, he took leave of Rabbi Adam and returned to the manor.

A few days later the squire was visited by a friend, one of the king's ministers. "You know, squire," the minister related, "something very strange happened to us the other day. As you know, our king invited the Prince of Moscow for a state visit. Elaborate preparations were made; a special palace was built for the occasion and furnished with precious things. Even a banquet was prepared. Then one day, the entire palace vanished into thin air. The king was perplexed. None of us could offer any explanation or find a solution to the mystery. But, to our relief, the palace returned within a day. Everything was exactly as it had been. The only things missing were two silver goblets."

The squire then produced the two goblets. "Take them," he said. "They belong to the king." The minister was puzzled, but the squire realized that he had witnessed a remarkable example of the power and greatness of his friend Rabbi Adam, the wonder-worker.

4

Search and You Will Find

Time passed and Rabbi Adam grew old. His son was a fine man, learned in the law and honorable in all his ways. Yet the aged rabbi knew well that his son Yehiel was not worthy to inherit his books and his powers. He lacked vision. He was more interested in material than spiritual matters. He was not concerned with the unseen world, nor did he believe in demons and evil spirits.

One night Rabbi Adam had a dream. "Hand over the writings to Israel ben Eliezer of Okopy," he was told.

When the rabbi lay dying, he gave his son careful instructions. "My good and faithful son, I know you will fulfill my last wishes. When I have been gathered to my fathers, take the holy writings that were the light of my life and hand them over to Israel of Okopy, the son of Eliezer. He will make proper use of the sacred mysteries."

"How will I find this man?" his son asked.

"Search and you will find," was his father's reply.

After his father's death, Yehiel, the obedient and sorrowful son, set out to carry out his father's last wishes.

As soon as Rabbi Yehiel arrived in Okopy, he began to look for Israel ben Eliezer. He assumed that Israel was a famous scholar, a saint, a sage. But to his surprise there was no rabbi called Israel ben Eliezer in Okopy. The only man in the whole town whose name was Israel and who was the son of Eliezer, was, of all people, the synagogue beadle.

Israel, the beadle, looked like a beadle and acted like a beadle. He wore coarse garments and carried out his duties to the letter. Every morning, his strong voice woke the people for the synagogue service. He brought water from the well, heated the oven, distributed the prayer books, cleaned the House of God.

Rabbi Yehiel found himself in a terrible dilemma. How could he hand over the keys of heaven and earth to a beadle? It was unthinkable. Yet Yehiel, a man of wisdom, knew that appearances could be deceptive. He decided to wait and to watch a little longer before making a decision.

So Yehiel appointed Israel his personal attendant. But although he never let the young man out of his sight, his close watch was not very rewarding. He began to experience a deep affection for Israel. He saw in him an honest and devout soul with a great love for God and man, though he was ignorant, unlearned, and unworthy. Yehiel knew his father had been a mystic, a man of vision who knew all things. How could this great father have made such a mistake? Yet it seemed to be a mistake. Patiently, Rabbi Yehiel waited and watched, watched and waited.

One night, Yehiel was awakened from his sleep. In the stillness of the night he heard a melody that moved him strangely and set every nerve in his body tingling with awe. Not since his father's death had he heard the Song of the Torah sung so sweetly. He sat up and looked around and behold, a remarkable scene met his eyes. He could hardly recognize his own servant. The servant who no longer looked like a servant sat in a holy haze amid the holy books. Israel bore himself like a prince, his eyes radiant and a crown of light upon his brow. His spirit hovered in the heavenly spheres and flew upward on the winged words of the Torah.

Then Yehiel knew that his father had seen a true vision and that a fitting heir had been found for his father's treasures. He entrusted the writings to Israel the beadle and returned home with a light heart. The holy books were in good hands, and his duty was well done.

—— 5 ——

The Singing Children

Rabbi Israel always remembered his father's last words and tried to put them into practice: "My son, fear no one except God!" The people in the village had loved and honored Israel's parents, and for their sake the villagers had taken care of the orphaned boy and treated him with great kindness.

When his own schooling ended, the youthful Israel went back to school as an assistant to the teacher. He loved his work. He was very fond of children, and the little ones were deeply attached to the tender-hearted young assistant. Every morning, Israel would collect them from their homes and lead them in a merry band to school. In the evening, he would escort them home and see each child safely to its mother's arms. The school was a long way off, but the boys and girls enjoyed their walk, and the distance was covered all too quickly, for Israel taught them to sing.

It was a pretty scene as he led the singing children to the school on frosty winter mornings when snow covered the fields like a newly laundered sheet. With joy in their hearts, the villagers would hear the song of the happy children. Even God in His heaven hushed the angels and bent down to listen. The songs were as precious and pleasing to Him as the chant of the priests in the ancient Temple of Jerusalem.

One person, however, gazed at the singing youngsters without joy. Satan was sorely displeased. He hated the lad Israel, and he hated the singing of the children. Those childish notes were planting the seeds of heavenly happiness on earth, and Satan was determined to put an end to this good work. So he came down to earth, disguised himself as a werewolf, and hid in the woods. Israel and his charges were passing through the forest without fear, without thought of danger, when suddenly out of the bushes sprang the werewolf and attacked the children. Panic fell upon the group. The little ones shrieked, wept, and rushed home to their parents in terror. Their fathers and mothers were terrified too. They felt they could no longer trust Israel to escort their children to and from school, and the joyful journeys ceased altogether.

Israel was very, very sad, and he did not know what to do. He loved the children and missed them very much. In his grief, he recalled the words of his father: "Fear no one except God." Then Israel felt strong and brave. He armed himself with a stout stick and went back to the parents. He spoke so winningly, so wisely, and so well that he persuaded them to entrust him once more with their children.

So Israel again conducted his singing charges to school. And again the werewolf attacked them. But this time Israel was ready for him. With his stick and his strength and his courage, the children's protector fought off the wicked werewolf and beat him until he fled for his life. After that, Israel continued to lead the children with confidence.

Eventually, Israel took the teacher's place and reorganized the Hebrew school, the *heder*. In those days the *heder* was a miserable place—a small, dark room where children huddled on hard benches or even squatted on the bare floor. School hours were long. The little ones had been awake since early in the morning and had been dragged or carried to classes that lasted until late at night. The teacher held a book in one hand and a rod in the other. He was a strict disciplinarian, and a child who was naughty or disrespectful soon felt the rod.

Israel's *heder* was different. His love and kindliness won the hearts of his little pupils. He would tell them stories from the Bible and the Talmud and tales of the sages of Israel, and they listened, enthralled, to his words. He never dreamed of raising his hand against his children. Nor was it necessary. Just one glance would hush unruly youngsters into silence.

And on earth and in heaven, the chant of the young voices carried happiness and delight.

— *6* —

Swords into Plowshares

The Carpathian Mountains, the great mountain range in Central Europe, were for many years the home of a band of robbers. It was led by Peter, who was nicknamed "Cutthroat." He had murdered a Russian officer in a drunken brawl and had been sentenced to exile in Siberia. He escaped from his captors and formed a band of robbers with other outlaws. They terrorized the beautiful wooded countryside. They were desperate and daring. The snowbound recesses and mountain caves afforded them a safe refuge. They ambushed travelers at the passes of Teregova, Vulkar, and Tursberg. Few travelers escaped them.

There was a price on the heads of the bandits. Special military missions were sent out to capture them, but the robbers were alert and elusive and were able to avoid being caught by the superior forces of the army. Unarmed travelers and caravans were easy prey for them. They robbed, they killed, they captured, and they demanded high ransoms for their hostages. They had no fear of punishment. The only one they feared was their leader, Peter. His word was law to them, and woe betide anyone who dared disobey or disagree with him.

One day the robbers attacked a large caravan. They killed the armed guards and anyone else who offered any resistance. A number of travelers were taken captive. The robbers were delighted with their day's work. They had found gold, silver, and copper vessels and a large amount of food. They sat down by a brook to make merry and to consume a well-earned repast.

The scenery around them was breathtaking. The mountains formed picturesque gorges, with high peaks seeming to reach the heavens. Suddenly, the bandits spotted a figure climbing to the top of a mountain. It was none other than Rabbi Israel, who was deep in meditation. He reached the summit unaware of the danger of falling down the precipice. "He is going to fall and be killed!" cried Cutthroat Peter. "He is going to his death," called out One-eyed Jack. They expected him to fall within seconds of his being spotted by them and to break his neck. They stopped eating and drinking. Their eyes were fastened on the figure of Rabbi Israel. Suddenly, the two opposite mountains joined together and became one, providing a level path for the rabbi to continue his walk in safety.

The robbers had never seen such a phenomenon. They realized that they were in the presence of a man of God, a miracle-worker. One-eyed Jack was not impressed: "He must be a magician who has put a spell on nature," he informed the others. He became determined to kill the rabbi one day.

The next day, on his return from collecting wood for the campfire, One-eyed Jack came across Rabbi Israel, lying in a field, fast asleep. Here was an opportunity One-eyed Jack could not miss. The "magician" was lying helplessly asleep in front of him. He did not hesitate. He lifted up his heavy ax and was about to strike Rabbi Israel on his head. His hands became numb. He dropped the ax, and he became rooted to the spot. The agile One-eyed Jack could not move. He stood still, like a giant statue. Terror stricken, he cried out for help.

His loud cry awoke Rabbi Israel. With surprise, he saw One-eyed Jack standing over him. "Help me, man of God! I am wicked and evil. I tried to kill you. I am a worthless creature!"

"No one is worthless," replied Rabbi Israel. "We are all the children of the living God, and one God has created us all."

"I am wicked, I deserve to die!" cried One-eyed Jack.

"God does not desire the death of the wicked," Rabbi Israel assured him. "His desire is that you should repent and become good, kind, and honest and never harm another human being. Promise that you will change your ways and leave the band of the robbers, and you will fully recover.''

One-eyed Jack faithfully and without any hesitation promised Rabbi Israel he would do all of that.

''Then,'' said the rabbi, ''turn your sword into a plowshare. Become a farmer. Till the soil and make amends for all your evil deeds.''

——— 7 ———

You Shall Not Be Greedy

Israel loved children and enjoyed teaching them. At one time he was the tutor of Yossel's five children. Yossel had a small shop that he leased from the local squire for thirty rubles per year. There he sold whiskey, vodka, and wine. He was not a learned man. He had been brought up in the small village, away from a Jewish environment. The High Holy Days he spent in the nearby town. But he wanted his children to acquire knowledge, and he was very happy when Israel agreed to teach them.

Yossel set aside a wooden hut near his shop where his children could learn, undisturbed by peasants and customers. Whenever he was free for a few moments, he would stand outside the hut and listen with joy to his children's voices reciting the prayers and the Holy Scriptures. He greatly cherished Israel, who was dearly loved by his young pupils. They were eager to learn and to hear from him the stories of miracles and wonders.

One day Rabbi Israel noticed that Yossel was very miserable and that his wife, Havah, was crying. He found out that a neighboring Jew, Hayim, had made a better offer for the shop. He had offered to pay double the rent and had even bribed the agent. The landlord could not resist accepting the higher offer, and Yossel had been given one week's notice to leave his home and business. "Where shall I go?" lamented Yossel. "As it is, we just manage to make a living. I have no savings. What am I to do?"

When Israel heard this, he immediately went to Hayim and begged him not to take away Yossel's home and livelihood. "It is against Jewish law to deprive a fellow Jew of his living. He has a large family and nowhere to go. He has lived here all his life. Please, do not commit such a terrible deed. Do not be greedy!"

Hayim not only would not listen to Israel, he was also insulting. "How dare you, a mere Hebrew teacher, tell me what to do? You stick to your teaching. It is not your job to give unsolicited advice." He almost threw Israel out of his house.

Hayim was summoned to the landlord's office to settle the matter. A legal document had been prepared. The landlord was very happy to receive such high rent for the shop. Hayim took the pen to sign the agreement. His hands became numb. He could not grip the pen, and it fell onto the desk. Hayim's fingers had become numb, and he felt very unwell. He had to return home without signing the lease.

Hayim was ill for three years. His wife took him to the city of Lublin to see doctors. They gave him many remedies, but none helped him. His wife had heard how famous Rabbi Israel had become and the many cures he had been able to bring about and decided it was time for Hayim to visit him. Rabbi Israel recognized him immediately and told him, "Three years ago you committed a great sin. You were envious of your neighbor Yossel. You plotted to take away his livelihood. He had never done you or anyone else any harm. You caused him and his wife great unhappiness and anxiety. Now, if you will ask his forgiveness and

donate one-tenth of your wealth to charity, you will recover completely."

Hayim made amends as the rabbi had directed him, and in a short
time he found himself restored to full health. He vowed never to be
greedy again.

— 8 —

Love and Marriage

Because of Israel's patience and gentle ways, the people of his
village came to love and honor him. Often they asked him to
settle local disputes, for he was a peacemaker by nature. One day
the little village was visited by Rabbi Ephraim, a renowned scholar and
talmudist. The rabbi had an argument with one of the villagers, and the
two took their quarrel to Israel. The teacher listened patiently to them,
questioned them carefully, and then gave his verdict. Rabbi Ephraim
was much impressed by Israel's understanding and good judgment. He
little expected to find so brilliant a man in so small a village.

"Israel," said Rabbi Ephraim, "I am convinced that the Almighty has
guided me to you. I have a daughter Hannah. She is a fine girl with a
good heart and a well-cultivated mind. Would you like to become my
son-in-law?" Israel readily agreed. The betrothal document was drawn
up and signed by the father of the bride and his chosen son-in-law, after
which Rabbi Ephraim departed.

On the journey home, the aged rabbi collapsed and died. His only son, Rabbi Gershon of Kitov, rushed to his side. He found the betrothal document among his father's possessions. Rabbi Gershon rejoiced that his venerable father had found a worthy bridegroom for his beloved sister. He had no doubt that the chosen husband was a man learned in the Talmud and a scholar of great repute. Hannah, too, had complete faith in her father. She knew how much he had loved her and how greatly he had desired her happiness. Her father's sudden death was a great blow, but as she mourned for her father, she found comfort in the thought of the unknown bridegroom. He must be a man of many fine qualities to have reached the high standards set by her father. Was he a rabbi? A famous sage? Weeks turned into months, and still there was no sign of the mysterious Israel.

Then one day, when Rabbi Gershon sat with other scholars in his study, a stranger entered and approached him. He wore the coarse garments of a peasant. "I am Israel ben Eliezer," declared the newcomer. "I am the affianced bridegroom of your sister."

Rabbi Gershon grew faint. He was no great judge of character. He did not have his father's insight and could not see below the surface. The presence of this man and the prospect of having him as a brother-in-law displeased him sorely. He thought Israel looked a most unsuitable husband for his young sister, who was a cultured and sensitive girl. Rabbi Gershon tried to engage the stranger in scholarly discussion, but Israel did not respond, and the anxious brother attributed his silence to ignorance or stupidity.

Gershon summoned his sister and counseled her earnestly and urgently to break the engagement. "This must be a terrible mistake!" he cried. "I cannot understand this strange action of our wise and loving father. What made him do such a thing? It would disgrace me to have such a man as my brother-in-law. It would break my heart to see you married to such a man. You deserve a better fate."

But Hannah could not be dissuaded. She felt instinctively that there was something noble about this gentle-mannered young man. Although he wore rough garments and seemed a common peasant, she knew in her heart that this was no ordinary bridegroom her father had chosen for her, almost his last act on earth. She looked into Israel's eyes and was ready to follow him even to the ends of the earth.

Willingly she married him, and she never regretted her decision. After the wedding, Israel revealed his true nature to her and told her of his great and secret destiny. Hannah brought joy and gladness into his life, and they shared many hardships and suffering. A great love grew up between them, and they lived happily all the days of their lives.

—— *9* ——

The Hidden Light

For many years Rabbi Israel and his wife, Hannah, lived in the Carpathian Mountains. Israel spent his time in study and contemplation. He loved nature and the wild countryside. The grandeur of the mountains filled him with a knowledge of the glory of God. He was always in the presence of God. He knew that the Almighty was not only in the synagogue or in the House of Study. The Divine Presence was to be found in every herb and every blade of grass. Rabbi Israel could understand the language of the birds and could even interpret the rustling of the leaves. He studied the healing properties of all the herbs.

He was fortunate in his teacher, who was none other than the Prophet Ahiya of Shiloh, the teacher of the Prophet Elijah. There in the solitude of the mountains, completely undisturbed, Rabbi Israel found peace of mind. He studied the writings of Rabbi Adam. He studied the teachings of the great masters of the *Kabbalah*. He acquired hidden knowledge and the divine mysteries were revealed to him.

His wife kept a little inn but there were few customers, and it was with difficulty that they were able to keep body and soul together. None of the customers had any idea of the true character of the landlord. Only his wife shared his secret. Only she knew of the secluded cabin in the mountains where Israel studied and prayed. Years passed, and the period of preparation came to an end. The time had come for Rabbi Israel to reveal himself. The Jews of Podolia and Volhynia were engulfed in an ocean of hatred, and their skies were overcast by thick clouds. A guide was needed to lead the bewildered children of Israel through the maze, to comfort them and to strengthen them. Rabbi Israel was ready to answer the call.

One day the renowned scholar Rabbi Naftali passed by the inn. He was warmly welcomed by the hospitable innkeeper and his wife. After resting awhile, Rabbi Naftali prepared to continue his journey. He was anxious to be home in time for the Sabbath. Oddly enough, the innkeeper begged him earnestly to stay the Sabbath. But his pleas were in vain. After all, the friendly host was just an uncouth peasant. The learned rabbi had no desire to spend the holy Sabbath in his company.

And so Rabbi Naftali set out on his journey. However, his coachman lost his way. They rode round in circles all day long, and as dusk gathered they were forced to return to the inn. Exhausted by the fruitless wandering, Rabbi Naftali was now compelled to spend the Sabbath at the inn. The great sage could not conceal his disappointment. He had looked forward so much to being home for the Sabbath. He had nothing in common with the landlord, as Israel had never betrayed by word or action his true self.

Confirming Rabbi Naftali's low opinion, Israel rushed the evening service and behaved in an uncouth manner throughout the Friday-night meal. He talked only about mundane matters such as the standards and prices of bricks and timber in Brody and did not once mention the Holy Scriptures. Rabbi Naftali felt very uncomfortable and out of place. He felt he had been forced to spend the Sabbath in such unconvivial company as a punishment for an unknown transgression.

On Friday night, Rabbi Naftali retired early. Although he was tired, he could not sleep. He felt strangely uneasy, and the Queen Sabbath brought him no peace. Then, in the stillness of the night, he heard a melodious voice intoning the Torah. At first he thought he was dreaming. He knew there was no one in the house but the ignorant landlord. His curiosity overcame his fatigue. He got out of bed and left the room. A strange sight met his eyes. He saw his landlord studying the divine mysteries. He beheld that his landlord was a man of God with the light of the Torah shining in his eyes. Though there was only one candle in the room, the place was as bright as if it were illuminated by a thousand lights. Rabbi Naftali looked around him. He could see only Israel, but he sensed that there were many others in the room. The heavenly angels, too, were listening to the words of the Torah coming from the lips of Rabbi Israel.

Rabbi Naftali saw his host seated on the floor, surrounded by a heavenly halo. Israel was reciting prayers and passages from the Book of Psalms in mourning for the destruction of the Temple. Israel cried out bitterly, "Look down from heaven and see how we have become objects of scorn and derision among the nations. We are regarded as sheep to be led to slaughter, to be killed, destroyed, and humiliated."

These words pierced Rabbi Naftali's heart, and he fainted. When he regained consciousness, Israel said to him, "This was not meant for your eyes. However, since you have witnessed this event, it must be the time, that at the age of thirty-six, I reveal myself. After the termination of the Sabbath, go to Brody and tell the people there that Israel, the Baal Shem Tov, is now able and willing to help and guide the Jewish people."

Rabbi Naftali now realized the purpose of his journey. He had discovered the new leader who was to guide and teach the House of Israel. The time of waiting was at an end. The hidden light had been revealed, and Israel became the leader and teacher of his people and the founder of the hasidic movement.

— 10 —

The Shepherd's Pipe

There was once a Jewish farmer who lived in a little hamlet miles and miles from any other village. There was no synagogue in the village since only a handful of Jews lived there, not even enough for a *minyan*.

On the great and solemn High Holy Days, New Year and the Day of Atonement, the farmer went to Medziborz, the nearest town and the hometown of Rabbi Israel, and there he spent the Days of Awe with his fellow Jews.

The farmer had an only son, David. He was a shepherd, just like his namesake, the king of Israel. He knew every hill and every valley in the countryside around his home, and he knew the meadows where the grass was richest and the brooks sweetest. He also knew the woods where wolves and danger lurked. He tended his flock tenderly and had a special name for each of the sheep. As he wandered over the hillside, David loved to play his favorite tunes on his pipe.

The days passed pleasantly for the young shepherd. He learned all he could about nature, and his heart was filled with a sense of nearness to the Creator of all the beautiful things he saw and enjoyed. Meanwhile, David's father grieved that his son was growing up without schooling, for David could not even read the Hebrew prayers. So his father engaged a teacher for him but, though David tried very hard, learning did not come easily to the shepherd boy. He just could not learn to read or even to recognize the letters of the Hebrew alphabet.

When David was thirteen, a *bar mitzvah* boy, his father decided that the time had come to take his son with him to the synagogue of Rabbi Israel.

The New Year had passed with all solemnity, and the people reassembled on the Day of Atonement. On this holy day, Rabbi Israel prayed with zeal and passion for his people. With tears in his eyes and a breaking heart, he implored Almighty God to grant the children of Israel a year of peace and happiness.

The congregation, too, prayed with sincerity and earnestness. Every single worshiper repeated the words of the ancient prayers. Everyone, that is, but David. He alone could take no part in the service, and a great anguish filled his young soul. He yearned to express to God his fears for his flock and his delight in the wonders of nature, his longing for learning, and his difficulties with his studies. But how could he, an ignorant shepherd lad, converse with God Almighty? The *mahzor*, the festival prayer book, was a closed book to him. He could neither read nor understand a word of it.

David had only one way of expressing himself—his shepherd's pipe. It had never failed him in the meadows and on the hillside. When he lifted the reed to his lips, the stern frown on his father's face held him back. Throughout the long and weary day he resisted temptation. But in the evening, as *Ne'ilah* time approached, he could no longer restrain himself. Neither the threatening looks of his father nor the imposing presence of the master could stop him. Suddenly, in the midst of the august assembly, he blew his pipe. The shrill notes vibrated through the

House of God. The congregation was stricken with amazement. David's father hung his head in shame, wishing the earth would open up and swallow him.

Only Rabbi Israel remained calm. He called above the heads of the people and summoned the boy David to his side. "My son," he said in a voice overflowing with love and joy, "the notes of your shepherd's pipe sounded to our Father in heaven as sweet as the music played by King David on his harp. For, with all your heart and might, you prayed in the only way you knew. The veils before the heavenly throne were pierced by the sounds of your whistle, and through these gaps my own prayers reached their destination. In your merit, David, God has inscribed us all in the Book of Life for this coming year."

—— *11* ——

The Mystery of the Rabbi's Laughter

One Friday night in Medziborz, Rabbi Israel sat at the Sabbath meal with his disciples. It was an awesome experience to share the Sabbath with the rabbi. The disciples felt the holiness of the day as never before as they gazed upon their rabbi, following his every gesture. They had so much to learn from his every word, from every action.

But Rabbi Israel was deeply absorbed in his thoughts. He seemed to be far, far away from the disciples who clustered around him. No doubt his spirit was soaring to the heavenly spheres. Perhaps he was communing with the angels. The silence grew deeper and deeper. Then suddenly the stillness was shattered. The rabbi smiled to himself—a radiant smile—then he laughed out loud, and his joyous laughter rang through the room.

The disciples were startled, almost alarmed. What was the reason for this strange burst of merriment? True, the rabbi was always joyful, but they could not remember any other occasion on which he had laughed so happily for no apparent reason. Naturally, they dared not question him, but their amazement grew as the rabbi laughed a second time and then a third time.

The next day, when the holy Sabbath had departed, the thoughtful rabbi gathered his disciples around him. "My children," he said, "you surely wish to learn the cause of my strange conduct last night. Come with me and the secret shall be revealed to you."

Quickly the carriages were prepared and the rabbi and his disciples drove together through the night. On they traveled, many miles. The horses' hooves barely touched the ground as they all but flew past distant towns and hamlets. At last, when the young men were beginning to think they would ride on forever in this whirlwind way, the panting horses stopped of their own accord in the center of a small settlement, the village of Opatow in the Ukraine.

What excitement there was in Opatow that night! The fame of the great rabbi had spread through every hamlet in Poland and Russia, and the people of Opatow knew all about him. They often spoke with wonder of the miracles he had wrought and never tired of relating the long chronicle of his good deeds. They knew that all who came to him found happiness and healing. The sick were cured at his touch, the lame walked again without stumbling, and the blind opened their eyes once more. The wise words of the rabbi comforted all who were in trouble, and they longed with all their hearts to meet him.

Yet how could the poor villagers of Opatow make the long and difficult journey to Medziborz? They had never even dared to hope for a meeting with the saintly one. Now a miracle had occurred before their very eyes. As they could not go to Medziborz, the great man of Medziborz had come to them. The news spread like a forest fire. The entire community went wild with joy and all of them, every man, woman, and child, rushed to the marketplace to catch a glimpse of the rabbi. The local rabbi welcomed the visitors. Rabbi Israel was moved by the warmth of the welcome, and he greeted the crowd affectionately. But his keen gaze swept the assembled people carefully, as if he were seeking someone he could not find.

"Where is Shapsei the bookbinder?" Rabbi Israel asked. The people looked at one another in amazement. Imagine the great rabbi knowing about Shapsei, humble little Shapsei, the bookbinder. Imagine the great rabbi noticing that Shapsei was not amongst them. For indeed it was so. Shapsei was a modest man. He hesitated to join the noisy throng. "Fetch the bookbinder!" commanded Rabbi Israel, and his word was law.

Forgetful of his dignity, the stout beadle rushed away with most unbeadlelike haste and soon returned with Shapsei. The leaders of the community respectfully made way for the man whom Rabbi Israel wished to honor, and the bookbinder stood face-to-face with the rabbi. No wonder Shapsei was bewildered and could hardly find his tongue. In all his fifty-six years, no one had ever taken notice of him. No one had ever paid him any attention, let alone respect. He had led a quiet life in the poorest cottage in the whole village. Now, for the first time in his life, he felt the eyes of his neighbors upon him. The villagers eyed him with awe.

"Tell me," came the voice of the rabbi, a voice so soft that it felt like a caress, yet so penetrating that even the people on the fringes of the crowd heard every single word. "Tell me, Shapsei, what happened last night?" At first, Shapsei hesitated; then, to his surprise, words flowed easily, and he began to tell his story.

"Rabbi, I am a poor working man, struggling hard to make a living and to feed my dear wife. I am a bookbinder without books to bind. The village is small, and few people can afford to have their books bound. I earn very little, and throughout the week we live on bread and water. Whatever I earn, I save for the holy Sabbath. Friday night is the only time of the week we eat a proper meal, with fish and meat and other delicacies. Last week, however, I earned nothing at all, and when Friday morning arrived I had no money to give my patient wife.

" 'My dear,' " I said to her gently, " 'I am very much afraid that we shall have to fast this Sabbath. I know we have kind neighbors. They are charitable people, and they would help us if we asked them. But we have always been proud. We have never asked for charity, for the gifts of flesh and blood. Let us remember this now and beg no favors from our neighbors. I am going to the synagogue. Put our largest pots and pans on the stove. Fill them with water. When the water boils, the smoke from the chimney will convince our good neighbors that you are busy with Sabbath preparations.' My devoted wife readily agreed, and I made my way to the House of Prayer.

"At the end of the service, everybody rushed home for the festive meal. I alone was in no hurry. I knew there was nothing festive in store for me. Slowly, very slowly, I walked home. I felt ashamed before the ministering angels who escort every Jew on the Friday night and bring God's blessings with them. Then, when I sadly opened the door of my little cottage, what a surprise awaited me!

"The Sabbath candles glimmered brightly. The table was beautifully laid. My *Kiddush* cup was filled to the brim with sparkling purple wine. Plates were heaped with fish and meat and the sweet white twisted loaves. This was no illusion.

"It was all real, very real. I concluded that my wife had not been able to resist temptation after all. She must have asked for charity, and our good neighbors must have responded very generously. I felt sick at heart, but I knew the good woman meant well, so I held my peace. I sanctified the Sabbath and partook of the delicious meal. I sang the Sabbath songs, the *Zemirot*, and recited the Grace after Meals.

"Then I turned to my wife and said reproachfully, 'But surely you should have known that I would rather starve than eat the bread of charity.' Her smile reassured me. 'My husband,' she replied, 'I did not disobey you. I did not ask for charity.'

'Then how did you pay for all this?' I asked in bewilderment. 'There was no money in the house.'

" 'When you left for the synagogue,' explained my wife, 'I was very miserable. I felt I had to do something in honor of the holy Sabbath. True, I could not go to the marketplace to buy food. But I could still clean up the house. And this I did. It was like the eve of Passover. I swept, scrubbed, polished until there was not a speck of dirt to be seen anywhere, and every floorboard shone. Then I tidied all the cupboards. And in one of the cupboards I found an old, old garment that you discarded many years ago. It was the robe my father gave you on our wedding day. There were a few silver buttons on the garment. I took these buttons to the goldsmith, and he gave me a few coins in return. With this money, I was able to prepare royally for the Sabbath.'

"When I heard this, my heart was filled with such thankfulness to our Father in heaven that I took hold of my dear wife and danced with her, a dance of pure happiness. And three times that evening we danced for joy together."

"I knew that," smiled Rabbi Israel, and his smile was as warm and gracious as the sun. "When you rejoiced, when you danced that dance of innocent joy, the supreme King of Kings, the angels, the archangels, and the whole of the heavenly court rejoiced with you and shared your happiness. There was merriment and laughter in heaven. And when I heard the laughter of the heavenly hosts, I joined in."

Then Rabbi Israel turned to his disciples. "This is why I laughed three times on Friday night."

— 12 —

The Undelivered Letter

A wealthy man named Avigdor once came to visit Rabbi Israel. He brought with him a large sum of money that he gave the rabbi to distribute among the poor.

"Is there something I can do for you in return?" asked Rabbi Israel.

"No, thank you, rabbi," replied Avigdor proudly. "I am very rich. I have made a fortune for myself. I have a luxurious mansion and many servants. I have treasures of gold and silver. I own huge estates. I have more than I need."

"A blessing, perhaps?" suggested Rabbi Israel with gentle persistence.

"Rabbi, I have no need of blessings. I have a large family that is in every way a credit to me. There is nothing I need, nothing I want."

The master pitied proud people. Avigdor's boastfulness grieved him deeply. He well knew that one day such pride would be brought low. "If I cannot help you," he smiled, "perhaps you can help me. Would you be good enough to deliver a letter of mine to the chairman of the charity committee in Brody?"

Avigdor lived in Brody, so he could hardly refuse such a small request. Rabbi Israel wrote the letter, sealed it in an envelope, and handed it to his departing visitor. Avigdor put the letter in the pocket of his coat and forgot all about it. He had so much on his mind—plans, property, projects, big business. No sooner was he out of Medziborz than Rabbi Israel and his request were forgotten.

Sixteen years passed, and the wheel of fortune turned full circle. Avigdor's luck deserted him. His forests caught fire and were completely destroyed. His fields were flooded and the crops ruined. His properties crumbled and his stocks fell in value. Disaster followed disaster. The overconfident merchant lost all he owned, and there was nothing he could do to save himself, or even to recover part of his fortune.

Creditors repossessed his beautiful house and took away all his possessions. Soon the former magnate was worse off than the most wretched pauper. To feed his starving family, he was forced to sell the very clothes off his back. Then one day, when he was just about to hand over an old coat to a dealer, he went through the pockets as a matter of routine and found a letter, a letter he had promised to deliver so many years ago. It rekindled old memories. Vividly, he recalled his visit to Rabbi Israel and his own arrogant attitude. Tears flowed from his eyes, and he resolved at once to discharge his long-delayed mission. He looked at the envelope closely. It was addressed to Mr. Zaddok, the chairman of the charity committee of Brody.

Avigdor rushed into the street; when he met one of his friends, he seized him by the arm: "Please tell me where I can find Mr. Zaddok." "Mr. Zaddok?" asked the friend. "Do you mean the Mr. Zaddok who has just been elected chairman of the charity committee?"

"Yes, I want to see him urgently," confirmed Avigdor. "Then you will still find him at the synagogue office being congratulated by the rabbi. A lucky man, Zaddok. Only this morning he was elected chairman."

Avigdor was anxious to know more about Zaddok, and his friend was ready to oblige. "Zaddok has been living in Brody all his life. He is a tailor. He was very unlucky at first and never had many customers. He earned a living by patching old clothes. He and his family lived a life of dire poverty. No one knew him. No one took any notice of him. He worked long hours and thought himself lucky if he earned enough money to buy a loaf of bread for his large family.

"Lately, however, things have changed for the better. Zaddok was introduced to the squire, who instructed him to make uniforms for his servants. The order was carried out to the squire's satisfaction, and more orders began to come in from all sides. He received a contract for five hundred uniforms and became rich. People began to look at him with respect. He was a kind and generous man, and his newfound wealth did not make him forget his former poverty. He began to take an active part in the affairs of the community, and this morning he was unanimously elected chairman of the charity committee."

Avigdor soon made his way to the synagogue office. Zaddok was busily sorting out notes from the poor who wanted his help. He opened Avigdor's letter from Rabbi Israel and read the prophetic words: "Dear Mr. Zaddok, the bearer of this letter, Avigdor, was once a very rich man, but he is now exceedingly poor. He has paid in full for his vanity and his pride. As you have this morning been elected chairman of the charity committee, please do all you can to help him. He has a large family to support. With the money you give him, he will once again be successful, and this time he will be better fitted for success. So that you should not doubt that these words come from me, I will give you a sign. Your wife is expecting a baby. Today she will give birth to a boy."

No sooner had Mr. Zaddok finished reading the letter than the door burst open. The beadle rushed in and cried, *"Mazel Tov* —good luck — Mr. Zaddok! Your wife has just given birth to a son."

Rabbi Israel's instructions were faithfully carried out, and Avigdor soon rose to a high position in the community. He used his wealth with wisdom and was highly esteemed by his fellowmen. But he always remained humble.

13

The Prayer Book

Menahem was very young when his parents and his brothers and sisters were murdered by a gang of wild and wicked peasants, the Chmielnicki gang. These savages spared no one, neither young nor old. Without mercy, without any human feeling at all, they killed and robbed and reveled in their devilish deeds. By some miracle, little Menahem escaped. In their mad rush to kill and plunder, the ruffians had overlooked the child fast asleep in his crib.

The squire of the village was a kind and considerate overlord. He looked after his villagers and took a real interest in their welfare. Menahem's parents had been his personal friends. He loved children but had no sons or daughters of his own, so he enjoyed the warm atmosphere of Menahem's parents' home. Jewish customs interested him, and Jewish food delighted him. The squire had tried desperately to save Menahem's family but was powerless against the murderous mob.

When the squire discovered that Menahem had survived, he was filled with joy. He took the child to his manor and adopted him as his son.

Menahem proved to be a contented child. His pleasant disposition filled the house with sunshine. He was happy at home and happy at school. He had plenty of good food, fine clothes, and costly toys. The squire even bought him a pony, and the spirited lad would ride gaily through the meadows, imagining that he was a nobleman fighting battles with knights in shining armor.

One day, however, Menahem quarreled with one of his school friends. Words led to blows, and Menahem emerged victorious from the scuffle. The friend was a poor loser. "What have you got to be so proud about?" he jeered. "You're not the squire's real son. You're only a Jew."

Menahem grew pale. Could this be true? He knew no other father but the indulgent squire. He must find out the truth at once. He rushed home and told the squire what had happened. Then he asked questions, many questions. At first the squire laughed and treated the subject as a joke. But Menahem persisted and would not be put off. So at last the squire related to him the whole tragic tale.

Then Menahem was filled with wonderment and sorrow. He made his way to the old inn, where he had lived as an infant with his ill-fated family. The place was in ruins. No one had lived there since the night of the murders. All that was left were sticks and rags and rubbish. Yet again and again Menahem returned to the ruins, drawn there as if by an invisible magnet.

Once, when he was wandering sadly through the rubble, he noticed something sticking out from under a pile of rubbish. It was a Hebrew book. He picked it up lovingly and turned the pages reverently. This was his mother's prayer book; the leaves still bore the imprint of her tears. When Rachel, his pious mother, had opened her prayer book, she also opened her heart. Tears would flow in copious streams from her eyes as she poured out her lamentations to her Heavenly Father.

Menahem treasured the book. It was his most precious possession, for it created a link with his parents, his ancestors, his people. Whenever he held the book in his hands, he tried hard to recall his mother. The years had dimmed the picture, and the memories were faint. But there were a few Jews in the village, and Menahem began to take a great interest in their activities. He learned about the Sabbath and the festivals and fast days. He found out that the Day of Atonement, the Sabbath of Sabbaths, the most solemn day of the Jewish calendar, was at hand. He noticed that all the Jews were gathering in the synagogue.

Menahem, too, made his way to the House of God. The worshipers were wrapped in white prayer shawls. They swayed to and fro, praying loudly and fervently in a language he could not understand. The lad was bewildered. He felt more alone than he had ever felt in all his life. He knew he was a Jew, yet he remained a stranger in the midst of his fellow Jews. He wanted desperately to be a part of them. He wanted to proclaim his Jewishness. And he did not know how.

Menahem then took hold of his most prized possession, his mother's prayer book. He opened the book and lifted up his voice: "O Lord of the universe," he cried in anguish, "I cannot read the prayers. I do not know the sacred language. Heavenly Father, be my guide, my teacher, my instructor. Take the book and say the prayers for me!"

"At these simple words," said Rabbi Israel, as he told the story to his disciples, "the angels wept for pity. The gates of mercy flew wide open, and the prayer of the little orphan rose, a rare and precious offering to the very throne of God."

—— 14 ——

Two Friends

Elias, a very rich man, once visited Rabbi Israel. His wealth had made him proud and conceited. Elias thought he had nothing to learn. The master looked at him and was filled with pity. This is the story the rabbi told his visitor:

"Many, many years ago, there lived in a certain town two Jewish families who were neighbors and good friends. Each family had a son, and the two boys, Tobias and Joseph, grew up together, studied together, played together. They swore eternal friendship. Years passed. The young men married and were soon settled in different countries. They were sad to part. At first they wrote to each other frequently and kept in close touch. But as time went on, they became absorbed in their work and in their families. The letters became infrequent and finally stopped. The two friends lost touch with each other.

"In the beginning both men prospered. They undertook many enterprises and succeeded in them all. But after a while Tobias began to lose large sums of money. He worked hard and tried hard. He started new ventures. But nothing helped. His debts piled up, and his creditors grew more and more pressing. Tobias became very poor. He sold his beautiful home and his furniture and even his clothes. But the sight of his children begging for bread was more than he could bear, and he decided, as a last resort, to approach his friend Joseph for help.

"Tobias borrowed money and made the long and tiring journey to the country where his childhood friend lived. Joseph was delighted to see him and gave him a very warm reception. The visitor was feasted and feted and made to feel very important. Soon Tobias opened his heart to his friend and told him of his troubles. Joseph's response came readily. He took half his fortune and placed it in the hands of his friend.

"Tobias was overwhelmed by this generosity. Joyfully he returned home and once again began many new ventures. This time, fortune smiled upon him, and he prospered. Everything he touched turned to gold. But wealth brought him no peace of mind. He could never forget the terrible days of poverty and was haunted by the fear of becoming poor again. He grew avaricious and miserly, consumed by a passion for money. The more he had, the more he wanted. Gold became his god, and silver his idol. He became hard and cruel. He lived a selfish life in which there was no place for God and no room for his neighbors.

"The wheel of fortune turned once again. The good friend Joseph who had been so wealthy now became wretchedly poor. Joseph was a man of spirit, and he hated the thought of asking for help, but circumstances forced his hand. He could see no solution to his problem, and the only man to whom he could turn was his friend Tobias. He was sure that Tobias would be glad to repay him for his generous act.

"So he set out to visit his friend, and after traveling for many days, he finally arrived at the house of Tobias. But no warm welcome awaited him. The servants refused to let him into the house, saying they were acting on their master's orders. Joseph sent desperate messages to Tobias. He reminded his one-time comrade of their great friendship and of the vows they had made to each other. He reminded Tobias that he had helped him in his hour of need. But nothing could move the miser, who turned a deaf ear to his friend's pleas.

"Poor Joseph suffered greatly. The ingratitude of the wealthy Tobias grieved him deeply. Joseph was weary, and his heart was full of sorrow. Friendship had proven false, and life had no more meaning for him. Soon afterward, brokenhearted, he died. Eventually, Tobias also died; his wealth could not bribe or stave off the angel of death.

"The two men were brought before the heavenly court: their deeds were examined and the events of their lives were related to the judges. The great Judge did not take long to pronounce the verdict. "Joseph, the true and generous friend, is to enter paradise, there to enjoy eternal bliss. Tobias, his false friend, must do penance for his sins and go to hell."

"Then something strange happened. Instead of being delighted with his reward, Joseph protested strongly. He had no wish for revenge. He could not bear the thought of his friend being punished. Passionately, he pleaded before the court on Tobias' behalf. 'What joy can there be for me in the Garden of Eden if my friend is not at my side?' Even the angels were moved by the nobility of this unselfish soul, and for Joseph's sake, the court agreed to give Tobias another chance.

"It was decided that the two men should be born again. Once more Tobias would have a chance to choose between a life of generosity and good deeds and the selfish existence of a miser. And so it came to pass. Joseph was reborn as the child of poor parents. As soon as the little boy was old enough to walk, he was sent to beg bread for himself and his starving family. Tobias, on the other hand, was born into a wealthy home. His life was one of prosperity and plenty.

"He grew up to hold a position of great power, lived in a great mansion, and employed many servants. But he was a man with a heart of stone. No poor person was ever permitted to cross his threshold. Then one day, a wretched beggar passed his gates. The servants were busy preparing a big banquet, so the door was left unguarded. The beggar was thus able to enter and went unhindered to the master of the house. Tobias was counting his silver and his gold coins. He started violently when the man crept in. 'What do you want?' he cried in anger. 'How dare you enter my house? Don't you know that beggars are not allowed in here?' "

" 'Bread,' moaned the beggar piteously. 'Just give me a morsel of bread. I am faint with hunger. No food has passed my lips for the last two days.' Tobias lost patience and struck the beggar, who collapsed and died instantly."

Elias had listened intently to Rabbi Israel's story. Now the master rose from his seat, towering above him. "Does this story mean anything to you?" thundered the rabbi. "You are the man. You are Tobias. You are the faithless friend. You are the miser. This is your second chance to make amends for your wickedness, your last chance. You were reborn to make atonement, but you forgot your good intentions. Go now, before it is too late, and share your wealth with others. Be kind and generous so that you may enter the world of eternity and be deemed worthy of rejoining the faithful friend who has suffered so much because of you and who saved your soul."

Pale with fear, Elias stumbled to his feet. "Master, I have sinned," he wept. "I will make amends. I will open my heart, and all that I have I will share with my fellowmen."

15

A Wonderful Gift

Solomon was an innkeeper. He leased his inn from the local squire, Count Potozky, who owned the whole county. Solomon lived above the inn with his wife, Berachah, and their five children. They employed a Hebrew teacher to instruct their children. The peasants liked Solomon, who was honest and a genial host. He made a good living and was happy and content. He paid his rent regularly and punctually.

Conditions soon changed. A band of Haidamaks, a group of brigands and cutthroats, started to terrorize the countryside. They waylaid and attacked travelers. They robbed and they killed. People were afraid to travel to the fairs. The roads became deserted. Even the local peasants were nervous to leave their cottages, and the inn lost its customers. Solomon's income dwindled. Before long, he did not even make enough money to feed his family, and he fell heavily into debt. He now owed two years' rent to the count, whose manager, Ivan, hated Jews and regularly came to demand the rent. He warned Solomon that unless the rent was paid by the first of April—the count's birthday—he would evict him from the inn and imprison him in the castle dungeon.

Solomon was desperate. He did not know what to do. He prayed, recited psalms, and became almost demented with worry. "What will happen to my poor children?" he wailed.

His wife, Berachah, who could no longer bear to witness his distress over the uncertainty of their future, advised him, "Why don't you go to see Rabbi Israel. He is known as a miracle-worker. People come to him from far and wide. Go to him! Maybe he can help you."

Solomon was a pious and learned man, but he was no follower of

Hasidism, the new movement led by Rabbi Israel. His wife, however, continued urging him. "What can you lose? We are in a desperate situation!"

So Solomon listened to his wife and made his way to the rabbi in Medziborz. The rabbi, after listening carefully, advised him, "Stand outside your inn next Sunday, and when a stranger approaches you and offers you an article, buy it. Do not argue. Then present it to the count on his birthday."

Solomon was very disappointed. He had expected the rabbi to bless him, to lay his hands upon him, to say a prayer or perform a miracle. All the rabbi told him was to buy something from a stranger next Sunday. The rabbi's advice did not seem to relate to his problems.

However, on the following Sunday he stood outside his inn as the rabbi had instructed him. A total stranger approached him. "Would like to buy a piece of lambskin?"

"How much do you want for it?" asked Solomon.

"One ruble," replied the stranger. Solomon possessed only one ruble with which to buy bread for his family. Nonetheless, as Rabbi Israel had commanded him, he bought the lambskin. He was sorry to spend his last ruble on the lambskin, which looked utterly worthless.

The first of April, the count's birthday, soon arrived. There was great excitement. All the local squires were making their way to the castle, bearing presents: paintings, horses, jewels, china and gold and silver ornaments. In great fear and trembling, Solomon, too, went to the castle, hesitantly carrying his gift, the threadbare lambskin.

At the entrance to the castle, Ivan, the manager, snatched the skin from Solomon and put him in the dungeon. "Look what Solomon, the innkeeper, brought you!" he said to the count, who was being showered with gifts by his family and friends. "A cheap piece of lambskin. He deserves to be put to death for such impertinence. Not only is he in debt for the last two years' rent but he dares to insult you on your birthday by giving you such a worthless present!"

"Yes, put him to death!" exclaimed the count's guests, all of them eager to witness an execution.

"One moment, my Lord!" cried out the count's cousin. "Before we put Solomon to death, let us closely examine the present he brought." He took the lambskin and turned it over. Suddenly they all noticed that it was a beautiful tapestry produced by skilled artisans. It depicted the count's genealogy, showing the family crest, the dates of the births and deaths of all his forebears, pictures of their military exploits, and all the medals and decorations they had received.

The entire gathering looked on in admiration and heaped praises on the gift. "Not even the Flemish could produce such a tapestry. We must reward Solomon for this most beautiful and thoughtful gift," decreed Count Potozky.

Meanwhile Solomon was languishing in the dungeon, preparing himself for death. He even recited the last confessional prayer and was ready to meet his Maker. To his surprise, he was taken to the count, who said to him, "Solomon, I do appreciate your wonderful gift. It is the most precious gift I have ever received. Your debt is canceled. You can remain at the inn rent free for the rest of your life. I shall always treasure your gift."

Solomon returned home, happy in the thought that he had heeded his wife's advice to visit Rabbi Israel.

— 16 —

The Great Savior

Rabbi Gershon of Kitov, the brother-in-law of Rabbi Israel, decided to settle in the Holy Land. Before setting out on the long and arduous journey, he went to see his brother-in-law to bid him farewell. Rabbi Israel's last words to him were, "Please do not forget to give my regards to the Prophet Elijah."

Rabbi Gershon traveled to Odessa, where he boarded a ship going to Istanbul. There he waited for a considerable time for another boat to take him to the Holy Land.

He eventually found a boat that was sailing to Jaffa. As it was midsummer, the Mediterranean Sea was calm and serene. There was no breeze. The boat was crowded with pilgrims.

After a week at sea, they anchored off one of the islands in the Mediterranean. The captain decided to stop there for three hours to buy fresh provisions. Most of the passengers disembarked and went to look at the sights on the shore. The ship was completely deserted except for Rabbi Gershon, who decided to remain aboard. In the hot midday sun he felt the urge to bathe in the sea. He undressed and jumped in. In his youth, Rabbi Gershon had been a strong swimmer and was used to the cold waters of the Dnieper River, but he had never experienced the calm and warm seas of the Mediterranean. He felt refreshed and became oblivious of time. He swam with the gentle tide for some distance around the island and away from the boat.

The three hours soon passed. The sailors and the passengers had returned to the ship. A siren was sounded and the anchor raised. No one noticed the absence of Rabbi Gershon. From a distance, Rabbi Gershon became aware that the boat was moving from its anchor, and he began to swim toward it, trying hard to reach it before it had gone too far. The sea was no longer calm, and he was now swimming against the tide. The boat sailed on, and Rabbi Gershon could not catch up with it. With all his strength he began to cry, "Help! Help!"

The sailors were busy with their tasks, and the passengers were on the lower deck eating the fresh provisions they had purchased on the island. Rabbi Gershon, with superhuman effort and with his last remaining strength, endeavored to reach the boat. But it was of no avail. By now he was so exhausted that he could no longer call out. He was just floating on the waves. He feared he would soon be submerged by the waves. He felt that his end was approaching and cried out with his last breath, "Hear O Israel, the Lord our God, the Lord is One."

To his relief, he saw a sailor throwing him a rope. He caught hold of it and was slowly pulled to safety. He found his clothes and dressed and in his exhaustion fell asleep on deck. He slept many hours.

When he awoke refreshed in the morning, he searched for the sailor to whom he owed his life. He wanted to reward him. He searched the upper deck, and he searched the lower deck. He asked the captain, giving a detailed description of the sailor. The captain had never heard of the incident and could not identify the sailor. For the rest of the journey, Rabbi Gershon tirelessly but vainly searched for his savior sailor.

When Rabbi Israel was later told this story, he remarked, "I am not surprised that Rabbi Gershon could not find the sailor who rescued him. It was none other than the Prophet Elijah, the redeeming angel of the House of Israel. It was he who saved Rabbi Gershon."

— 17 —

Who Deserves Paradise?

The disciples of Rabbi Israel were discussing in his presence the vexing problem of who deserves to go to paradise in the hereafter. What must a man do to achieve this goal? One disciple suggested that such a man would have to fulfill all the 613 commandments enumerated in the Five Books of Moses. Another felt that one so honored must be familiar with the *Kabbalah*, the mystical mysteries of the law, and with the nature of God and the soul. Another disciple stressed that only a man who was a great scholar and who was steeped in the Talmud and its commentaries deserved paradise. Another expressed the opinion that only a man who prays with sincerity and devotion will enter the Garden of Eden.

Rabbi Israel listened attentively to the lively discussion but did not join in. Just then a man passed Rabbi Israel's house. Rabbi Israel asked his beadle to call him in. The man entered the House of Study. He gave the impression of being an illiterate workman. His hair was disheveled. His robe was fastened with a thick rope, and on his feet were heavy boots.

"Please, tell us something about yourself," said Rabbi Israel.

"What is there to tell?" replied the passerby. "I am no scholar. My name is Shloimke, and I live with my wife and our eight young children in a small hut outside the town. I am a hosemaker by profession. In this I follow in my father's footsteps. He taught me all I know about the making of stockings. Every morning I go to the tailors' synagogue, where I pray and recite ten chapters of the Psalms. I work until late at night at making stockings. The only break I take is to attend afternoon and evening services. I am unable to study, but I listen to the scholars' discussions on the Torah. I have customers who come long distances to buy their stockings from me and at one ruble a pair. Only rarely do I go to market for materials. Usually merchants bring them to me, and I pay them promptly. I am not in anyone's debt. Yesterday, a man came to me and said, 'I wish to buy four pairs of stockings. Can you reduce the price?'

" 'No,' I told him. 'My charge is one ruble per pair. I do not overcharge, nor do I allow bargaining.'

"All the money I earn is divided into three parts: one-third goes to feed and clothe my family; another third is devoted to paying Hebrew teachers to teach my children Torah, and the remaining third I give to the poor and the needy. In my humble home there is always room for a poor man. I never let anyone go away empty-handed. Whatever I earn I spend. I do not, nor have I ever, saved any money. I do not care for riches. I have always been honest and have never cheated anyone. My word is my bond. My aim in life is to serve God and my fellowmen. I am an ordinary, ignorant Jew, and there is very little I can tell you about myself."

After listening to the man's recital, Rabbi Israel told his disciples, "Just now you were discussing who deserves paradise, and what qualities are required to enter it. There is no better example of one who deserves it than Shloimke!"

— 18 —

A Difficult Choice

Rabbi Jacob, a disciple of Rabbi Israel, once had a very perplexing dream. He dreamed he was in the presence of the heavenly court and was witnessing a trial. The accused was Zerah, the keeper of an inn near Medziborz. He was accused by the Heavenly Prosecutor of being dishonest and of giving short measure to his customers: he never returned belongings left behind at the inn; he did not pay his debts on time but postponed payment for as long as possible, in spite of regular visits by the creditors. He took care of his wealthy customers, for whom nothing was too good, but he ignored, and was unkind to, the poor. They were given sparse meals and made to feel unwelcome at the inn. At times, he would not even open the door to them and would scream at them, "I cannot afford to offer you hospitality. I have a living to make. Do not come again." The poor often went to sleep hungry and thirsty.

Zerah could offer no defense. The heavenly court declared him guilty on all charges, and he was condemned to die prematurely. Rabbi Jacob then pleaded eloquently on Zerah's behalf. He pointed out that Zerah had twelve young children, and who was there to look after them if he died?

After further consideration, the heavenly court decided to give Zerah a choice: would he prefer imprisonment and the loss of all his wealth or that one of his children forsake the religion of his fathers and become an apostate?

Rabbi Jacob went to see Zerah to tell him of this dream. "The choice lies entirely in your hands," he said. "You have to decide now. Are you willing to suffer imprisonment, or would you prefer one of your children to leave his faith?''

"Rabbi," replied Zerah, "I deserve to be punished. I am a sinner. Let me go to prison. Let me suffer poverty. Never, never, do I wish, God forbid, that any son of mine renounce the religion of his fathers."

Soon after that, Zerah was imprisoned and all his possessions were taken from him. He vowed that he would turn over a new leaf. He fasted twice a week and recited the whole Book of Psalms daily. He never complained about the terrible conditions of the prison. He accepted God's verdict. "I deserve my punishment," he told all his visitors.

Rabbi Jacob was deeply moved when he saw Zerah's plight. He traveled from town to town and collected enough money to free Zerah. He even obtained another inn for him. Zerah was now a changed man. His home was open to anyone in need. He was even given the nickname "Zerah, the true penitent."

—— 19 ——

A Dowry

When Leah was just six years old, her whole family was murdered by the cossacks in the town of Uman. As she was all alone in the world, Rabbi Israel and his wife Hannah adopted her. They looked after her and loved her as they did their own daughter, Adel. Leah and Adel grew up together and became loving and close friends.

The years soon passed, and Leah was betrothed to Joel, the son of a rabbi. She had met Joel for the first time at their engagement party. He was tall and handsome and had beautiful brown eyes. It was love at first sight. Rabbi Israel had told her that Joel was a fine scholar and, although only seventeen years old, was delivering talmudic discourses in the House of Study. Joel's father demanded a dowry of two hundred rubles to enable his son to continue his rabbinic studies after the marriage. Rabbi Israel readily agreed to the terms. The wedding day was then fixed for the Sunday following the Fast of *Av*.

As the wedding day approached, Leah, together with her adoptive mother and sister, was preparing her trousseau. Adel made the wedding dress, and the pious women of Medziborz were busy baking and cooking for the wedding banquet, to which the entire town was invited. It was regarded as a great *mitzvah* to help in the marriage preparation of an orphan.

The day of the wedding arrived, and the whole town crowded into the small synagogue. When everything was ready for the ceremony, Rabbi Israel turned to Joel's father and said, "Come! Let us go with Joel now to cover his bride with her veil."

But the father bluntly replied, "First I would like to see the two hundred rubles you pledged to give to Joel as a dowry."

"I am truly sorry," replied Rabbi Israel. "I have spent every single ruble I owned on the trousseau and to pay for the musicians and the jester. I have nothing to give you now, but we all have faith in the Almighty. He will surely not let us down!"

As Rabbi Israel finished speaking, a man edged out from the crowd that surrounded the two rabbis.

"The Almighty has not let you down!" he announced. "I have the money for the dowry."

"You have the dowry, Rabbi Leib?" asked Joel's father in surprise, recognizing the man, who was a penniless itinerant preacher. "From where could you have gotten all this money?"

"For the last five weeks," explained Rabbi Leib, "I have been traveling up and down the country to collect two hundred rubles, needed to free a man who had been unfairly imprisoned by the squire of Uman. This morning I went to the prison to hand in the money and discovered that the squire had canceled all debts and freed all the prisoners in celebration of the birth of his son and heir. So, I hurried back here to give the money to Rabbi Israel to distribute to any worthy cause."

"The Almighty has truly blessed this marriage," Rabbi Israel said to Joel's father. "Here is the dowry. Come! Let us not delay any longer. The bride is waiting for us."

The ceremony then took place, and Leah and Joel were married according to the laws of Moses and Israel. They lived many happy and contented years together.

—— 20 ——

The Thief

Simon was a devoted follower of Rabbi Israel. He was a wealthy merchant. He frequently traveled to Breslau, where he bought fabrics that he sold in many towns and villages in Podolia and Volhynia.

One day, Simon returned from Breslau with a wagonload of linens and silks worth more than one thousand rubles. On his arrival at his usual inn, Simon unhitched the horses and left the wagon containing the valuable merchandise in the courtyard. He had a hearty meal and fell fast asleep.

In the morning, after morning prayers, Simon had his breakfast and went into the courtyard to check his horses. To his amazement, he could not find the wagon or the merchandise. A search was immediately started, but there was no trace of his wagon and no one knew of its whereabouts. Simon was desperate. His entire wealth was contained in the wagon. Poverty stared him in the face.

In despair, Simon went to Medziborz to see Rabbi Israel and to tell him of his misfortune. The rabbi reassured him, "Do not worry. The wagon will be found. I am only sorry that the thief was a Jew."

Then Rabbi Israel called his scribe Rabbi Tzvi, and instructed him, "Go to the inn that is outside the town."

Rabbi Tzvi asked no questions. He went to the inn and there he found Simon's wagon with all the merchandise. He asked the innkeeper, "Where is the owner of the wagon?"

"He is praying," was the reply.

Rabbi Tzvi saw a man clad in a prayer shawl and phylacteries praying devoutly. He could hardly believe his eyes that a man who prayed so fervently could also be a thief. He approached him and said, "Three days ago you stole the wagon containing Simon's merchandise and hid it in a forest near Medziborz. As this is your first offense, I will not hand you over to the police. I know that you were tempted. Your wife is ill, and you need money to pay for doctors and medicines. You owe a lot of money to your neighbors. Your creditors are giving you no peace. They worry you daily. You also have six grown-up daughters of marriageable age, and you desperately need money for their dowries. Nonetheless, you have transgressed the eighth commandment: 'You shall not steal.' Repent and the Almighty will forgive you."

The thief was very surprised that he had been caught. It terrified him to hear that Rabbi Tzvi knew all about his circumstances. He immediately returned the stolen wagon containing all of Simon's goods. He went to see Rabbi Israel and begged to be forgiven.

Rabbi Israel told him that as punishment for stealing Simon's property, he must sell his own horse and wagon to provide for his family. He himself was to leave home and wander from place to place, begging for his sustenance for a whole year. Only then would he be forgiven for transgressing the eighth commandment.

——— 21 ———

The Invisible Rabbi

Count Ignacy Petroff was a nobleman who lived near Medziborz. He was a hard and cruel man. He made the lives of his tenants and servants miserable. He owned a very large estate, and the peasants working on it were treated like beasts. He would ride through the estate daily, and if he found a worker resting for a moment, he would have him whipped. He would order his fierce dog, Hadrian, to attack the peasants, and they would run for their lives when he approached.

The count was particularly harsh to the few Jewish families who lived on his estate. He was indifferent to their problems and used every pretext to make their lives difficult and almost unbearable. If one of his Jewish tenants failed to pay his dues, he had him dragged to the dungeon immediately. Neither the supplications of the tenant, nor the pleadings of his wife, nor the heartrending cries of his children would move him to pity. He was hated by both the peasants and the Jews. He was the terror of the neighborhood.

The Jewish tenants often related to Rabbi Israel the count's cruelties, and the rabbi would do his utmost to help them. He regularly collected money to save a tenant from the count's anger. He would ransom those imprisoned by the count, and he often intervened on their behalf with the governor of the province.

The count knew of Rabbi Israel's activities, and he hated Rabbi Israel very much. He regarded him as his enemy, and often boasted to his friends that he would gladly kill Rabbi Israel with his own hands.

One day, the count heard that Rabbi Israel was visiting the house of the governor. Here was an opportunity not to be missed. He loaded his gun and went to the governor's residence. He waited in the antechamber, drinking merrily with his fellow nobles.

When Rabbi Israel left the governor's study, he passed through the antechamber, where the count was drinking heavily. Rabbi Israel talked to some of the squires about the heavy taxes that had recently been imposed on the Jews, especially the taxes on salt, meat, and candles, and asked them to relieve the Jews of these additional burdens. Rabbi Israel departed after concluding all his tasks at the governor's residence.

Then the count's companions asked him, "Why did you not shoot the rabbi? Surely, you came for that purpose. You had a wonderful opportunity to get rid of him. Why did you miss such a chance? He was standing next to you. One bullet would have sufficed."

"I did not see him," explained the count. "Had I seen him, you can rest assured, he would not have left this house alive."

The assembled noblemen concluded that Rabbi Israel, who was known to be a miracle-worker, had been able to make himself invisible to the count on this occasion.

—— **22** ——

A Widow's Plight

Nehamah's husband, an innkeeper, had died in an epidemic that had ravaged the Ukraine. He had been barely thirty-six years old. He left his widow in a desperate situation. She had six young children and an old mother to look after. Her mother was frail and bedridden and in constant need of attention.

Nehamah had no choice but to take over the running of the inn. She worked very hard from dawn until midnight. She looked after her children, her mother, the customers, and the guests at the inn. She distilled whiskey and sold it to the peasants and to passersby. She was hospitable and generous. If a poor *yeshivah* student or itinerant scholar stayed the night at the inn, she would not charge him for food or lodging. She regarded it as her religious duty to be hospitable, and she often recalled the words of her late father, who used to quote: "Let your home be a meeting place for the wise and let poor people be members of your household." She employed a teacher for her children, and to listen to the children reciting the weekly portion of the law was her greatest pleasure.

In spite of her hard work, Nehamah always had a smile for everyone, and she never complained. She was highly regarded by Jews and non-Jews alike. All respected her honesty and integrity, and they knew that her word was her bond. Many peasants owed her money, but she continued to give them credit. She was regarded as a friend by all who knew her. If a peasant's child was sick, he would come to Nehamah for help with food and medicines.

Yankel, whose inn was a mile from Nehamah's, was very envious of her success. She was always busy. Her inn always had guests coming and going, whereas his was mostly empty. No matter how much he tried, he could not attract more visitors. They all preferred to stay with Nehamah, who prepared delicious food and made everyone feel at home.

Yankel was determined to get rid of Nehamah. He offered the landlord's agent a large bribe to double her rent. When Nehamah heard of Yankel's underhanded efforts to have her evicted from the inn, she went to see him. She pleaded with him not to deprive her of her livelihood. Without the inn, she would have no place for her children and her ailing mother to live. Yankel would not listen to her. He was determined to take over her inn.

In despair, Nehamah went to see Rabbi Israel, who told Yankel that it is against the Jewish law to wrong a widow. Rabbi Israel pleaded with Yankel, "Do not deprive her of her home and livelihood. She has six children to raise. Do not commit such a vile deed!"

Yankel would not listen to the rabbi. He went ahead with his plan and bribed the manager. A contract was prepared, and Yankel went to the manager's office to sign the contract. He was overjoyed. At long last he was to have his wish. He was about to acquire the very popular inn. He picked up the pen to sign. Suddenly, he was overcome by weakness. His hand could no longer hold the pen, and it slipped to the floor. He bent down to pick it up, but he could not move. His body had become paralyzed. He could not speak. He had to be taken home and became bedridden. When his power of speech eventually returned, he haltingly informed all who came to see him, "If only I had listened to Rabbi Israel! How wrong I was to try to harm a widow!"

—— 23 ——

A Valuable Horse

Rabbi Israel once stayed with one of his wealthy followers Zalman, who owned a large builder's yard and a nursery where the farmers bought seeds for their farms. He was also a moneylender. The gentry as well as the farmers regularly borrowed money from him.

On this visit, he took Rabbi Israel around his large estate and explained to him his many complicated business transactions. "Have you any horses?" Rabbi Israel asked him.

"Oh, yes," replied Zalman. "I have twenty horses in my stables. The best of them all is Nicolai, whom I bought three years ago. He is a real thoroughbred. He is willing to pull at dead weight and is an exceedingly active animal. He has a very finely arched neck, low shoulders, thick whiskers, a deep, round, barrellike build. He does the work of three horses. He carries timber up the hill and never tires."

Zalman then showed Rabbi Israel the numerous promissory notes in his possession and told him of the many people who owed him a lot of money. He picked out one note and told Rabbi Israel, "This note is from a man who owed me one hundred rubles. Unfortunately, he died penniless three years ago and this note is now worthless. There is no one who will pay it."

"Would you give me this promissory note?" asked Rabbi Israel.

"With the greatest of pleasure," replied Zalman. "It is just a worthless piece of paper."

Rabbi Israel took the note and tore it up. As they were speaking, one of Zalman's stable boys came rushing up and informed Zalman that the horse Nicolai had just dropped dead. Zalman could not believe this. "I saw him only this morning. He appeared to be in perfect condition. He was eating well. He was not ill. How could he die so suddenly and unexpectedly? What a mystery!"

"It is no mystery," Rabbi Israel informed him. "When the man who was indebted to you for one hundred rubles died, he was transformed into a horse to repay you the debt. For three years he served you faithfully. No task was too hard. He did all the work required of him. He has more than repaid you for the amount he owed you. By your giving me the promissory note and my tearing it up, his mission on earth was completed. His debt discharged, there was no further need for the horse to continue working for you, hence its sudden death."

— 24 —

Jonah, the Prophet

A very rich man by the name of Aaron lived near Medziborz. He was a fur merchant who regularly visited Leipzig in Germany and the fur fairs at Breslau. He bought many skins of lamb, mink, chinchilla, sable, and squirrel, which he made into garments for noble ladies. He also made coats lined with fur and fur hats for the cold winter days.

Aaron and his wife, Freidel, never were short of anything. They had been happily married for nearly ten years but had as yet no child. This was the only source of unhappiness for them. "Why do I work so hard and travel such long distances? What is the use of all my money if I have no son? Who will recite the mourner's prayer for me when I die? Who will be my heir?" grieved Aaron.

Freidel, too, very much longed for a child. She dearly loved children and was envious of her neighbors, who all had large families. She often played with their children, gave them sweets and chocolates, and bought them presents for their birthdays.

One day, Freidel suggested to her husband, "Why don't you go to see Rabbi Israel? He is a man of God, a known miracle-worker. People come long distances to see him, from Poland, from the Ukraine, and even from Prussia. We live so near him. Why don't you go to see the rabbi? What can you lose?"

Aaron was reluctant. He was of Lithuanian origin and was no follower of the new sect. He could not understand its ways. Freidel, however, continued in her pleas, and eventually Aaron went to see the rabbi.

Rabbi Israel's advice was, "You must change your profession. You must give up the fur trade."

"How will I earn a living?" replied the worried Aaron. "I have been a furrier all my life. I know no other trade. What will I do?"

"Lease an inn from Count Potozky. You will then be blessed with a son. Do let me know when he is born."

Aaron returned home, full of doubt. He had been told to give up the business with which he was familiar and to become a tenant of the count, who was known to be a Jew hater. No Jew was allowed to enter his lodge. He incited his fierce and furious dogs, Haman and Chmielnicki, to attack any Jew who ventured into his courtyard.

To Aaron's great surprise, the day after his return from his visit to Rabbi Israel, the manager of Count Potozky came to him and offered him the lease of an inn. Aaron accepted, and within a year his wife gave birth to a son, whom he named Reuben. Aaron forgot to inform Rabbi Israel of the birth.

Reuben was the apple of his parents' eyes. They satisfied his every whim. He became terribly spoiled. Nothing was too good for him. His every wish was immediately fulfilled. He became difficult to discipline. He could not concentrate on his studies, and no teacher could teach him. He made his teachers' lives miserable. He hid from them and played tricks on them. When the teacher was having a nap, he glued his beard to the desk and hid his snuffbox. He fought with and bullied his friends. Often he returned home bruised, with his clothes torn. His parents became very worried. He was nine years old but could hardly read or write. The neighbors complained about his rude behavior and called him "Esau." He made friends of the peasant boys and ran off to the forest for hours. His parents had longed for a child, and their wish had been fulfilled. But now Reuben gave them little pleasure. He was a constant source of worry and anxiety to them.

Aaron suddenly recalled that he had failed to notify Rabbi Israel when Reuben was born. He decided to do so now and to apologize to the rabbi for his lack of courtesy. He confided to the rabbi that he was no longer able to control his son and was helpless when it came to his education. "I feel so ashamed. What will become of him?"

Once again, Rabbi Israel was able to advise him. "Return to Leipzig and resume your former fur business. Stay away from home for a whole year, and your son will completely change his ways."

Aaron took the rabbi's advice and went to Leipzig, where he was welcomed by his former friends. He resumed the buying of furs and purchased a large consignment that had just arrived from Siberia. He loaded the furs onto a large wagon and set out to sell the skins in Vilna.

In the wintry weather, the coachman lost his way. As it was late on Friday afternoon, and as there was no sign of any human habitation,

Aaron worried as to where he would spend the Sabbath. At the commencement of the Sabbath, he descended from the wagon and began
walking in search of a place where he could spend the holy day. At long
last he saw a house in the distance. He summoned up his last strength to
get to it. To his great joy, he saw a *mezuzah* (small parchment on which
are inscribed two passages from Deuteronomy) by the front door and
Sabbath candles lit inside. He entered the house and found a ready
welcome. He was lavishly entertained by his host and almost felt a taste
of paradise.

After the termination of the Sabbath, Aaron's host said to him, "I am
looking for furs. I would like to buy your whole stock."

Aaron was only too pleased to sell him his wagonload of furs. Only
then did he ask for his host's name. "My name is Jonah. When you
return home, give my warm regards to Rabbi Israel."

His business had taken Aaron a whole year, and on his return home
he was pleasantly surprised to see the transformation of his son. In the
long absence of his father, Reuben had become subdued. He had helped
his mother run the inn. He had felt useful. There had been no one to
spoil him and no one to reprimand him. He had been given
responsibility and had acted in an adult way. Reuben was a changed
boy.

Aaron returned joyfully to Rabbi Israel, who asked him, "How is my
friend, the Prophet Jonah ben Amitai?"

25

The Opponent

In the city of Sharagrod lived three brothers: Issachar, Zevulun, and Gad. They were learned and pious and worked together in the family business. Issachar and Zevulun were devoted followers of Rabbi Israel. They often visited him in Medziborz and regularly spent the High Holy Days with him. Whenever Rabbi Israel visited Sharagrod, he would stay in the home of one of the brothers.

The youngest brother, Gad, unlike the others, studied in the rabbinical college of Vilna, and when he returned home he became a bitter opponent of Rabbi Israel. He continuously criticized the rabbi and mocked his followers. Their ways were strange to him.

The brothers were very close to one another and lived in great harmony. The only bone of contention between them was Rabbi Israel. Gad could not endure his brothers' admiration of the rabbi.

One day Rabbi Israel visited Sharagrod and stayed in the home of Zevulun, where he was made very comfortable. "How is your younger brother Gad?" the rabbi asked.

"Unfortunately, he is very ill," Zevulun informed him. "He was taken ill very suddenly. The doctor is worried and baffled. He cannot find the cause. Gad has no appetite and hardly takes any nourishment. He is confined to his bed, and all his strength seems to have gone from him. He is only thirty-nine years old and has a wife and nine children. We are all very worried about him."

"Would it be possible for me to spend the coming Sabbath in his house?" asked Rabbi Israel.

The brothers were taken by surprise at this strange request. Surely,

Rabbi Israel knew only too well that Gad was highly critical of him. Gad had never visited the rabbi and had always avoided him. Had Gad been well, he would never have allowed the rabbi even to enter his home, let alone spend the whole Sabbath there. Now, however, he was too ill to offer any opposition, nor was he fully aware of what was going on.

Rabbi Israel moved into Gad's house. He found the sick man listless and almost lifeless. He was unaware of what was going on around him. The rabbi's followers almost took over the house. An ark and a scroll of the law were brought over from the synagogue. The dining room was converted into a prayer room. People were coming in and out of the house to consult the rabbi.

Throughout the Sabbath, Rabbi Israel prayed with great fervor and devotion. He recited special psalms, and at the Reading of the Law offered a special prayer for Gad's speedy recovery. He even gave him the additional name *Chayim* ("Life"), for it is written in the Talmud that "a change of name is one of the things that cancels the fate of a man."

After the service, there was a slight improvement in Gad's condition. He indicated that he was very thirsty, and Rabbi Israel himself gave him some liquid. Gradually, almost miraculously, Gad improved. He whispered weakly to Rabbi Israel, "I now realize how wrong I was about you. You are truly a man of God. Please forgive me for opposing you. I was very foolish. I should have listened to my brothers. How can I ever thank you for all you have done?"

"Thanks are due to God, not to me," replied the rabbi. "He is the faithful Healer, and it is He who healeth the sick."

On his recovery, Gad became a devoted follower of Rabbi Israel, and the three brothers regularly visited the rabbi. "It is never too late to change one's mind. Better late than never," Rabbi Israel told them.

— 26 —

Measure for Measure

In Moldavia there lived a rich Jew by the name of Shahna. He owned not only a large farm but also a mill. Peasants from miles around would bring their grain to him to be ground. Some left their sacks of grain for days. They knew that Shahna and his wife, Frumah, were trustworthy and honest.

Frumah was a great help to Shahna. She worked very hard. She looked after the home, helped on the farm, and kept the business accounts. She was always busy and rested only on the Sabbath. One day she suddenly became ill and partially paralyzed. She was able to walk about slowly and she could speak, but she could not use her hands. She had to be dressed and even fed.

Shahna felt very sad. He could not bear to watch his wife's anguish. She was the mainstay of his life. He relied on her totally. The house, the farm, the business, all revolved around her. Suddenly, she had become completely dependent on others. He consulted the local doctor, who recommended a well-known physician in Vilna. He, too, could do nothing for her. She was given many drugs, and many ointments were applied, but there was no improvement. Her arms remained motionless.

One day Shahna heard of the miracles performed by Rabbi Israel. Shahna was told how the rabbi cured the sick, restored sight to the blind, and made the lame walk. He decided he would take Frumah to see Rabbi Israel.

"Help my wife, Rabbi! She means everything to me. She is so helpless now. Her life is full of suffering and hardly worth living. I am willing to do anything. I am ready to donate all my money to charity. I will help the poor, the orphan, the widow. Just help her recover, please!"

Rabbi Israel listened carefully to Shahna and asked him to remain in Medziborz for a while. Some days later, Rabbi Israel asked Shahna and his wife to accompany him on a journey. They traveled many miles and eventually stopped at an inn where they were made very comfortable.

After a hearty meal, Rabbi Israel asked the innkeeper to lock all the doors, close the shutters, and not allow anyone to enter. "If anyone knocks, do not open the door, but say that the inn is closed for the day."

The residence of the lord of the manor, Count Valentine Tolstoi, was some eight miles from the inn. He was a kindly man who treated his tenants fairly. He had no children of his own, and his heir was his brother Bogdan, a cruel and heartless man. Bogdan bore a grudge against the whole world, especially against his older brother, whom he disliked intensely. He regarded him as too weak in his handling of his tenants and looked forward to the day when he would succeed Valentine and extract as much as he could from the estate.

Bogdan was in league with the Haidamaks, a lawless band of robbers and cutthroats who devastated the countryside and terrorized the Jewish population. They killed and they maimed. No one, not even babies, was spared. Bogdan was one of the leaders of the Haidamaks, and Jews called him "Bogdan the Terrible." Bogdan saw little of his brother. They were very unalike and had little in common. Every meeting ended in a violent quarrel.

On the day of Rabbi Israel's arrival at the inn, Bogdan was paying one of his rare visits to his brother. He was very fond of drink and was hardly ever sober enough to walk. On this occasion he demanded, "Get me a horse! I want to go to the inn. I hear they sell good vodka." The count was only too pleased to get rid of his unwelcome visitor and eagerly supplied him with a horse.

Bogdan was so drunk that he lost his way to the inn. Meanwhile, the weather had changed. The sky had become overcast. Snow began to fall and turned to a blizzard. It was very cold. Bogdan had gone out for only a short ride and had not bothered to dress warmly. He was freezing. He was raging at the weather and his unfortunate loss of direction. With much endeavor and his last strength, he eventually reached the inn.

The inn had been closed on Rabbi Israel's instruction. Bogdan tried every door and every window. He knocked and he kicked the door, but everything was securely locked and bolted. The snow continued to fall. "Let me in!" Bogdan screamed through the locked door. "I am frozen stiff. I will die if you don't let me in!"

"I am very sorry," replied the innkeeper. "The inn is closed today by the express orders of Rabbi Israel."

"Who is this Rabbi Israel?" Bogdan demanded to know. "How dare he order you about? I will cut off his head as I did to the Rabbi of Uman!"

"Unbolt the door," Rabbi Israel advised the innkeeper, "and let him in."

The innkeeper did as he was told. Bogdan almost fell through the door. He was half-frozen. He had been exposed to the extreme cold for too long.

His limbs were frostbitten. He became violent. "Show me this Rabbi Israel and I will kill him here and now." He unsheathed his sword and lifted up his arm to strike down Rabbi Israel. He suddenly became rooted to the spot with his arm uplifted. He had lost all power of movement.

Rabbi Israel then turned to Frumah and told her, "Try to move your hands!"

To everybody's amazement, Frumah was able to move first her hands and then her arms. She was filled with joy.

"Help me!" cried Bogdan.

"I am sorry I cannot help you," said Rabbi Israel.

"Take pity on me!" repeated Bogdan.

"Did you show pity to the mothers and infants you killed and tortured mercilessly? Did you have compassion for any of the innocent people you butchered? They cried out to you for mercy. They begged you for pity. Now the Almighty has punished you. Frumah's illness has been transferred to you. You will remain paralyzed for the rest of your life. You will no longer be able to hurt or harm anyone."

Bogdan was taken back to the castle. For the rest of his life, he remained an invalid who could no longer inflict harm on the Jewish tenants on the estate.

27

The Frog

On one occasion when Rabbi Israel went for a long walk, he found himself outside the town in an unfamiliar area. There was no sign of life. There were no houses on the barren and rocky plateau where the soil was parched and dry. Few plants grew.

The long walk had made the rabbi hungry. He found a small stream. There he washed his hands and made the benediction: "Blessed are You, Lord of the Universe, who has sanctified us by Your commandments and has commanded us concerning the washing of the hands."

As Rabbi Israel sat there eating his snack, a large froglike creature suddenly appeared out of nowhere. It had remarkably well developed webs between its toes, which it used in hopping from place to place. Its nest was in the branches of a shrub that overhung the little stream. It had external gills and a long tail that it used for swimming. It had protruding eyes. It was catching and eating insects and worms. Its movements were sluggish. Its eyes had horizontal pupils. Rabbi Israel had never encountered such a large, almost man-sized frog.

To Rabbi Israel's surprise, the frog addressed him: "Holy rabbi, I am so happy to see you. I have been here so long that I had almost given up hope of ever seeing a human being, least of all a rabbi."

Rabbi Israel, who had been startled by the appearance of this creature, was now taken aback even more by being recognized by the frog, who continued his introduction: "My real name is Michael."

"How is it then," asked Rabbi Israel, "that you are now a frog?"

"This is my punishment. I used to be a very observant Jew. I was a timber merchant. I studied the Torah, and I observed all the commandments. I was called 'Michael the Pious.' One day I returned from the forest very tired. I had had a long, hard day on the Vistula, directing workers in the cutting down of trees and loading them onto large rafts. It was heavy work on an icy winter's day. When I returned home I was so hungry that I forgot to wash my hands and say the benediction for washing the hands before my meal. The rabbis rightly say, 'One transgression leads to another.' I started cheating my customers. I sold them unseasoned wood. I dismissed my foreman, Ozer, who had worked for me for twenty years. He had to go begging to feed his large family.

"My wife could not understand the change in me. Instead of spending my spare time in the House of Study, I spent it at the inn, playing cards and drinking vodka. I soon became known as 'Michael the Drunkard.' Our rabbi urged me to change my ways. He told me, 'Great is the power of repentance. Repent before it is too late.' His words fell on deaf ears. I took no notice. I went from bad to worse. I became hard and cruel. People who had known me from childhood thought a demon had entered into me. When I died, the heavenly court sentenced me to return to the world as a frog.''

"Why as a frog?" queried Rabbi Israel.

"A frog spends its life near water. As my first sin was to neglect washing my hands before eating, I was condemned to wallow in water for many years.''

Rabbi Israel's heart was full of pity for this sinful soul. "I wish I could help you," he remarked.

"You have already helped me," the frog assured him.

"I really have done nothing," replied Rabbi Israel.

"When I was condemned to become a frog," confided the erstwhile Michael, "I was confined to this uninhabited spot where no human being ever ventures and where no Jew ever utters a prayer. You were the first Jew to come here and say the benediction for washing the hands. By doing this, you have redeemed me. I have now been forgiven my sins, and my sufferings are at an end.''

Rabbi Israel noticed that the frog was now lying dead on the ground in front of him. Michael had returned to heaven.

—— 28 ——

The Rabbi and the Doctor

Rabbi Israel had become famous. Anyone in trouble would seek him out and be helped. The sick came to him in large numbers and found in him a natural healer. He dispensed herbs and lotions, of which he had learned during his sojourn in the Carpathian

Mountains. He also gave out amulets to keep away evil spirits. Above all, he gave his patients hope and confidence. He demanded no fees as the doctors did, and he never turned anyone away.

Rabbi Israel's medical activities aroused the hostility and enmity of the local medical practitioner, Dr. Krenk. He was a graduate of the famous medical schools of Paris and Padua. For many years he had sat at the feet of the great surgeons and physicians of Western Europe. Dr. Krenk was a very impatient man. The Jews regarded him as a nonbeliever and a heretic. He would visit the synagogue only on the High Holy Days. He wore European garments and went without a head covering. He spoke only French, Polish, or Russian and pretended not to understand Yiddish or Hebrew. He patronized the wealthy. Squires, counts, and Russian generals and officers were foremost among those seeking his help. He had no time for the poor, the old, and the needy. He treated them harshly. He screamed at them and often ignored them.

When Rabbi Israel settled in Medziborz, Dr. Krenk's practice began to decline. His waiting room was no longer crowded.

"Where are all the patients?" he would ask his wife, Mirabelle.

"Surely you know," she replied. "They all now go to Rabbi Israel. He is not concerned with fees. He helps everyone. The rich and the poor are all the same to him. His patients speak highly of him and say that he is able to perform miracles."

Dr. Krenk was fuming. "Who is this Rabbi Israel?" he screamed. "Where did he study medicine? Where did he get his formal training? Did he study diseases, their causes, frequency, treatment, and prevention? Did he graduate in Paris or Edinburgh?"

Dr. Krenk's anger knew no bounds. He grew even more provoked when he heard non-Jews tell him that Rabbi Israel made the blind see, the deaf hear, and the lame walk; that he had a special way with the insane and that he drove out demons. These reports infuriated Dr. Krenk. He called Rabbi Israel a witch doctor, a magician, a quack. He felt that Rabbi Israel should be burned at the stake. He vowed that he would kill the rabbi himself.

Although the two men had been living in the same locality for years, they somehow had never met. One day Leizer, a wealthy follower of Rabbi Israel, fell ill. Rabbi Israel prescribed an herbal remedy. As the patient showed no signs of recovery, Rabbi Israel tried another remedy on his next visit. When this did not have the desired effect, the family was concerned and called in Dr. Krenk. He carefully examined the patient and prescribed some medication.

"But I have already taken this medicine," protested Leizer.

"Who gave it to you?" inquired Dr. Krenk in astonishment.

"Rabbi Israel."

Dr. Krenk wrote out another prescription.

"I have already taken that, too," protested Leizer.

"Who gave it to you?"

"Rabbi Israel."

At that point Rabbi Israel entered the room, and for the first time the doctor met his great antagonist.

"Who taught you healing?" was Dr. Krenk's first inquiry.

"My knowledge," replied Rabbi Israel, "comes from the Almighty, who is the Faithful Healer. I am merely His messenger."

From that time onward, the doctor no longer abused Rabbi Israel, who had proved to him that medical knowledge does not originate from the medical academies of Edinburgh and Paris but from the Almighty Himself.

29

Heard Already

Rabbi Mendel was a poor Hebrew teacher in Medziborz. For twelve hours every day, from eight o'clock in the morning until eight o'clock in the evening, except on the Sabbath, he would teach his pupils *Mishnah* and Talmud. After a day's work, Mendel would spend hours in the House of Study, poring over the pages of the Talmud and its commentaries. He would daily immerse himself in the ritual bath, even in the winter when the water had turned to ice. He fasted twice a week, on Monday and on Thursday.

When Rabbi Israel settled in Medziborz, he made his home and Study House in the same street as Mendel's. Although he lived within a few yards of the rabbi's home, Mendel never visited him, nor did he become one of the rabbi's followers. Mendel, who had originally come from Lithuania, was strong willed and obstinate. He constantly heard stories of Rabbi Israel's manifold activities. He heard that Rabbi Israel drove out demons. He was told that the Prophet Ahiyah the Shilonite, who had lived during the reign of King Solomon and had foretold that Jeroboam would become king of Israel, would regularly reveal to Rabbi Israel the mysteries of the Torah. Mendel could hear the continuous comings and goings of wagons and chariots that brought followers from such places as Mezeritch, Berdichev, and Lublin. He saw invalids being brought on stretchers to be helped by the rabbi. On the Sabbath, he could clearly hear the songs and melodies coming from Rabbi Israel's house.

Mendel's wife, Blooma, very much wanted him to visit the rabbi. His friends urged him to follow her advice. But Mendel was not a man to change his mind.

One Friday night Mendel had a very vivid dream. He saw a vision of a beautiful palace set amidst gardens, orchards, and vineyards. He had never seen such a magnificent palace. It was far superior to the palace of Catherine the Great in St. Petersburg, which Mendel had visited some years ago. In his dream, Mendel approached the main gate, but it was firmly locked. He tried all the side entrances, but they, too, were closed. He walked around the building and looked through a window into a large room. There, he saw Rabbi Israel sitting at the head of a table surrounded by his followers. The Sabbath candles were burning, and on the table were many delectable Sabbath dishes. Though the windows were shut, Mendel clearly could hear the Sabbath table melodies. He then heard Rabbi Israel expounding on the weekly portion of the law. Mendel drank in every word. He had never heard such a wonderful exposition. It was so simple and true. He tried hard to memorize every single word.

When Mendel awoke, he could remember every detail of his dream: the palace, the gates, the room, the melodies. But one thing he could not recall. That was Rabbi Israel's talk, not one single word of it. He tried hard to remember, but in vain. Although Sabbath was always a day of joy for Mendel, this Sabbath brought him no joy. He was very troubled at not being able to recall one word of the rabbi's explanation.

Toward dusk, Rabbi Israel's beadle, Yomtov, came to Mendel's house and said, "Rabbi Israel invites you to the third Sabbath meal." This time, Mendel did not hesitate to follow the beadle. He entered for the first time the Study House of Rabbi Israel. There, the rabbi sat surrounded by his many disciples. Twilight had descended, and there was no artificial light in the room. Mystical melodies such as *Benei Hehalah* ("Members of the Sanctuary"), composed by the kabbalist Rabbi Yitzhak Luria of Safed, and *Yedid Nefesh* ("Beloved of the Soul"), a poem composed by Rabbi Eliezer Azikri of the sixteenth century, were being sung. Only pieces of *hallah* (loaves eaten on the Sabbath) and herring were being handed round. The sparse meal was supplemented by spiritual fare.

The room became silent when Rabbi Israel began to speak. He spoke very quietly, with his eyes closed. The words appeared to be coming from his heart. Mendel was listening intently to every syllable. This was the same talk he had heard in his dream the previous night. Soon three stars could be seen in the sky, signaling the end of the Sabbath.

"Mendel," Rabbi Israel addressed him, "why were you listening so closely to every word I said, when you had already heard it in your dream last night?"

At this Mendel realized how foolish had been his antagonism toward Rabbi Israel. From that day onward, he became one of Rabbi Israel's most devoted followers.

—— *30* ——

Trust in God

Simhah was a publican. He was a simple man, not learned but known for his great faith in God. His Hebrew name, Simhah, means joy, and he was a happy and contented man. He worked hard, but never complained. He was happy in his lot. He was a devoted follower of Rabbi Israel.

Simhah was overjoyed when Rabbi Israel and his disciples paid him a visit one Monday, which also happened to be the day of the new moon, the beginning of the Hebrew month, which Rabbi Israel regarded as a festive day. Simhah regarded it a great honor and privilege that the rabbi stayed in his house, especially on that particular day. He prepared a special banquet in his honor. During the festive meal, Rabbi Israel asked his host, "Tell me, Simhah, how much rent do you pay for the inn?"

"One thousand rubles a year," replied Simhah.

"Do you pay it weekly, monthly, or yearly?" inquired Rabbi Israel.

"I have to pay it all once a year."

"When is it due?" asked Rabbi Israel.

"It is due next Friday at twelve o'clock. Squire Natowski does not tolerate any delay. He expects the prompt payment of the rent. He is very unbending. Woe betide anyone who fails to pay him promptly. Five months ago my neighbor Mordecai Tzvi was unable to pay his rent. The squire was merciless. He would not wait one day. He threw Mordecai Tzvi into the dungeon, where he still remains. The pleas of his wife and children did not move the squire. He is heartless and devoid of pity. He loves only his two dogs, Titus and Nero. Nothing is too good for them. But he hates people, especially the Jewish tenants who cannot pay their rents promptly."

"Have you the money ready to meet your obligations?" asked Rabbi Israel.

"No, rabbi," replied Simhah. "This year has been an exceptionally bad year. There was little rain, and the harvest was poor. The peasants had no money to spend. I gave them food on credit, which they have not yet been able to repay. The Haidamaks have once again been ravaging the countryside. It was dangerous to be on the roads. Life has been very hard, and I do not have a single ruble at the moment. But I have faith. God will not desert me! 'The Guardian of Israel neither slumbers nor sleeps.'"

On Tuesday morning, Rabbi Israel decided to stay on at the inn for the rest of the week. The days passed quickly. Although the rent had to be paid by Friday morning, Simhah betrayed no anxiety. He behaved as though he had not a worry in the world. He spent his time looking after his guests and taking food to the dungeon for his neighbor Mordecai Tzvi.

On Thursday morning, Roman, the squire's agent, came to the inn to remind Simhah that payment was due the next day.

"Tell the squire not to worry. I still have a full day. Much can happen in a day. God's bounty is great."

Early on Friday morning, the agent, Roman, came again to the inn to remind Simhah that the day for payment had arrived. "Unless you settle your debt today, you will share the fate of your neighbor Mordecai Tzvi. I have orders to take you to the dungeon."

"It is only 8:00 A.M. I have until midday," Simhah assured him. "Why do you worry me unnecessarily? Tell the squire I will pay him, as I have done for the last twenty years. I have never failed him so far."

When Roman left, Rabbi Israel said to Simhah, "You have only four hours left. You still have not even one ruble in your possession. Where will you get such a large sum in a few hours?"

"I am a simple man," said Simhah. "I am not learned, but I trust in God. He will not let me down."

For the next four hours Rabbi Israel was full of anxiety. His heart went out to Simhah. What was to become of his wife and eight children if he were put in the dungeon? He had been so hospitable and did not deserve that fate.

Simhah, however, betrayed no anxiety. He carried out his usual tasks, bringing in logs for the fire and preparing the food for the Sabbath.

At ten minutes to twelve, with only ten minutes to go, a noise was heard in the yard, the sound of rattling wheels. A wagon had stopped, and three merchants entered the inn. They were well dressed and gave the appearance of wealth and prosperity.

Simhah welcomed them and asked, "What can I do for you? Do you wish to spend the Sabbath here?"

"What can you do for us?" replied one of the merchants. "We really need your help. We are timber merchants from Danzig and have been negotiating the purchase of his large forest with your landlord, Natowski. We have made him a very generous offer, but he has not yet agreed. There is great competition for the forest from merchants in Breslau. If you could use your influence with Natowski, we would give you a considerable sum of money for your help."

"I am always happy to help fellow Jews. I will certainly speak not only to Natowski but also to his agent, Roman, who will soon be here. But first I need one thousand rubles to pay my debt."

The merchants gladly handed him the money. At the stroke of twelve the squire's agent, Roman, entered the inn to tell Simhah that his time was up. He had the keys to the dungeon ready.

"I am so glad to see you," Simhah greeted him. "Let us go together to Count Natowski. I have the money ready for him."

The squire welcomed Simhah's prompt payment of the rent. He had just returned from a very successful hunt. His dogs had done him proud. He readily agreed to grant the merchants the timber concession. "If they are as prompt and reliable as you, I have no need to hesitate."

When Rabbi Israel took leave of Simhah, the rabbi congratulated him. "I am so pleased to have been here for the last five days. You have been a most genial host, and you have taught me and my disciples the true meaning of faith in God."

—— *31* ——

A Sweet Singer

Akiba, one of Rabbi Israel's followers, had an only son Benjy. They lived in a cottage many miles from the town. Akiba was a peddler and was away from home all week, selling household goods, kerchiefs, rings, and watches to the peasants. He wanted Benjy to have a good Jewish education. He did not want him to be brought up among the unlettered peasants. He could not afford to engage a private tutor, and the nearest synagogue was many miles away. Akiba approached Rabbi Israel for advice.

"How can I bring up my son to be a God-fearing Jew?"

Rabbi Israel offered to look after Benjy. Akiba was delighted. Benjy went to live in Rabbi Israel's home and was treated as one of the family. He was taught by the same tutor as were Rabbi Israel's children, Tzvi and Adel. The children played together happily. Benjy was not scholarly, but he was blessed with a beautiful singing voice. He had a natural gift, and once he heard a melody, he never forgot it. Everyone enjoyed hearing Benjy singing the Sabbath table hymns. At the termination of the Sabbath, he would intone the melodies "Elijah the Prophet" and "God of Abraham, Isaac, and Jacob." Rabbi Israel would listen to Benjy's songs and tell his followers that only the power of song can unlock the gates of the highest heaven.

One day, Benjy accompanied Rabbi Israel on a long journey. They stopped at an inn for rest and refreshment. The inn was crowded with peasants; there was hardly an empty seat. Benjy was sitting in a corner and humming one of his favorite melodies. Facing him sat a tall man with a black patch over his right eye and a crooked nose. He carried two revolvers and a long sword. He was a giant of a man with the look of a fierce robber. He caught hold of Benjy, almost holding him in the palm of his hand, and said to him, "You sweet little singer. Sing for me! I love your melody!"

Benjy was terrified. He loved to sing in Rabbi Israel's house. But this was not where he felt at home. The tall man frightened him. The man could easily have squashed him. Benjy looked to the rabbi for help and guidance. Rabbi Israel spoke quietly to him, "Do not be afraid, Benjy. Sing for him!"

Benjy's spirit revived, and he began to sing his favorite shepherd's song:

Rose, rose, how far you are,
Forest, forest, how vast you are.
Would that the rose were not so far,
And the forest not so vast.

All noise in the inn had stopped. Everyone was listening attentively to the sweet melody of the child. The tall man was touched. He took off a ring and presented it to Benjy. Benjy cherished the ring and always wore it on his finger.

The years passed. Benjy had grown up and married. He became a merchant and traveled regularly to Lodz, the Polish textile center, to buy fabrics from the mills. One day, on the return journey, he was attacked by armed robbers. They took away all his possessions, and after stripping him of his clothes, decided to hang him from the nearest tree. They pulled him toward the tree and put a noose around his neck. The robbers asked him what his last wish was and promised to grant it. Benjy asked to be allowed to sing his favorite melody. His wish was granted, and he sang his song.

"Rose, rose, how far you are." His voice was charged with emotion. He was thinking of his wife, Ethel, and his young children, of his old father, Akiba, and of Rabbi Israel, whom he regarded as his second father. How he would miss them all! His melodious voice resounded through the forest. All the brigands stopped to listen. His voice dominated them. The cook stopped cooking and the others stopped eating. They were all listening to his lovely voice. The leader of the brigands, too, heard the song. He came out of his tent and saw Benjy with the rope around his neck.

"Are you the little boy who sang for me at an inn many years ago?" he asked Benjy.

"It was me. You even rewarded me by giving me a ring, which I am still wearing," Benjy told him.

The chief brigand recognized the ring. He was happy to release Benjy. He restored all his possessions and accompanied him to the nearest town.

Benjy was delighted to return home and be reunited with his family. On being told the story of Benjy's adventure, Rabbi Israel remarked, "Great, indeed, is the power of song!"

—— 32 ——

The Importance of Charity

One day when Rabbi Israel was on his travels, he stopped at the humble home of one of his followers. Pinhas was a small shopkeeper who sold butter, eggs, and cheese. He worked hard but made a very poor living. He paid an annual rental of eighteen rubles for his store.

Pinhas was delighted to welcome Rabbi Israel. He greatly venerated the rabbi. Pinhas prepared the rabbi a meal of bread, butter, and cheese. He could not afford to buy either meat or fish.

On the day of his departure, Rabbi Israel said to Pinhas, "I urgently need eighteen rubles. It is for a very worthy cause, and it is a matter of life and death. I want to redeem an elderly Jewish captive who has been languishing in prison for nearly a year. He is now very sick, and unless he is set free, he will die of a fever."

Pinhas had no money in his possession, but he could not refuse the rabbi. He sold his horse and cart. He went to the pawnshop and pledged his gold watch, which had belonged to his late father, and his wife's silver candlesticks, which had been a wedding present from her parents. All together, he realized the eighteen rubles, which he handed to Rabbi Israel before the rabbi left.

Time soon passed. At the end of the year, Pinhas did not have enough money to pay the rent. There was nothing left to pawn. He was evicted from the store and moved to a nearby village. With the help of relatives and a few friends, he bought a cow whose milk he sold to the peasants and his neighbors. He struggled hard to make a meager living.

When the squire's cows became sick and gave no milk, his servant went to the village to buy from Pinhas some milk for the household. The squire was delighted with the milk. He had never tasted such rich and well-flavored milk. He called Pinhas and expressed his delight to him. "Your milk pleases me very much. It has a wonderful flavor. From now on you will be our only supplier of all the butter, cheese, and dairy products we need in our establishment."

Pinhas was pleased. He acquired several more cows and began employing workers to help him in the making of cheese and butter. His reputation spread, and people came long distances to buy from him. They knew they could rely on him to provide high-quality, fresh dairy products.

Pinhas prospered and expanded. He raised chickens and sold their eggs. He bought a piece of land and built an inn where weary travelers found a warm welcome. He bought a distillery and produced whiskey to sell at the inn. He became wealthy and was able to redeem the pledges from the pawnbroker.

One day, Rabbi Israel came by, and again he stayed with Pinhas. Pinhas was very happy to see the rabbi and entertained him lavishly. "Had I not given you the eighteen rubles last year, I would still be struggling to make ends meet," he joyfully told Rabbi Israel.

"By giving me the eighteen rubles, you performed a great religious deed. You saved a fellow Jew from certain death. So great is the power of charity that it bestows blessings upon him who gives!"

—— 33 ——

A Tenth Man

Rabbi Israel was once again on his travels. It was raining heavily. Alexis, his faithful coachman, was doing his best. The weather was against him. The horses were tired and weary. Alexis was helpless. He knew he could go no farther. Rabbi Israel realized Alexis' predicament. It was midday on the eve of the Day of Atonement. It would now be impossible to reach the nearest town in time for the holy day. Reluctantly, the rabbi decided to remain in the village for the Day of Atonement.

He stopped at a small inn and inquired of the landlord, Zelig, "Will there be a quorum of ten males for the service tonight on this night of nights?"

"Certainly," replied Zelig. "Now that you have arrived, we shall have nine, and Uri, who lives only one mile away, will be coming as he has done for the last few years. He is very reliable."

Rabbi Israel prepared himself for the holy day. He donned a snowy white robe, which is called a *kittel*. The dining room of the inn was converted into a place of prayer. Candles were lit, and the nine Jews, covered in their prayer shawls, assembled. But there was no sign of Uri. Just as the festival was about to commence, a woman arrived. She was Uri's wife. She informed the gathering that her husband had met with an accident. He had broken his leg, and it was, therefore, impossible for him to get to the village.

"What shall we do?" asked Rabbi Israel. "We need another Jew to make up the quorum. Is there any other Jew living in this area?"

Zelig informed him, "There is one. He is the local squire, Sorrel. He is an apostate. He used to be a peddler, selling his goods to the villagers. The widow of the former squire fell in love with him. Her outstanding beauty dazzled the peddler, and he converted to Christianity to marry her and become the squire. Some two years ago the woman fell off her horse and died within days. Since that time he has been living all alone in the manor house, which he rarely leaves. No one ever sees him. He has become a recluse and an eccentric."

Rabbi Israel listened intently. "He is a Jew. The rabbis say, 'A Jew, though he commits a sin, remains a Jew.' I am going to ask him to join us on this most solemn day of the year."

"Please, Rabbi," Zelig entreated him. "Do not endanger your life. His dogs are fierce and attack all strangers. People are terrified to approach the manor."

Rabbi Israel was not to be dissuaded. Straightaway, he left for the lodge. His first encounter was with the fierce dogs. To everyone's amazement, the dogs were docile and did not even bark at his approach. Sorrel left his room and addressed Rabbi Israel: "What can I do for you?"

The squire had not been to the village for a long time. It had been several years since he had seen a Jew. Rabbi Israel reminded Sorrel of his own father, who had been a devout Hebrew scholar with a long beard and sidelocks. "Tonight is the eve of the Day of Atonement. We are nine, and we need you to join us to make up the quorum. The doors of heaven are wide open tonight. The scholarly and the unschooled, the saint and the sinner, all have equal access to God. In fact, it is believed that the truly repentant can reach a higher level than those who, never tempted, have never sinned."

Almost docilely, the squire followed Rabbi Israel to the prayer hall. There he was given a prayer shawl and a festival prayer book. The ark was opened. A scroll of the law was taken out and carried reverently around the prayer hall. Rabbi Israel intoned the traditional words: "By the authority of the court on high and by the authority of the court below, with the divine consent and with the consent of this congregation, we hereby announce that it is permitted to pray with those who have transgressed."

All the next day the squire remained standing by the ark. Images of his pious father, Enoch, and his learned grandfather Zalkind came to him. He recalled how much the Day of Atonement had meant to them. He recalled how much grief and sorrow his conversion had caused his family, how they had cried out to their Heavenly Father. They had mourned him for seven days and had torn their garments as if he were dead.

The climax of the holy day, the *Ne'ilah* service, the service of the closing of the gates of heaven, had arrived. The ark containing the Torah scrolls was opened and remained open throughout the final hour of the day of prayer, the last opportunity for prayer and repentance. The sun went down. The long day waned. Together, with one voice, the worshipers uttered the affirmation of God's unity: "*Shema Yisrael, Adonai Eloheinu, Adonai Ehad*"—"Hear O Israel, the Lord our God, the Lord is One!" The Jews chanted the responses their ancestors had made during ceremonies in the ancient Temple: "Blessed be the name of His glorious kingdom forever and ever!" Rabbi Israel repeated seven times the words the Israelites had uttered when the Prophet Elijah confounded the worshipers of Baal on Mount Carmel: "The Lord He is God."

Squire Sorrel, by now weak from fasting and prayer, cried with them, "The Lord He is God!" He fell to the floor as the *shofar* rang out loud and clear that the day of "joyful weeping" was over. His soul had departed.

Rabbi Israel said of him, "He was a true penitent. His repentance has been accepted. He has returned to the fold."

34

The Wedding

One Wednesday morning, Rabbi Israel and three of his disciples set out on a mysterious journey. "We shall spend the Sabbath in Berlin," announced Rabbi Israel quietly. The disciples looked at one another in surprise. They knew that Berlin was hundreds of miles away. It was a journey that would take at least ten days. The students were, however, too well trained to ask questions. They knew that Rabbi Israel could work wonders.

That evening they stopped at an inn where they spent the following day. The rabbi seemed in no particular hurry. It was not until late on Thursday evening that they continued their journey. Then, with lightning speed, they flew through the night. As dawn broke, they entered Berlin. Quickly, they made their way to the Jewish quarter. There, a terrible scene met their shocked gaze.

The streets were filled with weeping men and women, wedding guests whose enjoyment had turned to grief. A wedding had been arranged for Friday. The guests had arrived. The feast was ready. The wedding canopy had been erected, and the musicians stood with their instruments poised to make merry music. Then, suddenly, there was tragedy. The beautiful young bride had collapsed and, moments later, died.

"Take me to the bride," ordered Rabbi Israel. Quickly, the people led the rabbi to the house of mourning and to the sorrowing parents. The dead girl was their only child, the light of their eyes. Rabbi Israel lost no time. "Take the bride to the cemetery and place her in a grave," he commanded. "Hold her wedding gown in readiness. Set up the canopy by the graveside and assemble the wedding guests."

His orders were obeyed without argument. The bride was placed gently in the open grave. The canopy was set up nearby, and those who had come to celebrate now stood about in tears. Rabbi Israel gazed intently upon the bride. All held their breath as they watched. Then, in the presence of them all, a miracle took place. The bride stirred and opened her eyes. Loving hands lifted the maiden out of the ditch and dressed her in her bridal gown. The rabbi himself conducted the wedding ceremony and blessed the revived bride and her rejoicing groom.

At the banquet that followed, the bride told of her unearthly experience. "My new husband was married before. His dead wife was a dear friend of mine. I was very fond of her and of her children. She was ill for a long time, and I went every day to look after the household and feed the little ones. One day, the sick woman called me to her bedside and said, 'I know that I am going to die. I want you to promise solemnly that you will not marry my husband.' I was very young then and never considered that I might one day wish to marry him. Besides, the important thing was to comfort and to soothe the sick woman. So I promised. Soon afterward, she died.

"Some years went by, and my heart went out to the neglected children and the lonely widower. My love for the living was stronger than my promise to the dead. I became betrothed to him. On the morning of the wedding, the spirit of my friend came to me. She summoned me to appear before the heavenly court. There I stood, alone and frightened, accused of breaking my promise. I was guilty, and I had no defense. Then Rabbi Israel became my advocate. He pleaded for me so eloquently, so passionately, that the heavenly court acquitted me and allowed me to return to earth."

—— 35 ——

The Magician

From time to time Rabbi Israel and his disciples visited the home of Velvel, one of his devoted followers. Velvel was always happy to welcome Rabbi Israel. Once when Rabbi Israel arrived, the place was filled with bustle and excitement. Servants were rushing to and fro, busily preparing for a banquet. But the host stood among them in a daze, sorrow stamped upon his brow. Moved by his distress, Rabbi Israel asked him what troubled him, and the man was only too ready to unburden his heavy heart.

"My wife has given birth to a son," he said, "and tomorrow the child will enter the Covenant of Abraham. It should be a day of great rejoicing, but I am filled with dread. I tremble for the life of the child. I have already lost two children, infant sons, who died when they were eight days old. I wish this third infant had never been born," wept the anguished father. "My wife will not survive another bereavement."

Everything was ready for the circumcision. A special chair for the Prophet Elijah was prepared. Thirteen candles corresponding with the thirteen times the word *covenant* (*brit*) occurs in the biblical chapter dealing with circumcision, were lit. All of Velvel's relatives and friends had arrived. A festive meal was being prepared. But would they be able to enjoy it? Would the baby survive the night?

Rabbi Israel grew grave. He realized that the baby was indeed in great danger. "Please, do not worry, and tell your wife to stop worrying!" Rabbi Israel assured Velvel. "We will save your baby. Tomorrow the circumcision will take place. No harm will come to him. You will both live to see his *bar mitzvah*, his wedding, and his good deeds."

Rabbi Israel prepared for battle. He placed an amulet containing a protective text at the head of the bed of the nursing mother and her infant. It contained twelve simple letters, the sign of the zodiac, the months of the year, and the words *Shaddai Kera Satan* ("the Almighty annuls the design of the Satan [and protects the baby against the designs of the demon Lilith]").

He placed two of his disciples near the cradle and charged them to watch diligently over the child and to make certain no harm befell it. To their surprise, the rabbi gave them a sack and told them to hold it open by the side of the cradle. Should anything fall into this sack, the disciples were to close it securely and to send for him immediately. "Be very diligent," the rabbi enjoined them. "Remember, a human life lies in your hands. Do not fall asleep, even for one second! Tonight is *Wachnacht* ("a night of watching"). The Satan is striving to harm the child in order to prevent the religious rite of circumcision from taking place."

Faithfully, the disciples kept vigil all through the long, dark hours.

They did not relax for one instant. They recited verses from the Book of Psalms, especially Psalm 91: "You shall not fear the terror of the night, nor the arrow that flieth by day nor the pestilence that stalketh in darkness." Though the windows were closed, the candles in the room flickered, and some even blew out. The disciples continued their watch and the recitation of the Psalms.

They heard eerie noises and saw many frightening shapes during the night. Then, just before dawn, they heard a soft, low hiss. Like a thief in the night, a huge black cat, its great eyes green with evil, made its way stealthily to the cradle of the sleeping baby. When it was about one foot away, the creature crouched and sprang. But the trap was well laid. Instead of reaching the cradle, the cat landed in the sack.

The disciples were startled; they had hardly expected this. Certainly, they had never dreamed they would spend so many hours only to catch a cat. Still, Rabbi Israel's instructions were clear. Though the cat fought madly, the men quickly tied up the sack and held it firmly. Rabbi Israel was summoned, and when he came he carried a big, strong stick. With this stick, the rabbi gave the cat a sound beating. For this was no harmless household pet. This was a magician in league with the devil and the demons.

In the morning, to the parents' delight, the baby was found to be well. Rabbi Israel and his disciples participated in the festive meal following the circumcision. A messenger then arrived from the lodge. The Squire Konstantinovich demanded that Rabbi Israel come to see him immediately.

"Please, Rabbi, do not go!" Velvel begged him. "He is a renowned magician. He dabbles in witchcraft and black magic. He casts spells. He befriends spirits. He can walk over fire without being burned. He practices ritual murder. He can foretell future occurrences, such as earthquakes, floods, and fires. He is a great menace!"

Rabbi Israel was unafraid. "I am not afraid of his magic and his witchcraft. I will go to see him, as he requests."

When the rabbi arrived at the lodge, he was taken to see Squire Konstantinovich. The squire was lying on his bed. His face was bruised, his body was battered, his ribs were broken, his eyes were swollen. He was covered with bandages. He was moaning and groaning. "How you beat me last night!" he cried. "You took me unawares," conceded the squire. "I was totally unprepared for your assault. You are a greater magician than I. You must be using abracadabra charms."

"I am no sorcerer. I do not practice magic or the black arts. I believe in God and carry out His commandments. I had no desire to kill you but merely to put an end to your murderous designs. If you promise me you will no longer use your evil powers to harm the innocent, God will forgive you and you will recover your health. Know that the power of good is mightier than the power of evil," declared Rabbi Israel.

The squire was forced to acknowledge the greater power of God. He faithfully promised Rabbi Israel to turn over a new leaf and to be particularly kind to the tenants on his estate.

——— 36 ———

A Performing Bear

The Jewish community of Medziborz was worried. Three weeks before the festival of Passover a nine-year-old boy, John, disappeared. John was no stranger in the Jewish quarter. He would fetch firewood from the forest. He would act as *Shabbat Goy* (do jobs that were not permitted to Jews on the Sabbath) and help out as a stable boy in Rabbi Israel's house.

After John's sudden disappearance, his family and friends searched for him in the forest and by the river, but there was no trace of him.

The rumor soon spread that the Jews had killed him and were using his blood in the preparation of *matzot* (unleavened bread) for the festival. This baseless accusation was known as *blood libel* and was the cause of much Jewish persecution throughout the ages. The Jews of Medziborz soon discovered that it was the chief of police, Martov, who was spreading the rumor. Martov was unhappy about the large number of Jews who were settling in the area, and the disappearance of John gave him a heaven-sent opportunity to get rid of them.

"He was last seen at the house of Shlomoh Zalman, the Jewish ritual slaughterer," Martov told John's parents. "He must have been killed there."

On the Sabbath before Passover, known as the "Great Sabbath," a large number of Jews turned up at the synagogue of Rabbi Israel to listen to his customary talmudical discourse. To everyone's surprise, Rabbi Israel got up from his seat, removed his prayer shawl, and walked out of the synagogue. A number of his congregation followed him. They found him standing outside the home of the chief of police, watching a gypsy making a bear perform tricks. The large brown bear rose up on his hind legs and did all sorts of antics, to the delight of the onlookers. The gypsy threw a large ball into the air and the bear caught it. He hummed a tune and the bear danced to it. Almost the whole town, including the chief of police, stood watching this performance. Suddenly, the bear stopped acting and rushed into Martov's house. It began sniffing and moving a rug. This revealed a door leading to a cellar. The bear then continued down the stairs into the cellar and emerged carrying a large and heavy sack. When the sack was ripped open, the murdered boy John lay revealed.

The peasants were outraged. They set the house of Martov on fire while he escaped through a back door. He was later caught and killed by the boy's family.

Meanwhile, Rabbi Israel had, returned to the synagogue. "Now I can safely commence my discourse. The bear has saved us from a great calamity. The Almighty employs many messengers to save the House of Israel."

——— 37 ———

Two Socks on One Foot

Many years ago, a wicked man called Abuyah lived in Constantinople. There was no sin that Abuyah had not committed. He hardened his heart against the cry of the poor and the oppressed. He even dealt in human cargo with slave traders. Manacled together, without food or water, the helpless captives were carried across the sea to a life of bitter servitude. Abuyah often heard their groans, but there was no pity in his heart. The battered, overloaded vessels were at the mercy of the storms, and in many instances, the wretched slaves perished in the cruel seas.

The fame of Rabbi Israel had by then reached even the city of Constantinople. Abuyah visited Rabbi Israel, with startling results. It was as if the rabbi had given him a new soul. Abuyah no longer dealt with the slave traders. Instead, he became a friend of the slaves. He frequently ransomed them, took them home, and fed and clothed them. Rested and restored, the rescued slaves would be sent safely back to their families. The more Abuyah did, the more he wanted to do to help his fellowman. The sins he had committed lay heavily upon him, and he wanted to atone in full. Every year he visited Rabbi Israel, who guided him in the paths of righteousness.

Abuyah had no children. He longed desperately for a son. On one of his visits to the rabbi, he confided, "Rabbi, you are my spiritual father. You have shown me the error of my ways. You have brought me to repentance and have caused me to change my sinful way of life. If only I had a child, my most heartfelt desire would be realized!"

The master had pity on him. "Abuyah, your wife will give birth to a son before long," he promised. "But remember to come and see me on the very same day he is born."

Abuyah was very happy indeed when Rabbi Israel's words came true and his wife gave birth to a son, whom he called Benjamin.

At once, Abuyah made his way to Medziborz to tell the rabbi his good news. He was full of thanks to God and deeply grateful to the rabbi. He found it strange that Rabbi Israel did not share his happiness. The rabbi remained silent, deep in thought. At last he spoke. "Abuyah, I see a black cloud hovering above you. On the day your son reaches his thirteenth birthday, he will drown. You have not fully atoned for the agony you caused the helpless slaves. Many of them were drowned, and the souls are crying out for revenge."

Abuyah was very frightened. "Rabbi," he pleaded fearfully, "help me! You prayed for me before, and your prayers were heard. A son was granted to me. Do not allow me to be deprived of my newly found happiness!" Rabbi Israel was very moved. "On no account are you to allow your son to go near the water on the day of his thirteenth birthday. In case you forget this warning, I will give you a sign. The day on which you put two socks on one foot will be the day of mortal danger to your boy."

Abuyah returned home. His son, Benjamin, grew into a fine lad. He was handsome and fearless. He was also a good student. Learning came easily to him. He was good at sports and learned to swim at an early age.

Even when the water was icy, young Benjamin loved to splash about in it with his playmates.

The years passed quickly and the day of Benjamin's thirteenth birthday, his *bar mitzvah*, drew near. This was the day he would become a full-fledged member of the House of Israel. The boy and his parents eagerly looked forward to the great day.

The day arrived at last. It was hot, humid, and sunny. Benjamin longed for a cooling dip in the sea. He dressed quickly and ran down to the shore.

Benjamin's father, too, rose early. There were preparations to be made for the ceremony and the banquet. Many guests were expected. Abuyah began to dress hurriedly. But somehow he fumbled, and everything seemed to take twice the usual time. Finally, he could not find his second sock. He searched on the bed and under the bed. He ransacked the room, and still he could not find it. He summoned his servant. "Where is my sock?" he demanded. "Who took my sock?" The servant stared at him in amazement. "Why, sir," he stammered, "you are wearing two socks on one foot!"

Suddenly, Rabbi Israel's warning came vividly to Abuyah's mind. He recalled the solemn words the rabbi had uttered thirteen years ago. "On the day when you put two socks on one foot," Rabbi Israel had said, "your son will be in mortal danger."

"Where is Benjamin?" cried his frantic father in a voice of anguish. "He has gone down to the shore for a swim," replied the astonished servant. Abuyah knew that this was the moment when his son's life was in danger. He rushed down to the sea and caught his son just as he was about to dive into the cool waters.

"Come home," he commanded, keeping a grip of iron on his son. Benjamin protested vehemently. "I am so hot, Father! Please let me swim awhile. Just to cool down!" His father ignored Benjamin's entreaties. Benjamin had never seen him so determined and unyielding. In spite of his weeping and pleading, he was taken home and locked in his room. His father remained firm in his decision and stood guard outside Benjamin's room the whole day. Only when night came did Abuyah unlock the door and lovingly release the boy. The danger had passed, and Benjamin's life had been saved.

To the end of his days, Abuyah worked for the poor and helped the needy. He always remembered with a grateful heart that he had been rescued by Rabbi Israel, who had guided him from being a sinner into the paths of mercy and loving-kindness.

---- **38** ----

An Evil Decree

At one time a man arose who brought misery and misfortune upon the Jews of Poland. His name was Jacob Frank, and his followers were known as Frankists. Calling himself a messiah, this false prophet hurled vile accusations at the rabbis and the holy law. It came as no surprise when this man who had so wickedly abused the Jewish faith became a Roman Catholic and continued to persecute the Jews even more viciously. Publicly, he declared that the Talmud contained heresies, and the enemies of the Jews were only too pleased to believe him. They decreed that all copies of the Talmud be burned in public.

This evil edict came as a crushing blow to the Jewish people. A Jewish home always had a volume of the Talmud, and it was the ambition of every Jewish family to possess a complete set of these bulky tomes. For the Talmud is the lifeblood of the Jews, and it is studied by both rabbis and laymen. In its pages Jews find laws and legends, commandments and customs. In its pages Jews have found hope and comfort in the darkest days of persecution. Even little children are inspired by the adventures and the stories of the sages. At the age of seven or eight, boys are introduced to the Talmud and "learn to swim in the sea of the Talmud."

The decree of "Burn the Talmud" came just before the High Holy Days. The Jews were desperate and tried by every means within their power to make Bishop Dembovski of Kamenetz-Podolsk change his mind. They sent delegations. They begged, cried, pleaded. It was no use. Like Pharaoh, Bishop Dembovski hardened his heart and turned a deaf ear to their agonized pleading. With heavy hearts, the Jews gathered in their synagogues and prayed with bitter tears to their Father in heaven. Prayer was their secret weapon. It had never failed them in the past, and they hoped earnestly that it might save them this time.

Rabbi Israel realized that the Jews could not survive without the Talmud. He had spent his whole life warring for the House of Israel, and he had never had a worthier cause. The Jews looked upon him as their heavenly pleader, and he resolved not to fail them.

The Day of Atonement brought large crowds to Medziborz. Rabbi Israel's followers left their homes, their shops, their farms, and assembled around him. The master was delighted to see his people. A general is powerless without his army, and a rabbi, too, needs supporters to strengthen him in his struggles and to fight by his side.

There was an air of expectancy in the synagogue. The evil decree hung like a black thundercloud over the congregation. The soldiers were already breaking into Jewish homes and removing the holy books. Cartloads of books were already making their way to bonfires at Kamenetz-Podolsk. The decrees of Bishop Dembovski were immutable and could not be altered. Yet the people believed their revered rabbi could and would intercede for them. He was their only hope.

Rabbi Israel stood near the reader. All through the service he swayed in tense, silent paroxysms of ecstasy and anguish. Even those who had been with him many years had never witnessed such devotion. For twenty-four hours, without a pause, Rabbi Israel communed with God in the presence of the people. When the reader came to the phrase, "Open the gates of heaven," Rabbi Israel repeated it again and again. Suddenly there was silence. Rabbi Israel's eyes were closed. Although he stood among his disciples and followers in Medziborz, his soul had risen into the highest heaven. The reader's voice was hushed. The service was halted. The worshipers were terror stricken. There were often unusual incidents in Rabbi Israel's synagogue, but never had there been such a feeling of suspense. Like prisoners in the dock awaiting sentence, the congregation stood, all eyes on the motionless rabbi. Time seemed to stand still, and two hours passed before Rabbi Israel emerged from his trancelike state.

Then, to everyone's relief, the master opened his eyes. "Open the gates of heaven!" cried the reader once again. "Open the gates of heaven!" repeated Rabbi Israel in a strong, confident voice. The worshipers felt in their hearts that the battle had been won and that the gates of heaven were indeed open.

After the Day of Atonement, Rabbi Israel shed the sadness that had clothed him like a garment, and this change was reflected in the people. Tears and fears gave way to songs and dances. Then Rabbi Israel gathered his faithful disciples around him and told them the story of his great adventure.

"It was the fault of Satan, the evil one, the accusing angel. He is our enemy, the enemy of everything that is good and noble. He wanted to destroy the Talmud, the holy law that is our inspiration. He realized we could not live without the teachings of the rabbis and the traditions handed down through so many centuries. Without the sacred Talmud, our body would grow faint and our soul would languish. So the evil one planted the wicked idea in the mind of Bishop Dembovski and the evil decree was declared. Then Satan managed to close the gates of heaven and lock them so securely that none of our prayers could enter. In vain we pleaded. However earnestly we prayed, our prayers could not rise before the great and merciful Judge. That is why the decree was not lifted, even though we cried to our Father in heaven on the holy New Year, all through the Ten Days of Penitence and on the Day of Atonement itself. I felt that my prayers were not reaching their high destination. There seemed to be an iron wall between me and the Creator. I could not understand this, and a feeling of desolation came over me.

"Then the reader reached the prayer, 'Open the gates of heaven,' and at that moment I saw the light. It came to me like a flash that there was some barrier at the very gates of heaven. This obstacle stood in our way and was the cause of all our misery. I went up into the heavenly sphere and I looked at the gates. They were indeed locked and barred. No one, nothing, could get through. Having found the cause, I was determined also to find the cure. I examined the gates again. They were massive and strong. Why, the lock alone was almost as big as the city of Medziborz. There was nothing I could do to force open the great gates. I refused to give up, for the holy Talmud was in danger, so I went farther into holy high heavens.

"I sought out my heavenly teacher, the Prophet Ahiyah of Shiloh, and pleaded for his intervention. He was anxious to help, but he, too, was powerless to unlock the gates. I grew desperate. It was getting late. Time was running short. The Day of Atonement was nearly over. 'Do not despair,' said the prophet. 'Have you already forgotten the words of the rabbis: "Even when the murderer's sword hangs over his neck, even then a man should not give up hope." Come, let us together petition the Messiah. He may be able to save us.'

"Quickly we made our way to the court of the anointed Savior of Israel. I was granted an audience, and I poured out my unhappy heart. I told him of the troubles of his people, of their sufferings and their struggles, of the enemies who attacked them from within and the enemies who attacked them from without. And to crown it all, I cried with passion, 'As if the cup of bitterness were not already full, Bishop Dembovski of Kamenetz-Podolsk is about to burn the holy Talmud, the delight of our soul. The children of Israel beat their breasts and weep and pray, but their prayers have not been heard. The gates of heaven have been barred against them and our entreaties cannot rise before the Almighty. O Savior of Israel, the Lord's anointed, help your unworthy servant to help your unhappy people.'

"The Messiah was filled with sorrow and wept many bitter tears when he heard of the misfortunes that had afflicted his beloved children. He was determined to rescue them. He gave me two Hebrew letters, mystical letters fraught with secret power. With these two letters anything was possible and miracles could be performed. With my new knowledge of the divine secrets, I shattered the unbreakable locks. The gates of heaven opened wider than they had ever opened. The prayers of the people of Israel rushed in, a great torrent of tears and entreaties, a stream of love and devotion and sincerity. At once, our loving Father in heaven granted the wishes of His children. The evil decree was annulled, and the Talmud was saved. Then Satan retired from the scene, thwarted and sullen. And I returned to earth, my dear disciples, tired but triumphant. The battle was over and the victory ours!"

39

Deserves a Child

In the little town of Tulchin there lived an orphan, Bezalel. His parents had been murdered by the cossacks, and the community looked after him. He was a very attentive pupil but no scholar. He could barely read his prayers. He was apprenticed to a blacksmith, for whom he worked very hard. When the blacksmith died, Bezalel took over the workshop. As he was very skilled, both nobles and peasants used his services.

Bezalel had married Shifrah, another orphan, who had worked as a servant in Tulchin. They were very happy and worked hard. They would have been the happiest couple in the world, if only they had had a baby. They were still childless after ten years of marriage.

After a hard day's work, still black from the smithy, Bezalel would spend some time in the House of Study, where he enjoyed listening to the talmudical discussions of the scholars.

Melech was Bezalel's best friend. Bezalel had often stayed in Melech's house as a young boy and had been treated like one of their own children by Melech's parents. They all grew up together and loved one another. When Melech married, he moved to a neighboring town. He had a little boy called David, who was chubby and good looking and loved by all.

Melech leased a plot of land from the priest Dimitri Andreievitch, a Jew hater. Every Sunday morning he incited his congregation against the Jews. He told them that the Jews had killed their founder and that they still killed Christian children and used their blood for the preparation of unleavened bread for Passover.

One year, Melech experienced financial difficulties. There had been a cholera epidemic and many people had died. There was a drought. Every drop of water had to be brought from a neighboring village. Melech could not pay his rent. This was an opportunity Priest Dimitri Andreievitch could not miss. He took young David hostage and told Melech, "Unless you pay your debt within the next seven days, I will have David baptized."

David was taken to live in the priest's house and forced to eat nonkosher food. When he refused, the priest beat him. Melech was desperate. He needed two hundred rubles to save his beloved son from the clutches of the priest. But who could lend him such a large sum? Unless the money was paid, David would be baptized. His last hope was his friend Bezalel. Bezalel was not a rich man; he had no cash at his disposal. But to help his friend, he sold his house and workshop to raise the money with which to redeem young David. To survive, Bezalel became a peddler, traveling through the countryside, selling small goods to the peasants. The thought that he had saved David kept him going.

When Rabbi Israel heard of Bezalel's self-sacrifice, he was very moved. "Surely," he said, "Bezalel and his wife deserve a child of their own!" And he prayed to the Almighty on their behalf.

The following year Shifrah gave birth to a son, whom they named Jonathan. Their happiness was now complete.

40

One Sin Leads to Another

Rabbi Israel was once walking with his disciples on the outskirts of Medziborz. When he was young, he had enjoyed roaming the countryside, and this feeling for nature never left him. To walk with Rabbi Israel was an education. He knew the language of the animals and the birds. He knew by name the flowers of the field and the healing properties of the herbs.

As they walked, the rabbi spoke to his disciples of the dangers of sin. "One sin leads to another," he said. Then they spotted a wagon being driven toward them. Rabbi Israel left his disciples and approached the driver, with whom he spoke very earnestly for a while. Then the rabbi returned to his companions, and they continued their walk.

Rabbi Israel's action puzzled the young men. What had been the object of the conversation? What did the rabbi tell the stranger? Who was the stranger? A sage in disguise? The Prophet Elijah? Or maybe one of the thirty-six secret saints for whose sake the world exists?

Later on, one of the disciples, Rabbi David, followed the wagon and pressed the coachman to tell him what had transpired. The coachman was pleased to tell his story.

"I am neither a rabbi nor a scholar. I am Sholem, and I live in Vitebsk. My best friend is my neighbor Shiyah. For generations, a strong bond of friendship has existed between his family and mine. Shiyah and I are about the same age. We attended the same school and now attend the same synagogue. We have no secrets from each other. We share our joys and our sorrows. We spend every free moment together, and we are almost inseparable. We are always in and out of each other's homes. In twenty years, not a cross word ever passed between us. Our friendship was as pure as it was unselfish and as cloudless as a summer's day. The townspeople nicknamed us 'David and Jonathan.'

"Shiyah and I are both married. I own a small village store, and Shiyah became a peddler. He would travel from village to village selling his wares—kerchiefs and trinkets, soap and children's wear—to the peasants. Often he would stay away for several weeks at a time. The local shopkeepers, the baker, the butcher, and the grocer always sold to Shiyah's wife on credit. When he came back he would pay his debts, buy new stock, leave money for his family, and go on his travels again. I missed him very much and always looked forward to his homecoming.

"Often I helped Shiyah's wife and family in his absence. I lent them money and food and was happy to be of service to them. The day of his return was always a holiday for me. We went on long walks and had talks together. I loved listening to his stories of his adventures.

"On one occasion Shiyah stayed away for nearly three months. He had never been away so long. His wife and children and all his friends were filled with anxiety. Naturally, I helped them out with money and food. We were overjoyed when at last Shiyah returned safely. His journey had been very successful. He had sold all his merchandise and brought back nearly three hundred rubles.

"On the following day he invited me and some other friends to a special party. He told us of his many adventures in distant places. It was a very happy occasion, and we enjoyed our reunion. His wife brought cakes and wine. We ate and drank and made merry. Late at night my friend, tired after the long journey, fell asleep, and I took my leave. Just as I was leaving, I noticed a small brown leather bag, bulging with money, lying on a small table by the door. 'How careless and trusting Shiyah is!' I exclaimed. 'Imagine, leaving such a big sum of money exposed! I had better take it home for safekeeping and return it to him in the morning.' So I took the bag away with me.

"In the morning, I was rudely awakened. My wife rushed in with terrible news. 'A calamity has befallen Shiyah,' she cried. 'Somebody has stolen his money!'

"Shiyah's wife and children were searching for the money everywhere. I was going to tell her that I had taken the money into my safekeeping and was about to return it to the rightful owner. I opened my mouth but somehow I could not utter a word. Quickly, I got dressed and rushed over to my friend. He had aged overnight. I hardly recognized him. All the gaiety had gone out of him.

" 'Woe is me!' he wept. 'What shall I do? All my money is gone! How will I pay my debts? How will I live? For three months I suffered misery and hardship. Is this my reward?' My heart went out to him. I wanted to confess to him. I wanted to return the money, but somehow I felt ashamed, and I did not have the courage to admit my guilt. I was afraid that people would not believe me. They would misunderstand my motives and brand me a thief. So I held my peace.

"Shiyah suffered terribly. The whole town soon knew of the loss. Creditors besieged him with threats and pressing demands. They even accused him of fraud. 'It is only a fairy tale,' they said. 'He has made up the story of the stolen money in order to avoid paying his debts.'

"The local rabbi was consulted. On the Sabbath, before the Reading of the Law, the rabbi appealed to the community to help Shiyah and appealed to the thief to return the stolen bag. I found it harder and harder to confess. I could not even bring myself to tell my wife about it. I felt utterly ashamed. I could not sleep at night. I did not know what to do. My conscience was troubling me. How could I have harmed my best friend?

"Shiyah had no money to purchase new stock. No one would give him credit. Starvation stared him in the face. Who would trust him now? How would he be able to provide for his family?

"I was so distressed that I decided to leave the town. I was sure that no one suspected me. When I reached Medziborz, I stopped for a while. Rabbi Israel came toward me. He greeted me with these words: 'Sholem, Sholem! There is an eye that seeth all things! How could you commit such a terrible crime? To steal from your best friend! Must you continue in your wickedness? You have already caused enough trouble for your friend and his family. Go back and return the money! I know that Shiyah, who is kindhearted, will forgive you. No harm will come to you. If you repent and restore the money, God, too, will forgive you. Great is the power of repentance.'

" 'But Rabbi,' I protested, 'no one will believe me. They will call me a thief.'

" 'Fear not,' Rabbi Israel reassured me. 'If the people refuse to believe you, I myself will come and testify for you. I know that your motive was good. There is no evil in you.' I felt as if a heavy load had been lifted from my back. I now realized that my secret was no longer a secret. Rabbi Israel gave me new courage and new strength. 'Return the money immediately, and you will be forgiven. It is never too late to repent.'

"I am now going to return the money to my friend."

The disciples nodded their heads sagely. Now they understood why Rabbi Israel had said, "One sin leads to another."

—— 41 ——

A Sorrowful Sabbath

Rabbi Israel loved to take his disciples on long drives, and the disciples loved to travel with him. Accompanying the master was always an adventure. One day Rabbi Israel, accompanied by three of his disciples, set out on a long journey, so long that the disciples

thought it would never end. The horses were as usual under the control
of the experienced coachman, Alexis. With lightning speed they passed
towns and villages, woods and fields. They were caught in the middle
of a blizzard, and the roads became wet and slippery. Rabbi Israel was
deeply submerged in thought and did not guide them. Alexis lost his
way, and it was well past midday on a Friday in the winter when they
found themselves too far away to reach town before the commencement of the Sabbath.

The carriage halted outside a small inn, in distant and unfamiliar
countryside. The weary travelers alighted and sought shelter at the inn.
They knocked. A man dressed in rabbit skins opened the door and
asked them abruptly, "What do you want?" The innkeeper was surly
and unfriendly. He had never heard of Rabbi Israel or his great deeds.
He spoke rudely to the master and his disciples and refused to let them
enter. It was late Friday afternoon, nearly time to light the Sabbath
candles. It was too late to look for other lodgings. Earnestly, the
disciples pleaded with the innkeeper and begged to be allowed to stay
the Sabbath. The innkeeper listened, unmoved, to their entreaties, and
only when all four of them were in despair did he grudgingly consent to
let them in.

"Why do you pick me?" asked the man angrily. "We are poor folk.
We cannot accommodate so many people. We cannot entertain you in
the manner to which you are accustomed. I do not know your ways.
You probably take a long time praying. I pray quickly. I eat quickly. If
you want to stay here, you will have to follow my ways."

Rabbi Israel did not reply. They had no alternative but to accept the
man's conditions. They entered the house. The rooms were bare. There
was hardly any furniture. They could see no tangible preparations
being made for the Sabbath.

"Is there a pool here, or a stream where we could immerse ourselves
in honor of the Sabbath?" the rabbi asked.

Once again he received a curt and abrupt reply: "Did I invite you to my house? Did I send for you? Why did you come? What else would you like? I do not welcome visitors, especially those who make so many demands."

What a Sabbath that was! It was a terrible ordeal. The innkeeper gabbled the evening service, which the rabbi loved to recite slowly, dwelling meaningfully on every word. The innkeeper would not allow them to sing any of their melodies. "I am hungry," he announced. "I have not eaten the whole day."

The table was a plank of wood. There was no wine for *Kiddush*. The innkeeper cut up a large black bread and gave a piece to each of the travelers. He then gave them some lukewarm lentil soup and a plate of potatoes. He piled his own plate so high that there was little left for his guests. Once again, he would not let them sing any Sabbath table melodies. "The candles will soon go out," he warned them, "there is no time to waste!"

All the while, the innkeeper abused his chief guest and heaped insults upon him. The disciples saw with grief the misery of their master. The glory had departed from him, but he accepted the insults with resignation, neither protesting nor complaining. Never before had the disciples endured so melancholy a Sabbath.

There were no beds. The innkeeper gave each one a bundle of straw, and they made themselves as comfortable as they could on the bare floor. The fire in the stove soon went out, and the room became bitterly cold. They spent a most uncomfortable and almost sleepless night.

The host awoke them early. "No time to waste," he told them. He recited the morning service very quickly, as fast as lightning. There was no quorum, so they could not read from the Scriptures. For their lunch he gave them a dish made of beans, onions, carrots, and potatoes, which had not been cooked properly. As they were famished, they ate this with relish.

All were relieved when three stars could be seen in the heavens to show that the Sabbath had terminated. But their sufferings were not yet over. The innkeeper, who had been so reluctant to let them in, was now even more reluctant to let them go. "The horses are lame," he said on Sunday. "The carriage is broken and is being repaired," he said on Monday. He raised so many objections and put so many obstacles in their way that they were forced to remain in his house for another three days. Only on the fourth day did the hard-hearted peasant permit them to depart.

As they stood on the threshold ready to leave, the mistress of the house suddenly appeared. They had not seen her throughout their days at the inn, as she had stayed in a back room. She approached Rabbi Israel.

"Honored Rabbi, do you recognize me? My name is Feige. Many years ago I came as a little orphan girl to your house and became a servant to your wife. I was very young and careless. One Sabbath I broke a valuable dish. Your wife lost her temper. She scolded me. She called me awkward and clumsy. She even pushed me away. I had no one to speak for me and to take my part. You sat there at the table in the same room, but you did not raise your voice to protect me. I wept and cried out to the Almighty God, the Father of all orphans. My cry pierced the heavens. God took my part. It was decreed in the heavenly court that in punishment for your silence, you should forfeit your share in the World to Come."

As if they had been turned into stone, the rabbi and his disciples stood motionless, scarcely breathing.

Then the woman's lips curved in a sweet smile and her eyes were filled with gladness. "I grew up and left your service and married. My husband is not the coarse peasant he seems to be. In truth he is a saint and a sage. When he realized the evil fate that was in store for you, he prayed night and day, without pause, for the annulment of the terrible decree. His prayers were answered. He was told that the only way to save you was to cause you misery for a single Sabbath. For this reason, he grieved and abused you and pretended to be rude and inhospitable.

He is really a kind and considerate person. You have suffered much, but better one Sabbath of suffering than an eternity of anguish.''

Rabbi Israel agreed with her. He had atoned for his transgression, and once more heavenly peace reigned in his heart and shone from his brow.

—— *42* ——

The Messiah

Jews believe with heart and soul in the coming of the Messiah, the Redeemer. In the darkest days of persecution, they have found comfort and strength in the hope that the Messiah may come at any moment to deliver them from their enemies and to begin an era of peace and plenty for all mankind. In the days of the Messiah, all the nations of the world will be united and all nature will be in harmony. The prophets painted glowing pictures of the time when "the wolf shall dwell with the lamb and the leopard shall lie down with the kid; and the calf and the young lion and the fatling together." Jews have always prayed for the Messiah. Every day saints and sages strove by fasting and self-denial to hasten his coming.

Rabbi Israel loved his people dearly. He could not bear to see their sufferings. Passionately, he prayed for the coming of the Redeemer, and his disciples joined in his prayers for the speedy redemption of Israel. Among his disciples, one man stood out above all the others. He was Rabbi David Firkes, a scholar and a sage. He had many great qualities, but his finest possession was his voice. When Rabbi David prayed, he poured out his whole heart before the Heavenly Maker in tones that emanated from his soul. The voice of Rabbi David had great power—the power to move men to repentance and angels to tears.

One day, Rabbi David stood before the reader's desk and his mind was sorely troubled. Jewish people were being attacked on all sides. Their lives were bitter and their anguish almost beyond endurance. Every day brought new tales of woe. Massacre followed massacre. As Rabbi David thought of all the suffering of his people, he became convinced that only the Messiah himself could save them. He felt that he had a unique opportunity for bringing about the coming of the Promised One. While he would pray before the master and the whole community on the Day of Atonement, he would seize the chance, and he would pray with such fire and such passion that the Almighty would listen to him and permit the Messiah to come down to earth.

Rabbi David prepared himself very carefully. He fasted regularly. He purified his mind and his body. He engrossed himself in the study of the sacred book of the *Zohar* and the works of mysticism. At midnight, he would rise from his couch and lament the destruction of Zion and the exile of the Divine Presence. Anxiously, he counted the hours to the day of the great trial.

The Day of Atonement arrived. The synagogue was crowded. The whole community was assembled. All the disciples were there, and Rabbi Israel stood in his accustomed place. As the people waited in awed silence, the voice of Rabbi Israel rang through the synagogue. "Who will officiate at the reader's desk?" asked Rabbi Israel in a challenging voice.

A tremor of amazement ran through the synagogue. What kind of question was this? For years, Rabbi David had been their favorite reader. There was no one who could possibly take his place. To Rabbi David himself, Rabbi Israel's words sounded like a death sentence. He was dressed in a white garment and stood ready to mount the platform. But again Rabbi Israel asked, "Who will chant the service for us today?"

David's face was whiter than his garments. Instinctively, the devout congregation realized that they were the spectators of a drama beyond their understanding. The long moments of silence seemed like hours to the people assembled. Then Rabbi Israel himself broke the silence. He turned to Rabbi David and said, "If there is no one else, let Rabbi David officiate!"

Humbled and ashamed, Rabbi David began to intone the service. But his heart overflowed with fear, and there was pain rather than passion in his voice. This was no mighty advocate who would storm the gates of heaven. It was all the unhappy man could do to concentrate on the service.

When the fast day ended, Rabbi David entered the master's room. "Tell me, my teacher," he entreated, "what fault have you found in me? Why did you shame me before the whole congregation? Did I not prepare myself carefully? Did I not fast and pray with all my heart and soul?"

"Dear Rabbi David, my beloved son," replied Rabbi Israel. "I have found no fault in you. You are very dear to my heart. Yet you wanted to hasten the coming of the Messiah, and that would be against the will of God. In order to save you from divine displeasure, I was forced to humble you. It was that very note of suffering and uncertainty that crept into your voice and into your prayers that saved you, my son. You were guarded from sinning against God in your attempt to disturb His well-laid plan. Be comforted, my dear David. You shall continue to be my reader on the Day of Atonement. You shall be the messenger who transmits our continuing prayers to our Father in heaven."

43

True Love

Rabbi Israel's house was a place of refuge. It was open to all, and anyone in trouble went straight to the master. Some sought the rabbi's advice on their money problems, others complained of harsh overlords, some came because there was illness in the family and begged him to pray for a quick recovery. People asked for help, for guidance, and for a blessing. And they all left his presence comforted.

One woman came to Rabbi Israel again and again. She prayed for a son with all her heart and soul. Although the years passed and her prayers were not answered, the woman refused to give up hope, and one day her faith was rewarded. Rabbi Israel said to her, "Next year a child will be born to you."

And so it came to pass. A new life began for the happy mother. She devoted all her energies to bringing up her son, determined to give him the best of everything. When the child was five years old, she brought him to Rabbi Israel and, like Hannah in the Bible, dedicated her son to the service of God.

The boy grew up in Rabbi Israel's house, and the master loved him as if he were his own son. The boy was a brilliant student and was endowed with a noble character and a princely bearing. Many of Rabbi Israel's disciples looked with favor upon the youth and wanted him as a husband for their daughters. But the rabbi declined all offers. Instead, to everyone's surprise, he chose for the boy a poor young girl, the daughter of a humble villager. The rabbi himself arranged the wedding. He provided the bride's dowry and invited all to a fine wedding feast. Rabbi Israel officiated at the wedding. At the festive meal he related the following story.

"Many years ago there lived a powerful ruler. His country was large and prosperous. He was a mighty warrior and emerged victorious from every battle. His word was law, and his command was obeyed without question. But power brought him no happiness. He wanted a son and heir to the throne, and this was the one thing that power and wealth could not obtain for him. Neither ministers nor magicians could comfort the anxious king, although they knew he would willingly give up half his kingdom to the man who helped him realize his dearest wish. Then one day one of the ministers came to the king with a wicked plan.

" 'Your majesty,' he said, groveling before the king, 'in your kingdom there are many Jews. They have a God who is mighty and most powerful, an unseen God who works great wonders. This unseen God listens to the prayers of the Jews. Force the Jews to pray for you. Pass a decree forbidding them to practice their faith until a son is born to you. Then they will entreat their God to have mercy upon them, and He may well hearken to their prayers.'

"Willingly, the king agreed and passed the evil decree. The Jews were extremely troubled. Only at the cost of their lives could they observe the Sabbath or study the holy law. A great cry went up to heaven. One of the saints was so moved by the sufferings of the innocent people that he volunteered to return to earth to end the troubles of the House of Israel.

"A year passed and a son was born to the king. The ruler's joy knew no bounds. Celebrations were held throughout the land. In the palace, courtiers feasted and caroused for many days. The royal father was happy once more and again took an interest in his great kingdom. But he forgot all about the Jews and the undeserved punishment he had imposed upon them. The cruel decree against them was not canceled, and the birth of the prince made little difference to their sufferings. They were still forbidden to observe their religion. They still had to meet in dark places to hold their services. Though they managed to conceal their faith outwardly, secretly they continued to fulfill the Jewish law in every detail.

"The prince grew into a fine, handsome lad. He was intelligent and had a great passion for knowledge. He soon grew tired of his teachers, who could not keep up with him. They could neither satisfy his curiosity nor appease his love of learning. So the king searched his kingdom for new teachers for his son. One day he heard of a sage who was renowned for his scholarship. The monarch invited him to live in the royal palace and to supervise the prince's education.

"The king's invitation was accepted on one condition: the teacher requested one hour of freedom each day, an hour in which he would be at liberty to do exactly as he wished, unwatched and undisturbed. This wish being granted, the sage came to live at the palace and soon won the confidence of the young prince.

"All day long they studied together, and for the first time in his life the lad felt both respect and affection for his tutor. For the first time, he felt that he was really advancing the acquisition of the knowledge his soul craved.

"Every day, for one hour only, the sage left the prince, shut himself in his room, and permitted no one to intrude or to interrupt his solitude. The boy's curiosity was aroused. When one day he hid himself in his tutor's room, he beheld a strange scene. He saw his tutor wrapping himself in a big white shawl and winding black cords with little black boxes around his left arm and around his head. He then closed his eyes and swayed to and fro, muttering strange-sounding musical tunes. The prince was too awed to interrupt.

"Later, he confessed what he had done and begged for an explanation. His tutor explained that he was a Jew and that he prayed to the great God of Jews, the God of all mankind, the one and only God. A new world now revealed itself to the prince. The more he heard of this God, the more he wanted to know about Him. In Judaism, he found the answer to his prayers. He begged his teacher to help him become a true Jew. So master and pupil fled the palace together and took refuge in a faraway country. There, the prince learned to be a true Jew. He entered a rabbinical college and became its finest pupil.

"In due course, the prince married the daughter of the head of the college, and the young couple lived together very happily. This happiness, unfortunately, did not last. The prince began to grieve over his wasted youth as a pagan. He died when he was barely twenty years old, and his young wife, brokenhearted, died soon after.

"It was decreed in heaven that the two lovers should be reborn and enjoy a long life with all the happiness they deserved.

"That is why," concluded Rabbi Israel, looking lovingly at the young couple, "I rejoice at this union of two souls. My children, experience all the joy and happiness of which you were deprived in your first lives!"

—— 44 ——

Act of Faith

In Rabbi Israel's hometown, Medziborz, there lived one of his most devoted disciples, Rabbi Wolf of Kitzes. While other disciples had scattered to far corners of the country, Wolf could not bear the thought of leaving the rabbi. He had received many tempting invitations to distant communities but had declined them all. Rabbi Israel's house was his second home, and to be near the rabbi was his greatest joy.

Rabbi Wolf was a fine scholar, but he was very poor. His most precious possession was his only child, his daughter, Esther. Esther, a beautiful girl, was betrothed to a very diligent student at the rabbinical college at Brody. His name was Hillel. Rabbi Wolf was well satisfied with his future son-in-law, who knew one thousand pages of the Talmud by heart. He knew that Hillel was a worthy husband for his beloved daughter, and he rejoiced at the prospect of her being happily settled in a home of her own. She was a good, obedient daughter, and he was sure that she would make a loving and dutiful wife.

Yet the date of the wedding could not be fixed. Rabbi Wolf simply did not have any money. He could not afford to give the promised dowry of three hundred rubles. He did not even have the money for the wedding dress, let alone for the wedding banquet. Nor could he provide a home for his scholarly son-in-law. Rabbi Wolf grew very sad. Every day his wife, Leah, anxious for her daughter's sake, harassed him with reproaches and questions. "You spend the entire day with Rabbi Israel. Why does he not do something for you? He helps strangers. Surely he could help you too. The children have been engaged for nine months now. It is high time the wedding date was fixed. How long must we wait?" Thus the woman worried, and Rabbi Wolf listened with pain but made no reply.

Then one day Rabbi Israel said to him, "Rabbi Wolf, the festival of Passover is approaching. When is your daughter, Esther, getting married? Have you decided on the happy day?" In this way Rabbi Israel gave his faithful disciple an opening to unburden his heart. Rabbi Wolf thought of his wife's daily nagging and of his daughter, waiting so patiently and trustingly.

"Oh, Rabbi," he wept, "I am in great trouble. I have no money. How can I fix the wedding? I need at least five hundred rubles to cover expenses. I have to settle the dowry, to buy a home, and to provide a banquet. Where am I to find this money?"

"Rabbi Wolf, Rabbi Wolf!" Rabbi Israel answered reproachfully.

"Have you lost faith in God? Is He not able to provide you with all your needs? Is the hand of the Lord powerless to help you? Are you, my dear disciple, of so little faith?"

Rabbi Wolf remained silent. He knew that he deserved this rebuke.

"Wolf," continued Rabbi Israel, "let the wedding take place on the thirty-third day of the *Omer*, on Lag b'Omer, the scholars' feast."

At once, Rabbi Wolf began to make the preparations. He sent invitations to all his colleagues and to all the students of the talmudical college in Brody. Esther ordered her wedding dress, and arrangements were made for the wedding feast. But as the days passed, Rabbi Wolf grew more and more anxious.

On the day before the wedding, Wolf was still penniless. Where would he get the money to pay for the dress, the festive food, the musicians? He felt like a thief. He pictured the creditors descending on him, demanding payment he could not make, and his honest soul quivered at the thought. He plucked up courage and approached the master. Rabbi Israel greeted him warmly. "Calm yourself, Wolf! I know that tomorrow is the happy day. Is everything prepared? Your daughter is a very fortunate girl. Great things are in store for Hillel, her husband-to-be!"

"But Rabbi," murmured Wolf fearfully, "how can I go through with it? Tomorrow everyone will want to be paid. How can I face them all? Only a miracle can save me now!"

Rabbi Israel remained unruffled. "Surely you have not given up hope?" he inquired. "The Lord never fails those who trust in Him!"

Rabbi Wolf returned home. The house was filled with excitement. Leah was busy with elaborate preparations, and Esther was trying on her wedding dress. Only Rabbi Wolf felt no real joy. How could he raise the dowry within twenty-four hours? He knew only too well that Isaac, the bridegroom's father, was a hard man. He was scrupulously honest, and his word was his bond. Isaac always kept his promises, and he expected others to do so too.

Rabbi Wolf rose early on the morning of the wedding and set out for Rabbi Israel's house. On the way there he was accosted by a stranger, a man who seemed greatly distressed. "Can you please help me?" he asked. "I have been traveling all through the night from Kossov to see Rabbi Israel. My daughter, my only daughter, is very ill. The doctors have abandoned all hope. Please take me to Rabbi Israel! I have heard so much about him. He is my only hope now. He and he alone can save my child!" Hastily, Rabbi Wolf conducted the man to the master.

Rabbi Israel welcomed the stranger, and before the man could utter a word, the rabbi held up his hand. "First," he commanded, "I want you to listen to this story.

"There was once a wealthy timber merchant who was very successful in his business. Every year he took his timber to Prussia, where his regular customers paid him promptly. One year he was exceptionally lucky. He sold his entire stock at the great profit of forty thousand rubles. Well satisfied, he bought fine presents for his wife and only daughter and set out on the homeward journey. His driver, Ivan, drove with great speed through deserted countryside and dense forests. The merchant, being tired, fell fast asleep. Suddenly, he woke up with a jolt. The coach had stopped. Ivan, his trusted driver, stood over him with an ax in his hand. 'Your money or your life!' he demanded. The merchant saw murder and greed in the peasant's eyes. Here was a chance to come into the possession of forty thousand rubles—an absolute fortune! For such a sum there was nothing the peasant would not do! The merchant handed over the money without protest. However, Ivan was not satisfied. 'I cannot let you go,' he snarled. 'If I spare your life, you will inform against me. I shall be arrested and sent to Siberia. I have no choice—I must kill you!'

"The merchant realized that he was in grave danger. Desperately, he prayed to God. 'If you deliver me from this danger and enable me to return to my home in peace, I will, in gratitude, devote one-tenth of my money to charity.' With all his strength, he cried out for help. Then something wonderful happened. Horses' hooves were heard galloping toward them. It was the forest police. They were approaching fast. The terrified robber took to his heels with the police in pursuit. They soon caught up with him, and the merchant returned home safely. He prospered greatly, but he quickly forgot his vow."

"Oh, Rabbi," cried the stranger, rising from his seat. "I am that sinful merchant. It was I who was thoughtless and forgetful. But I will fulfill my vow now! I will devote one-tenth of my wealth to the poor. All my life from now on, I shall be charitable and openhanded. But honored Rabbi, pray for my daughter! Save my only child!"

Rabbi Israel was overjoyed at these words. "Give five hundred rubles to Rabbi Wolf," he commanded. "His only daughter is getting married today. The Mishnah tells us that 'dowering the bride' is a *mitzvah* that profits a man both in this world and in the next. Go in peace, stranger. Your daughter is already feeling better and will soon be restored to perfect health."

Rabbi Wolf's worries were over. Never had Medziborz seen so magnificent a wedding. The whole town joined in the festivities. Esther looked like a queen, and the groom glowed with holy joy. But no one was as happy as Rabbi Israel and his disciple Wolf. They sang and they danced until dawn. Then Rabbi Israel took Wolf by the hand and said to him, "Now know, my dear friend, that a man must never give up hope. Have courage! Have hope! Trust in God with all your heart, and all will be well with you!"

—— *45* ——

The Inheritance of My Fathers

In the town of Zloczov, where the famous Rabbi Yehiel Michael resided, lived a man called Joseph. He was a hardworking and honest bookkeeper and lived in a quaint old house that had been owned by his family for many generations. The house was surrounded by a very large plot of land, and Joseph and his two sons spent every spare moment growing vegetables, tending the fruit trees, and caring for the shrubs and plants. They were very successful gardeners and managed to produce enough fruit and vegetables to feed the family throughout the year. Every Friday, before *Shabbat*, Joseph took round some of his produce to the rabbi's house.

All his adult life Joseph had worked for two brothers, Asher and Dan, who were importers and exporters of cloth and textiles. They often traveled to Lodz, Danzig, and Breslau, leaving Joseph in charge of the large warehouse. Deliveries arrived daily, and Joseph recorded every item in large ledgers. The two brothers greatly relied on his conscientiousness and his honesty.

Joseph was a devout follower of Rabbi Yehiel Michael and listened rapturously to the rabbi's discourses and tuneful melodies every *Shabbat*.

One day after his employers, Asher and Dan, had returned from a successful business trip, they summoned Joseph to their office. "Joseph," the elder brother, Asher, said, "we have decided that we need to extend our houses and enlarge our gardens. Now, as your house is situated between our two homes, it seems a good idea to buy your house. We, of course, shall provide alternative accommodation for you and your family, and pay you a fair price, let us say, three hundred rubles.''

Joseph was absolutely stunned. How could he possibly give up his family home and his beloved garden? He categorically and instantly rejected their offer. Like the biblical Naboth, the neighbor of Ahab, king of Israel, he replied, "I was born and bred in my house, the home of my forebears. My father lived and died there. My sons were born there, and I hope that one day, when I am gone, they will live there. The garden is an important part of my life. 'God forbid that I should give the inheritance of my fathers to you!' "

Dan and Asher were outraged at Joseph's reply, which they regarded as unreasonable and impertinent. They immediately dismissed him from his post.

Poor Joseph was desperate. All his life he had been a bookkeeper, and he knew no other profession or trade except for his gardening skills. However, the Gentile farmers would not employ a Jew. In the small town of Zloczov there were no other openings. He tried everything. He worked as a peddler, he did odd jobs in the market, and he even helped the synagogue beadle with some menial tasks. Soon, he owed money to all the local shops and could not even afford to pay the tuition fees to the Hebrew teacher who was preparing his son for his *bar mitzvah*.

Joseph's wife, Feiga, could bear it no longer. She was ashamed and tired of having to borrow from her neighbors and of preparing stews with only the vegetables grown in their garden and the meat bones that the local butcher kindly donated.

"What is the use of having a house," she moaned and nagged, "if we cannot feed our starving children? Go to Asher and Dan and sell them the house. Then they will then give you back your job and we can live properly again."

Joseph was very reluctant to do this, but when he saw his sons walk barefoot to school, as there was no money even to repair their old shoes, it was the final straw. He swallowed his pride and cap in hand went to his former employers. He informed them of his change of mind and his willingness to accept their offer of three hundred rubles for his property. But Asher and Dan turned out to be hard and vindictive and refused to abide by their original offer. "The property has gone down in value in the last few months, so we are only able to give you one hundred fifty rubles, which we cannot pay you for some months. However, we shall give you and your family living quarters in one of our properties in the town, and you can have your job back."

Sadly, Joseph signed the deed of sale for his property. In a few days he moved out of his family home into a small cottage, returned to his old post, and worked very hard. But he was a broken man. Although his financial problems were solved, he became melancholy and depressed. He missed his old home, especially the garden. After a few months he became unwell. When he died soon after, his family felt that the cause of his death had been a broken heart.

After his death, Feiga went to the brothers and asked for the money that they owed her for the property. She was given all kinds of excuses. "We have no money now!" "Our clients are bankrupt!" "We have to pay heavy taxes!"

In despair, Feiga went to Rabbi Yehiel Michael and poured out her heart to him. Straightaway, the rabbi summoned the brothers and ordered them to pay the widow.

"How much do you owe this woman?" the rabbi demanded. "One hundred and fifty rubles," they replied. "Only one hundred and fifty rubles for such a large house and such a large garden?" asked the rabbi. "Let me see the bill of sale!"

The rabbi examined the document very carefully and saw that in their greed and haste, the brothers had not changed the original price they had offered Joseph.

"The sum stated here is three hundred rubles and not one hundred fifty," the rabbi stated. "You must pay it immediately, and remember that God is the Father of the orphans and the Protector of the widows."

Asher and Dan had no choice but to pay the three hundred rubles to the widow. Feiga and her sons were able to live well on the money, and Joseph could rest in peace at last.

46

The Right Answer

Rabbi Wolf, one of Rabbi Israel's disciples, was preparing for his journey to the Holy Land. Rabbi Israel and Rabbi Wolf were devoted to each other, and it was hard for them to part, even for a short while. "My dear Rabbi Wolf," said Rabbi Israel, "I shall miss you very much. But I can understand your yearning for the land of Israel, the land of our fathers. Go in peace, and may God be with you! I have just one word of advice for you: remember the saying, 'O wise men, be heedful of your words.' When the time comes, my dear disciple, think carefully and give the right answer."

Rabbi Wolf was somewhat puzzled by this counsel but promised to do as Rabbi Israel asked. With his teacher's blessing, he set out on the long and arduous journey. At first everything went smoothly. He arrived safely at Istanbul and managed to get passage on a ship. The journey was pleasant, the sea calm, and he spent his time peacefully in prayer and study. Then, on the third day, the ship was tossed to and fro in mountainous waves by a great tempest. The captain and his crew tried desperately to save the vessel and its passengers. In an attempt to lighten the load, they threw the cargo overboard. With great difficulty, they managed to steer the ship to a little island. There the passengers went ashore, and the sailors began to repair the boat.

Rabbi Wolf wandered aimlessly around the island. Absorbed in holy thoughts, he lost his way and found himself in the midst of a dense forest. He could see no way out. He had no idea in which direction to go. He heard the cries of wild animals and all the strange, frightening sounds of the forest. It was late on Friday afternoon, the Sabbath was approaching, and the rabbi was getting quite worried. How could he celebrate the holy Sabbath alone, in the middle of a wood?

As he paused, perplexed, he saw an old man coming toward him. The stranger had a long, white beard and was clad in white garments. "Rabbi Wolf," he said, addressing the astonished disciple by name. "Be not afraid. The holy Sabbath is near. Come with me. You shall be my guest, and we shall spend the day together." Rabbi Wolf had been brought up in the house of Rabbi Israel, and he was used to surprises. The gentle tone and the kindly face of the stranger reassured him, and he had no fear. Gratefully, he accepted the timely invitation.

The host led his guest to a large house nearby, and there they spent the Sabbath together. He was a most learned man, a stimulating companion, and Rabbi Wolf enjoyed every minute of his stay. They sang Sabbath melodies and discussed the holy law. So it was altogether a wonderful day for Rabbi Wolf, almost like a foretaste of the World to Come.

On Saturday night, after the Sabbath had ended, the stranger guided Rabbi Wolf back to the shore. The ship had been repaired and the passengers were all on board. The vessel was about to sail. "Tell me, Rabbi Wolf," asked his host, "how do the Jews fare in the many countries where they have been scattered?"

"The Almighty be praised, they are well," replied Rabbi Wolf politely. "Our Father in heaven neither slumbers nor sleeps. He does not desert His children."

Rabbi Wolf sailed away and in due course reached the Holy Land. When he at last returned to Medziborz, Rabbi Israel greeted him with great warmth and affection. But there was sadness, too, in Rabbi Israel's eyes. "Oh, Rabbi Wolf," he said, "you failed me in the moment of trial. Did I not beg you to be heedful of your words? But alas, you did not give the right answer to the most important question you will ever be asked. Your host on the island was none other than our Father Abraham. Every single day he pleads with the Almighty on behalf of the children of Israel. He is our finest advocate. Had you thought carefully before you rushed to reply to his question, you would have told him the truth. You should have related all the troubles that beset the children of Israel, their great suffering and their many sorrows. For the bitter night of exile has lasted too long and the dawn is long overdue. Had Abraham been told the true story, he would have had new weapons with which to storm the gates of heaven. You had a rare opportunity, but you forfeited your chance. You forgot my parting advice to you: 'O wise men, be heedful of your words.' "

—— 47 ——

The Scholar and the Carpenter

Rabbi Israel loved his students and tried hard to help the young men overcome their failings. There was one particular failing that Rabbi Israel deplored above all others: excessive pride. The rabbi believed that the ideal person was humble in his own eyes, and this humility raised him in the eyes of his fellows. To illustrate this point, Rabbi Israel often told his followers the story of the scholar and the carpenter.

Once a great scholar lived next door to a poor carpenter. Although they lived so close to each other, there was no contact between them. It was as if they dwelt in different worlds. The scholar dedicated his days and nights to the study of the Torah, and the synagogue was his second home. The carpenter, on the other hand, worked away at his bench all day long, struggling to support his family.

Early each morning, before the break of dawn, the two neighbors would leave their homes. The scholar, Rabbi Joshua, would make his way to the synagogue, where he would spend the rest of the day in prayer and study. Uri, the carpenter, would go straight to the work-shop and start his toil, amid sawdust and wood shavings. Often Rabbi Joshua and Uri would meet or pass each other. The scholar held his head high. He despised his neighbor and would not stoop to greeting or even acknowledging the existence of the ignorant workman. Rabbi Joshua considered that he had nothing in common with a man like Uri, even though the carpenter was a devout Jew. Rabbi Joshua considered himself the better man and did not deem the carpenter worthy of his attention.

Uri was no fool. He knew well that his learned neighbor despised him, and he felt that he deserved this contempt. He looked up to Rabbi Joshua in sincere admiration and paid him the highest respect. He was very proud of his learned neighbor and would always stand aside to let the great man pass.

At the age of eight, Uri had been forced to leave school, as his father could no longer afford to pay the fees of a Hebrew teacher, and Uri then joined his father in the workshop to learn the trade. A good friend took pity on the earnest lad and taught him to read the Hebrew prayers and to put on his phylacteries on his reaching *bar mitzvah*. Uri often wished he had the time to study, but his whole life and energy were spent in earning his living. He worked until late at night, and then the poor man was too tired to go to the synagogue. He would have fallen asleep on the benches had he gone.

Only on Sabbath afternoons would the carpenter make his way to the House of God. He loved to hear the discourses of the *Maggid*. He thirsted to listen to the parables, the legends, and the wise sayings. Listening to the wondrous words opened a new world to him, and for one brief moment the carpenter tasted the sweetness of knowledge. He felt all the more respect for Rabbi Joshua, the scholar who had drunk so deeply at the fountain of wisdom.

The years passed. The scholar died, and the carpenter died, and both men came before the heavenly tribunal.

"What did you do with your life on earth?" the great Judge asked Joshua. The scholar replied with eloquence. With many fine words he told of his long years of study in the talmudic colleges and in the Houses of Study. He described how he had spent his days and his nights studying the word of God and seeking true understanding. He recounted the number of his disciples. He assured the court that he had faithfully observed the Torah and all 613 commandments.

The Heavenly Judge was favorably impressed. Rabbi Joshua had a very fine record. All his good deeds and all the hours he had spent in poring over the Talmud were piled on the scales of judgment. They were heavy, and it seemed certain that Rabbi Joshua would soon be conducted to his well-earned place in paradise.

Suddenly, the prosecuting angel spoke. He had examined the scholar's life and had found one failing in his almost sin free record. "Rabbi Joshua despised his neighbor, the humble carpenter," thundered the accusing angel. The court was horrified. The sin, this one "little" sin, was set against all his good deeds already on the scale, and the balance tilted. Not all his pious acts, not all his scholarship could balance his sin of contempt. Rabbi Joshua forfeited his share in the World to Come.

Next, trembling and fearful, the carpenter approached the Heavenly Judge. Movingly, the defending angel told of Uri's constant struggle for existence, of his great respect for knowledge and learning. What could the prosecuting angel say? Uri had lived his life revering God. He had always honored the Torah. He had respected his neighbor. The prosecutor remained silent.

With love and tenderness was Uri led to a golden throne.

48

Just Reward

After many hours of traveling, Rabbi Israel and his two disciples needed a rest. It was snowing and icy cold. The coach stopped at an inn. It was dilapidated, and many of its windows were broken. Its garden was overgrown with weeds. Though it looked deserted, Uzziel, its Jewish innkeeper, welcomed them. "Make yourselves comfortable. You look tired and hungry. My wife will soon have a good meal ready for you. It is such an honor for me to have visitors. Very few coaches stop here, as the inn is rather out of the way to the town."

Uzziel instructed his wife to prepare a meal for the guests. "How can I prepare a meal when I have nothing in the house?" she complained. "We ourselves have had hardly anything to eat for days. Where will I get the food to provide meals for three people?"

Uzziel rushed to his nearest neighbor and borrowed some money to buy food. His wife fetched firewood from the forest and lit the stove. Soon, a meal was on the table. Uzziel made up beds for the visitors and provided them with blankets and pillows from his own bed. He and his wife slept on the bare floor.

Rabbi Israel and his disciples stayed at the inn for three days. Uzziel continued borrowing money to provide their meals. His guests were not short of anything. Uzziel never complained about his poverty, nor were his guests aware that he had to borrow from his neighbors or that his wife had had to pawn her wedding ring to feed them.

On his departure from the inn, the rabbi blessed them. "May the Almighty reward you for your kindness and hospitality!"

Life continued for Uzziel and his wife in the usual way, except for the fact that he was now in debt to many people. One day there was a knock at the door, and Uzziel thought it was one of his creditors coming to collect. However, it was Garin, an old peasant he had known all his life. "Give me a drink, Uzziel!" Garin demanded. "I feel terrible. My daughter and my son-in-law threw me out of the house. I have done everything for them. I gave them a home, my farm, my cow, and my horse. I have worked hard for them. My son-in-law drinks all day long, and it was I who looked after the farm. Now they have had enough of me! They begrudge me food and drink. He insults me and wishes me dead. My daughter has no heart. She allowed him to throw me out of my own home, and they both shouted 'Don't ever come back!' Let me stay here, Uzziel. I will pay you for my board and lodging."

Old Garin settled in very happily. He loved Jewish food. He played with Uzziel's children and helped around the house. After some months Garin said to Uzziel, "I am very happy here. My daughter has not even troubled to inquire whether I am dead or alive. I never want to return there. I have some money I do not need at the moment. Take it! Buy a small farm and I will work for you."

Uzziel acquired the farm and sold its produce. He, with the help of Garin, prospered. One day, Garin's daughter and son-in-law caught hold of the old man and told him, "You have stayed with the Jew long enough. He will rob you and leave you penniless." They persuaded him to return home with them. The following night, Uzziel heard a great commotion outside his window. It was Garin's son-in-law, leading a large cow.

"The moment we brought him home, Garin died," the son-in-law informed Uzziel.

"Did he say anything before he died?" inquired Uzziel.

"His dying wish was that we give you his cow!"

Uzziel continued to prosper and, for the rest of his life, he welcomed the poor and the stranger into his house.

—— *49* ——

Power of the Psalms

There was once a very wealthy man named Alexander. He lived in a large house and was attended by many servants. One of them was a most pious man whose name was Nathan. All day long, while Nathan worked or rested or ate his meals, the words of the Psalms were on his lips. He was respected by his fellow workers, and even Alexander took pleasure in the songs of his servant.

One day, Alexander decided to give a magnificent banquet to which he invited all his friends and relatives. The servants worked very hard to prepare the house and the elaborate meal. The singer of the Psalms, too, worked very hard. He loved his master and he enjoyed his work. On the day of the great banquet he felt so exhausted that he fell fast asleep in the middle of a verse of his favorite psalm. When his master called him, he did not hear. Alexander then went to Nathan's room to check and found him asleep. He grew angry and rebuked him. "How dare you sleep at such a time, you lazy good-for-nothing!" he stormed. Abashed, Nathan roused himself and went back to his duties.

As Alexander was leaving Nathan's room, a stranger approached him. "Sir, I have a matter of the utmost importance to discuss with you. Be good enough to follow me." Alexander hesitated. This was no time for business. He had no wish to follow the stranger. The house was already full of guests, and more were arriving every minute. He had many things to attend to and did not want to keep his friends waiting. But the stranger towered over him, and somehow Alexander felt forced to obey.

Without protest, he followed the stranger. Outside the house a carriage waited. The stranger opened the door, and a mystified Alexander got in. They drove off in silence. The coachman drove swiftly through strange country, and at last he drew up before a great mansion. The two passengers alighted and entered the house. There was no one to be seen. The house seemed deserted.

At last they found themselves in a huge, empty room. Suddenly, the door opened and many people crowded in. Three tall, stately looking men with long, white beards, in judges' robes, took their places at the head of the table. By their side, Rabbi Israel seated himself. The chief judge broke the silence. "David, king of Israel," he called, "step forward and state your case. What is your complaint? Why have you called us together in this way?"

King David rose and came forward. "I am making a complaint against Alexander," he declared. "He has a servant, an honest, hard-working man. Every day and every moment of his life this man is chanting my psalms. His melodious voice reaches the highest heavens, and I rejoice in my eternal resting place because my words are recited with such sweet sincerity in the world below. This faithful servant was insulted by his master, Alexander. I demand that Alexander be punished. The cry of the humble servant must be heard and avenged."

Then Rabbi Israel rose. He was acting as counsel for the defense. "Alexander is not a bad man," he pleaded. "There is no man on earth who is perfect. Even you, King David, the Lord's anointed, did you not commit a sin? But you repented, and the Almighty pardoned you. Do not harden your heart against my client. All his life he has honored the Torah and feared God. You do not desire a righteous man to be cut off in the prime of his life. Forgive him, O compassionate one!"

Rabbi Israel's eloquence won the day. Alexander was forgiven and acquitted. A moment later he found himself back in his own house at the banquet. He left the table and sought out his servant, who was hard at work, and humbly begged his pardon. Nathan willingly forgave him, and once again his sweet voice brought joy and holiness into the house, and he rejoiced to the end of his days.

—— 50 ——

Who Is Wise?

In a certain town there once lived two wealthy men. Each had a son. One of the sons was very clever and ambitious, the other happy-go-lucky and unpretentious. Despite their different characters, the two young men were great friends. There came a time when both fathers, having lost their wealth, became so poor that they could no longer support their children. Simon, the simple son, became a shoe-maker. Nathan, the clever one, went out into the the world to make his fortune.

Simon married a neighbor's daughter and settled down contentedly. He was an honest, hardworking man. The townspeople liked and trusted him and brought him plenty of work. The shoemaker was a cheerful fellow. He enjoyed his life and sang merrily as he hammered away at the boots and shoes. His work was not very exciting, but he was satisfied with his lot.

Nathan, meanwhile, traveled through many countries. He visited Poland, England, Spain, and Italy. He studied many sciences and became skilled in various arts. He was a fine goldsmith and an excellent physician. But his skill and knowledge brought him no happiness. He sought perfection in all things and could never reach the high standards he set for himself. Even his medical knowledge brought him grief, for he was blamed—and blamed himself—when his treatments failed.

After many years, Nathan decided to return to his native town. His arrival caused great excitement, for everyone had heard of his great achievements. Nathan's parents were no longer alive, and the visitor lodged at the local inn. Not feeling comfortable there, Nathan accepted warmhearted Simon's offer to stay in his home. So the simple shoemaker and the sage lived together. The shoemaker was always cheerful, the sage always sad.

"Would that you could become as happy as I am," said the shoemaker to his friend.

"I can become as you are," replied the other proudly, "but you can never become as wise and learned as I am."

Unexpectedly, the king invited the two friends to appear before him. The shoemaker was overjoyed at the honor and set out for the court at once. The king liked his straightforward approach and trusted him instinctively. So Simon, whom he appointed mayor, conducted the affairs of the town with justice and integrity. He was promoted again and again and finally became the king's chief adviser. Then the king built a fine palace next to his own for his loyal counselor.

Nathan had responded differently to the royal summons. He had meditated, delayed, pondered, and delayed further. "Does the king really exist?" he philosophized. "Did the king himself command you to invite me?" he asked the messenger.

"No," replied the messenger. Nathan convinced the messenger of his belief that there was no king, and together they traveled the country in search of the truth, a pair of scoffers without faith in anything or anyone. After some time, the two arrived in the capital city, where there lived a great mystic, a master of God's Name, a man respected and beloved by all the people. Him, too, they mocked and derided. Their behavior infuriated the townsfolk, and the two travelers were arrested and brought to trial.

Minister Simon recognized his old friend and set him free. But Nathan's latest experiences had taught him nothing. He still doubted the existence of the king and the powers of the master of God's Name.

One day, when the two friends were dining together, a messenger burst in and told the one-time shoemaker that the devil requested his presence. Simon was terrified. He rushed to the master of God's Name for help. The holy man gave him the strength and courage to defeat the evil one. The sage had received the same summons. He did not belive in the existence of the evil one. Boastingly, he offered to subdue the powers of evil, but they were too strong for him. He was vanquished by the devil and disappeared from the face of the earth.

Once again, Nathan's faithful friend Simon came to his aid. He enlisted the services of the master of God's Name, and the holy man rescued the sage from the snares of Satan.

Only then did Nathan realize that there were forces in the universe of which he knew nothing and against which he was powerless. He learned that a wise man must know to cast down his eyes and to say humbly, "I know nothing."

51

Alef Bet

Rabbi Israel yearned for the land of Israel, the Holy Land, and his dearest wish was to set foot on its sacred soil. Twice he tried to make the journey, but each time there were obstacles in his way, and he was unable to reach his destination. Then one day, Rabbi Israel decided to try once more.

For the third time he set out from Medziborz on his pilgrimage to the Holy Land. This time, he was accompanied by his daughter Adel and one of his disciples. The three pilgrims traveled for many days, and after many strange adventures they arrived in Istanbul. There they were fortunate in finding a ship going to their destination. They eagerly embarked on the last stage of their difficult journey.

The heart of Rabbi Israel was filled with joy. At last he would visit the Holy Land. He would enter Jerusalem, the City of David. He would weep, as his ancestors had wept, at the Wailing Wall, the sole remnant of the glorious Temple. He would stand by the tomb of King David, the sweet singer of Israel. He would see the holy cities of Safed and Tiberias. He would wander through the Promised Land, and every stone, every valley, and every tree would hold mystical meaning for him. Every minute of the journey seemed like an hour to the impatient traveler, and daily his yearning increased.

The days at sea passed uneventfully, and the ship steadily got nearer and nearer to the land of Rabbi Israel's dream. Then, on the fourth day of the journey, pirates attacked the ship and captured the passengers and crew. Rabbi Israel, his daughter, and his disciple were among the prisoners. They were bound in chains, and Rabbi Israel's sadness knew no limits. He was so near the Holy Land and yet so far from it.

"Rabbi," pleaded his disciple in anguish, "you are the Master of God's Name. You heal the sick, you raise up the fallen. People say there is no problem you cannot solve, no burden you cannot lighten. Your power extends to heaven as it does to earth. Rabbi, save yourself and rescue us from this fearful danger!"

"Alas, alas!" lamented Rabbi Israel. "I am powerless. There is nothing I can do. I have forgotten all I ever knew!"

"All?" exclaimed the disciple in horror.

"Yes, all," the rabbi replied sadly. "My mind is blank. I cannot remember a single passage of the *Zohar*, the Book of Splendor. I cannot recall a single verse of the Holy Bible. I cannot recollect a single word of the Talmud or the *Mishnah*. I have forgotten every phrase in the prayer book, the *siddur*. Could I but recall a single passage, we would all be safe!"

His disciple gazed at him in pity and fear. He had never seen his revered rabbi in such distress. "Is there nothing, nothing at all, that you remember?" he begged.

Suddenly, a flame flickered in the rabbi's eyes."Yes!" he cried joyfully. "I am beginning to—I remember—a few letters of the Hebrew alphabet. Come, my son and my daughter, let us say together, *Alef*, *Bet*, *Gimmel*, *Dalet*. . . ." Before they had reached the fifth letter, the rabbi and his companions were miraculously back in Medziborz. Pirates, prisoners, and chains had vanished like a fleeting dream.

Why had this happened? Why had heaven intervened to prevent the master from reaching the Holy Land for which he longed? The fate of many worlds was in the balance. The time appointed for the coming of the Messiah had not yet arrived. Had Rabbi Israel set foot in the land of Israel, nothing could have delayed the coming of the Redeemer. The Rabbi had been deprived of his knowledge for a crucial moment so that the world would have to wait until the Messiah was ready to come.

The great rabbi was not able to save the world by his wisdom, for all his learning had left him. He was saved by the simple letters of the alphabet—letters learned by every little Jewish child. For it is a hasidic belief that a man need be neither a saint nor a scholar to obtain an audience with the King of heaven. If a man were but to recite the letters of the Hebrew alphabet with passion and sincerity, his prayers would soar straight to his Heavenly Father and God would look down upon him with mercy and loving-kindness.

—— **52** ——

Take No Notice

From time to time, Rabbi Jacob Aryeh Guterman of Radzymin, on visits to Warsaw to "take the waters," would go for walks in Krasinski Park. The chief of the Warsaw police, Colonel Josef Alexandrowitch, and his wife, who lived near the park, also went for walks there, enjoying the trees and shrubs and the beautiful flowers, roses, rhododendron, and chrysanthemums growing in the gardens.

One day, on his daily stroll, the colonel encountered the rabbi, who was accompanied by a number of his followers. He lost his temper and shouted out, "Jews go to Palestine!" He then ordered the Polish parkkeeper Janusz to forbid the rabbi to enter the park, saying, "We cannot allow the Jews to spoil our beautiful gardens. Next time they come, don't let them enter!"

Janusz highly respected the rabbi. He had heard that he was a miracle-worker who cured the sick, made the lame walk, the blind see, and exorcized demons. He knew that the rabbi was held in high esteem by both Jews and Gentiles. He did not have the heart or the courage to insult and upset the rabbi. At the same time he was terrified of the chief of the police, who was known for his cruelty and viciousness. He delighted in tormenting, torturing, and whipping prisoners in the Paviak prison, especially Polish patriots who had rebelled against czarist rule.

When Janusz next met the rabbi, he told him of the colonel's orders and asked him what he should do. "He will have me dismissed from my job and put in prison. He is heartless and cruel."

"Don't worry, Janusz," replied the rabbi. "Take no notice of him. His days as chief of police are numbered. He will not trouble you much longer."

The colonel became infuriated when he saw the rabbi emerge from the park the following day, and he said to his wife, "It seems that Janusz ignored my instructions. I am going to punish him for being insubordinate. I shall whip him within an inch of his life!"

Janusz lived in Mokotov, just outside Warsaw. The colonel ordered his coachman to drive him there. "We have no time to waste. I must teach this rebellious Pole a lesson. Drive faster," he yelled. The coachman knew his master well and drove as fast as he could through the narrow cobbled streets of the Old City.

"Faster, faster!" screamed the colonel. The roads were covered in snow and very slippery. Near the Pionatovka Bridge, the coach crashed headlong into an oncoming coach. The coachman was killed, the colonel badly shaken and injured by splintering glass. Emerging from his coach with difficulty, the colonel saw the passengers of the other coach: the deputy chief of the military forces, General Assoroff, and Sergei, the only son of the governor general, were both lying dead in a pool of blood on the ground.

The colonel became very frightened. This was not the first time that his recklessness had resulted in such an accident. He could well imagine the reaction of the governor, General Paskowitch. In order to avoid public disgrace and dismissal, the colonel and his wife escaped to Austria that very night.

Good Janusz was delighted to have listened to the rabbi's advice. He remained in his post for many years and was happy to allow both Gentiles and Jews to enjoy the splendors of the park.

—— 53 ——

Pride Has a Fall

Yeruham was a wealthy man. He had a large textile business. He imported materials from Poland and sold them throughout the Ukraine. He employed many people. He was a kindly person and very charitable. No one left him empty-handed. He could always be relied upon to give a generous donation. He also provided visitors to the town with lodgings. He was very devout and studied the Talmud daily. He had just one failing: he was too confident and too sure of himself. He was overconfident of his virtue and his ability to resist temptation.

One day, Yeruham received a visit from Rabbi Israel. As was his custom, Yeruham told the rabbi of his wealth, of his business affairs, and of his many acts of charity. "I am very happy," Rabbi Israel told him, "that you are doing well and that you have been blessed with wealth. This is indeed a sign of grace. You can do so much good. Remember, Yeruham, that we are all flesh and blood and that we must not be proud. A proud man is as sinful as if he denied God. The reason man was created on a Friday is that if he becomes too overbearing, he will be told, 'The gnat was created before you!' "

That night Yeruham dreamed that one day he received a visit from the squire and his son. They were in a merry mood. Yeruham offered the squire vodka. He drank a whole bottle and became so drunk that he fell to the floor fast asleep. "Let him sleep in my house," Yeruham advised, "and tomorrow, when he is sober, he can go home." He had the squire taken up to a bedroom to sleep off his drunkenness.

The squire did not wake up the following morning. His son found him dead. "You poisoned my father," he accused Yeruham. In vain did Yeruham protest his innocence. The police were called in. He was arrested and sent to Minsk in chains. After languishing in jail for weeks, he was put on trial and sentenced to be hanged. The following day, he was taken to the gallows. A large fire broke out in the marketplace. The whole town was soon ablaze. There was great commotion. Everyone was rushing to get buckets of water to put out the fire. In the midst of this excitement, Yeruham escaped. He reached the forest, where he wandered about for several days. At last, he came to a small farmhouse. The farmer took pity on him and gave him some bread and water. The farmer was getting on in years and required a handyman, one to fetch water from the well.

Yeruham now became a water-carrier. He carried heavy buckets from the well to the farm. Sometime later, he became aware of a number of policemen searching the area for the escaped murderer. Once again he ran away and found shelter in the forest, where he was exposed to the danger of wild beasts.

Yeruham woke up covered with sweat. He was relieved to find that it had all been a dream. He felt that Rabbi Israel had been right in warning him of the sin of pride. He searched out the rabbi and confessed to him, "I have been very foolish, Rabbi. I now realize how true it is that we are all flesh and blood. It is not for us to be proud of our achievements but to be thankful to Almighty God for His many blessings!"

54

No Reward

Hanan was very poor. He could not make a living. He worked hard and tried many jobs, but he was not successful. His children had no shoes and were dressed in other people's castoffs. On the edge of the village stood a derelict inn. It had not been inhabited for several years. Rainwater came through the thatched roof and leaked through ceilings. It was overgrown with shrubs and thistles. It was used as a dumping place for rubbish by the peasants and villagers. The landlord was only too pleased to let it to Hanan for a very nominal rent.

Hanan and his wife worked hard to make it habitable. He mended the roof, cleared the rubbish, painted the walls, and generally made it into a home again. Despite all their hard work, few people came to stay there. Coaches did not pass there. It was too far off the main road.

On one of his journeys, Rabbi Israel made a detour to visit the inn. Hanan prepared a festive meal in the rabbi's honor. Before the meal, Rabbi Israel said to Hanan, "On my way here I lost my snuffbox at the edge of the forest. Please, go and find it for me! We shall eat later."

Hanan went to the forest to search for the rabbi's snuffbox. He suddenly heard the agonized cry of a human being: "Help me, help me! I am dying." He followed the cry and found a wounded man lying on the ground with his horse dead beside him. "I was attacked by a robber. He killed my horse. He robbed and wounded me. He took away all my possessions, even my signet ring, which had belonged to my late father." Hanan bound up the stranger's wounds and took him to his home, where he attended to him. He also called the *feltsher* ("barber-surgeon") to attend to the man's injuries. Rabbi Israel instructed Hanan to give the meal that had been prepared for him to the wounded man and not to take any recompense for the services rendered.

Upon his recovery, the stranger introduced himself to Hanan. He was General Gregory Ivanowitch, the governor of Minsk. He promised to send Hanan five hundred rubles as a token of his gratitude. When Hanan refused, the general increased his reward to one thousand rubles. Once again, Hanan declined this kindness with the words, "I do not wish to be rewarded for a good deed."

The governor was soon restored to good health and departed in a hired coach. Rabbi Israel also took his leave, asking Hanan for a contribution to charity. Hanan handed over to the rabbi all the money he had. He left himself nothing with which to buy fresh supplies for the inn.

The next day, a peasant came to the inn to buy a drink of vodka. Hanan, who had no vodka, gave him a glass of plain water. The peasant swallowed it in one gulp and expressed his appreciation to Hanan: "Your vodka has a wonderful flavor. I have not tasted such vodka for many years."

Hanan realized that the water had miraculously been transformed into vodka. The fame of Hanan's vodka soon spread. The inn became very popular. It attracted not only the peasants but also merchants on their way to trade fairs.

One day two merchants stopped at the inn. They took a private room and drank heavily. They had an argument, and a drunken quarrel ensued. One of the merchants picked up a knife and stabbed his roommate. When he realized that he had accidentally killed his partner, he was terrified and told the villagers that Hanan had robbed his friend of one hundred rubles and had killed him. Hanan was seized by the peasants and taken to Minsk, where he was thrown into a dungeon.

In vain did Hanan protest his innocence. No one believed him. He was put on trial and sentenced to be hanged in the marketplace. The whole town turned out to watch the hanging. Hanan was brought out of his prison. He was taken to the marketplace, and the noose was

placed around his neck. At that particular moment, the governor of
Minsk arrived to supervise the execution.

The governor looked at the condemned man and immediately recognized him as the one who had saved his life. "Why are you hanging
him?" he demanded to know. Hanan's accuser came forward. "He is a
murderer. He killed my friend and robbed him of one hundred rubles.
He deserves to hang," he said, lifting his hand to point his finger at
Hanan. The governor then noticed that the accuser wore a ring that had
been removed from his own hand when he was attacked in the forest.

The governor immediately ordered the release of Hanan. "He not
only saved my life, but he even refused one thousand rubles that I
offered him as a reward. He is neither a murderer nor a thief. It is the
merchant who is the killer and the robber. He even wears on his finger
the ring he took from me."

The merchant was hanged, and Hanan was set free to return home.
He pondered on Rabbi Israel's wisdom in advising him not to accept a
reward for a good deed, for its reward lies in the deed itself.

——— 55 ———

The Dangers of Boasting

There lived in Berdichev a wealthy man named Lieber. His
greatest pleasure was to be hospitable to strangers. He set aside
rooms in his house, specially built to provide free lodging for the
poor. Whoever entered his house was given food and a donation.

Lieber had many servants, but he himself would serve the poor. They would share his meals, and he would treat them as members of his household. He enjoyed watching them eat and be satisfied. He was highly regarded in the community. He had only one fault. He liked to boast about his hospitality. Wherever he went, he would tell of how he looked after the poor and how pleased he was to be able to do this. He would constantly tell Rabbi Israel of the good deeds he performed daily. The rabbi often advised Lieber to be more modest in proclaiming his good deeds, but his pleas were to no avail. The rabbi also told Lieber to take note at all times of his dreams.

One night Lieber had a dream. In it, he found himself before the heavenly court. He was highly praised for his charitable work. The accusing angel, however, pointed out his love of boasting and his lack of humility. He was sentenced to death. Rabbi Israel pleaded on his behalf, and the court decided to test Lieber.

It was on Friday afternoon, when Lieber was almost ready to welcome in the Sabbath, that a poor man arrived. "You are welcome," Lieber greeted him. "We shall have a meal after the evening service."

"No," replied the visitor, "I am starving. I want to eat now."

Lieber complied with the man's wishes and he was given food. His appetite was extraordinary. He appeared insatiable. He kept demanding more food and finally fell fast asleep. When he got up in the morning, instead of going to the synagogue, he continued demanding food. He devoured everything edible in the house, and Lieber had to borrow food from his neighbors. Throughout the Sabbath, the guest continued eating without respite. Despite all these unreasonable demands, Lieber did not complain but kept supplying more and more food.

After the termination of the Sabbath, the man informed Lieber that he was none other than the Prophet Elijah. He had been sent to earth to test Lieber. He had passed the test. He had never lost his temper and had always been ready to satisfy the excessive demands for food. As a reward for his patience, the heavenly death sentence would not be carried out, but for the next two years Lieber was to become a wanderer and go from town to town begging for his bread.

Lieber clothed himself in old garments and left his comfortable home to go begging, as had been decreed. He lived on the crumbs of bread given to him by kind townspeople. He slept on the bare floors of synagogue hostels. He suffered the cold and sometimes nearly froze to death. He often helped out with menial tasks, carrying water from the well to different homes. He helped to chop wood to light the fire in the synagogue. After one year of living rough, he became unrecognizable. He had aged considerably. He was constantly worrying about his wife and family, whom he missed very much. He fretted that his business, which had been left unattended, would no longer supply them with the means for survival.

The two years eventually passed and Lieber returned to his home. He found that his family and business had been well taken care of in his absence. He regretted deeply his previous boastfulness and determined to change his ways.

Lieber awoke from his dream. He felt very shaken by his dream experiences and realized what Rabbi Israel had meant by his advice to take note of his dreams.

—— 56 ——

Every Man Has His Day

Fishel, the innkeeper, had a Gentile servant, Kusciosky. Kusciosky's parents had died when he was very young, and Fishel had brought him up. He worked for Fishel, who treated him like a member of his family. He was very willing. No work was too much for him. He could speak Yiddish and was popular with Jews and Gentiles. He was also eager to improve himself. He learned to read and write. Nehemiah, the tutor to Fishel's children, taught him arithmetic and bookkeeping.

One day Rabbi Israel visited the inn, and Kusciosky went out of his way to make him comfortable. He even went from house to house to find ten men to make up a quorum for prayers for the rabbi. On taking his leave from Fishel, Rabbi Israel advised him, "Look after Kusciosky! Treat him kindly. One day you may be in need of him."

One day, a Polish nobleman from Pultava came to stay at the inn. He was very impressed with Kusciosky's willingness to be of service and with his knowledge of men and affairs. He offered him the position of manager of his vast estate of hundreds of acres of farmland.

Kusciosky moved to the estate near Pultava, where he soon became indispensable. He kept the accounts, managed the estate, and controlled the different activities of the household. He was honest and fair and popular with the tenants and the servants. He abolished the hated custom of whipping the servants. He regularly visited the tenants. They all felt that they could confide in him. He would arbitrate in their disputes, and all accepted his judgment with good grace.

The elderly nobleman was a great hunter. On one of his hunting expeditions, he fell off his horse and broke many ribs. He was in agony for three months and later died as a result of the accident. His widow, who, like her husband, had come to treasure Kusciosky, married him after a period of mourning. He thus became the master of the entire estate.

Kusciosky now traveled about the country and one day passed the inn of his early mentor, Fishel. He had not been in touch with him for many years, but he very much wanted to see his old master, who had been so kind to him. He longed to tell him of his good fortune. Fishel, alas, was no longer there. "Where is Fishel?" Kusciosky asked the new landlord. "Fishel left here four years ago. He fell into debt. He could not find the money to pay the rent. He became a beggar, and no one knows his whereabouts."

Kusciosky made further inquiries but could find out little more than that Fishel was constantly on the move. He decided to announce that he was giving a free banquet to all beggars. Everyone was welcome. Each would be given a donation in addition to a festive meal. This offer spread like wildfire through the begging fraternity. Beggars came from all directions to claim their largess. Kusciosky scrutinized every beggar but could not find no trace of Fishel.

One day, just as the company of beggars were sitting down to their meal, an unkempt old man in tatty garments joined them. He looked famished. He walked with a limp. Just the same, Kusciosky immediately recognized his former master. He embraced him and assured him that all his troubles were now over. He would find him a position on the estate. He would provide him with a home for his family. He would even build him a small synagogue.

Fishel then recalled the words of Rabbi Israel, who had told him many years ago, "Look after Kusciosky. Treat him kindly. One day you may be in need of him!"

—— 57 ——

A Swift Recovery

Rabbi Israel was returning home after a long absence. As he was nearing Medziborz, he realized it would not be possible for him to reach home before the commencement of the Sabbath. He decided to spend the holy day in a small village. A man by the name of Shahar, who knew the rabbi, offered him hospitality. "We are honored to have you spend the Sabbath with us. We shall do our best to make you comfortable. Unfortunately, there are only eight Jews for prayer in this village. Therefore, we do not have the required quorum. Now that you are here with us, we shall be nine. We shall still be one man short!''

Rabbi Israel was not unduly concerned. "Do not worry, Shahar. We shall have ten men this evening. Prepare a room for the service."

Shahar fetched a scroll of the law from the synagogue, which was closed throughout the year. The eight villagers turned up for the service, as did Rabbi Israel, all dressed in their Sabbath garments. "Is there no other Jew living in this area?" Rabbi Israel asked. "There is one, Meir," replied Shahar. "He lives around the corner but became housebound three years ago. He is paralyzed and has lost the power to move. He stays in bed all the time."

"So there is another Jew in this village," commented Rabbi Israel. "Shahar, you take my hat and my staff and go to your neighbor. Place my hat on his head and put my staff in his right hand and say to him, 'Rabbi Israel wants you to come now to make up a quorum for the Friday-evening service.' "

The villagers were smiling. They all knew that the man was incapable of using his legs. He had not even attended his daughter's wedding, nor had he gone to his father's funeral. The doctors had indicated there was no hope of his ever walking again.

Shahar did not question Rabbi Israel. He took the hat and staff and went off to find his neighbor. To everyone's amazement, the moment Shahar placed the rabbi's hat on the invalid's head and his staff in his right hand, Meir rose from his bed and followed Shahar, unaided, to his house. When he arrived there, Rabbi Israel joyfully began to intone the *kabbalistic* melody:

Come my beloved with a chorus of praise,
Let us welcome the Bride Sabbath, the Queen of days.

Rabbi Israel turned to Meir and told him, "You are now fully recovered. Faith is all powerful. It can even make mountains move."

58

The Magic Mirror

Rabbi Israel was a great admirer of the Moroccan kabbalist Rabbi Hayim Ibn Attar, whom he regarded as the "Western Light." He was eager to meet him. His work *Or Ha-Hayim*, a commentary on the Five Books of Moses, is still venerated by the followers of Rabbi Israel.

The Jews who lived in Morocco suffered much. Hussain, the vizier to the sultan Mohammed, was a very intolerant man. He hated the Jews, whom he called "nonbelievers." The building of new synagogues was forbidden. Jews were not allowed to ride on horses but had to use mules. They could not carry swords. They had to dress in a special way and wear yellow patches on their sleeves as well as yellow head coverings. They were confined to special quarters, known as *mella* or *hara*. Heavy taxes were imposed on them. Often the *mella* was sacked and the Jews imprisoned. Heavy ransom was demanded. It was the vizier's intention to impoverish the Jews and eventually to expel them from the country.

Hussain was corrupt and dishonest as well as greedy. No amount of money satisfied his rapacity. He even sold military secrets and the plans for the fortification of Moroccan strongholds. He was ready to betray his master to his master's archenemy, Abdel Malik of Algeria, for a large sum of money.

Sultan Mohammed trusted Hussain implicitly. Many of Mohammed's ministers complained to him about the vizier's ruthlessness. They informed him that Hussain was building himself a magnificent palace, made entirely of marble, and that he employed a large band of armed guards, who owed allegiance only to him, to watch over him day and night. The sultan was warned that his vizier was plotting against him.

The sultan was a simple and trusting man. He could not believe that his vizier would act in such a deceitful way. He thought his ministers were jealous of Hussain's achievements. He dismissed all their accusations as nonsense and gave the vizier even greater powers.

The Jews were very unhappy. Not a day passed without new restrictions that made their lives even more unbearable. They appealed to Rabbi Hayim for help. "Please, Rabbi, help us. The vizier is a second Haman. We have been expelled from Spain and Portugal. Are we going to be expelled from Morocco, too?"

The following week the sultan made a state visit to Meknes. The entire community welcomed him. It was the sultan's seventieth birthday. He was showered with presents. Rabbi Hayim, too, gave him a present on behalf of the Jewish community. It was a small mirror encased in a golden frame. "Why are you giving me this mirror?" the sultan asked him. "Am I short of mirrors?"

"This is no ordinary mirror, Your Grace," explained Rabbi Hayim. "It has great magical powers. If you look into it and concentrate, you will see in it things happening far away. Although you are now in Meknes, the mirror will show you what is going on in Fez, in Agadir, and even in Casablanca. It will reveal to you anything you wish to know."

The sultan gazed at the mirror. He saw the vizier Hussain entering his private chamber in Fez, opening his safe, and removing from it precious jewels and gold ornaments. He also saw the vizier handing over state documents to an agent of the emir of Algeria.

The sultan's eyes were opened at last. He realized how foolish he had been to trust his vizier, who was not only a thief but also a traitor and was probably at this very moment plotting to take over the kingdom.

The sultan immediately ordered the arrest of the vizier. Under torture, the vizier admitted his many crimes. He was sentenced to death and was beheaded in public.

The Jews of Morocco were very grateful to Rabbi Hayim for having saved them from another Haman.

59

A Lonely Festival

Rabbi Israel had one son, Tzvi, and a daughter, Adel. Adel was highly regarded and loved by her father and would accompany him on many of his journeys. She married Yehiel Michael, one of her father's most learned disciples. He came from Germany and was nicknamed "the German." They were blessed with two sons, Baruch and Moses Ephraim, who in turn became rabbis.

After a few years of marriage, Yehiel Michael asked Rabbi Israel's permission to visit his parents in Germany. "I have not seen them or my brothers for several years. My parents are now old, and I would like to spend two weeks with them."

His father-in-law gave him permission but urged him, "Take with you your *shofar* (ram's horn), a festival prayer book, and your *kittel* (white garment)."

"It's only just after Passover," Yehiel Michael replied. "I hope to be back before the festival of Pentecost. Why would I need a ram's horn?"

Yehiel Michael departed. He was joyfully welcomed by his parents and his brothers. He never tired of telling them about Rabbi Israel and his teachings. The family was impressed. Yehiel Michael was a changed man. He prayed with such great devotion and fervor.

Two weeks later, Yehiel Michael bade farewell to his family. He decided to return by sea via Riga. A stormy sea and violent storms damaged the ship. The captain and his crew were able to take the damaged boat to an island, where all the passengers disembarked. Weeks passed, and the boat was still unseaworthy. The rudder could not be repaired, and a new one had to be ordered from Hamburg.

Yehiel Michael felt very lonely. There was not a single Jew living on the island. He had been allocated a hut by the seashore. Before too long he realized he would have to spend the High Holy Days on the island. On New Year's Day he donned the *kittel* and blew the prescribed one hundred sounds on his ram's horn. He prayed earnestly and with depth of feeling.

His unusual behavior aroused the curiosity of the islanders. They stood outside his hut watching his odd gesturing and listening to his strange prayers. The ruler of the island, when informed of this peculiar visitor, also came to observe. Speaking in German, he inquired who Yehiel Michael was. "I am a Jew," he proudly proclaimed. "I serve God, the Creator of heaven and earth."

The ruler, who had never met a Jew before, had believed that all Jews had large horns and that they poisoned wells and killed young children. "I can see that you are a God-fearing man. I wish many more Jews like you were living on my island!" he told Yehiel Michael.

The ruler found Yehiel Michael passage on another ship and gave him many presents to take home. On his return to Medziborz, Yehiel Michael went to thank Rabbi Israel, his father-in-law, for his advice to take with him his *kittel*, the ram's horn, and the festival prayer book.

60

A New Leaf

In distant Constantinople, the city of the sultans, there once lived a very wealthy Jew named Azriel, who was most charitable. Like Abraham's, the doors of his house were open wide to all. He fed the hungry and he clothed the ragged. All he asked in return from his guests was that they relate stories to him. He loved hasidic legends and was particularly grateful to anyone who told him a story relating to Rabbi Israel.

Once, a certain Rabbi Simeon was traveling through Turkey. Simeon had been one of the most devoted disciples of Rabbi Israel, and there had been a strong bond of affection between them. Before Rabbi Israel died, he gave Simeon his final instruction: "Travel the world and tell the Jews all you have witnessed." Faithfully, Simeon discharged his duty. He journeyed to many lands, and everywhere he brought comfort and courage to the Jewish inhabitants.

The fame of Azriel and his great love of hasidic stories had reached the ears of Rabbi Simeon. He visited Azriel and was warmly welcomed and invited to spend the Sabbath in Azriel's house. On Friday night, after the festive meal, excitement mounted. Many people assembled in Azriel's house, looking forward to hearing the master's greatest story-teller, who happened to be in their midst. What a treat there was in store for them! All eyes were on him. Rabbi Simeon stood before them at the head of the table and got ready to relate the wondrous legends of Rabbi Israel to them. Then something very strange happened. He faltered. He began to stammer. His mind went blank. He could not recall a single incident, however hard he tried. Poor Rabbi Simeon felt ashamed and humiliated; he felt like an imposter. The crowd around him felt sorry for him.

The following day, filled with fresh courage, the rabbi again stood up, ready to narrate a tale that would enthrall the assembled. By now they were even more eager to hear what he had to say. A strange excitement filled Azriel, the host. But once again Simeon's memory failed him. His mind went blank. It was as if all his knowledge had been wiped from his memory. Simeon was grief stricken. He felt that the Holy Spirit had departed from him.

As soon as the Sabbath was over and three stars could be seen in the sky, Rabbi Simeon took his leave of Azriel and quickly mounted the carriage that was to take him back to the Ukraine. Just as the carriage was about to start, the rabbi suddenly remembered a story, and he realized he had been restored to grace. He jumped out of the carriage and rushed into the house. When Azriel saw the expression on Simeon's face, he at once led the way to his study, and there the rabbi told him the following story.

"Many, many years ago, I accompanied Rabbi Israel on a journey. We traveled to a distant land and arrived at our destination at midday. We made our way to the Jewish quarter. To our surprise, there was not a soul to be seen. All the shops were shut and the houses were shuttered. The marketplace was deserted and the synagogue was locked. We approached the nearest inn and knocked urgently. It was only with the greatest difficulty that we persuaded the landlord to open his door and to give us shelter.

"The frightened innkeeper told us a terrible tale. He related that the Jewish community was in mortal danger. The bishop, an enemy of Israel and more wicked than Haman, was preparing to address the villagers and to incite them to attack the Jews. He liked to stir up mad passions in the common people, and wherever he passed he left a trail of blood and pillage. The Jews of the town had gone into hiding in their cellars and fearfully awaited a cruel death at the hands of the murderous mob.

"Rabbi Israel remained calm. 'You men of little faith, have you no trust in the Guardian of Israel, who neither slumbers nor sleeps?' he asked reproachfully. He then turned to me and said, 'Simeon, faithful disciple, go to the bishop and say to him, "Israel ben Eliezer wishes to speak with you." ' I must confess I was not very anxious to face the wicked man, but the rabbi's voice gave me strength.

"I quickly made my way to the bishop's house. I was just in time. He was preparing to set out for the marketplace, where the people waited impatiently for his signal. 'I must see his lordship face-to-face,' I told his attendant boldly. 'It is a matter of life and death.' At last I was brought before the brutal bishop. I looked him straight in the eye, delivered my message, and returned unharmed to the master.

"Soon afterward, a timid knock was heard on the inn door. The bishop, magnificently attired in his ceremonial robes, had come in answer to the rabbi's bidding. Rabbi Israel and the bishop retired to a private room, and there the two men spoke earnestly. After some time the bishop left the house. 'Rest assured, all will be well,' the rabbi comforted the innkeeper. 'Tell the Jews they may take down their shutters. The bishop will cause no more trouble to the community.' Rabbi Israel smiled a secret smile, and we returned home shortly afterward."

Azriel listened to the story with rapt attention, hanging on every word as if his life depended on it. "My dear Rabbi Simeon," he said, "I was that bishop. My story is a sad one. My parents died when I was very young. I was left alone in the world, with no one to help me or guide me along the right path. I wanted power, and I got lost in the tangled maze of my own ambitions. I became a high-ranking officer of the church.

"Filled with hatred, I stretched out my hand against my helpless brothers, my own people. I persecuted them without mercy. Then one night Rabbi Israel, the Master of God's Name, appeared to me in a dream. From that moment onward my peace of mind was shattered. My conscience began to trouble me. He aroused within me emotions that I never knew I had. My dead parents, too, appeared to me in a vision and rebuked me for my sins. But I resisted all these impulses. I went on preaching hatred and murder until my hands grew scarlet with the blood of my people. Only when you came to me with the message from your rabbi did I realize I could resist no longer.

"I went to the master and begged him to save my soul and to set me on the road to repentance. Rabbi Israel spoke to me kindly and wisely. He advised me to leave my home and to settle in Turkey, where I could return to the faith of my fathers. 'Do penance,' he urged. 'Live a good life, do charity, be humble. When you have paid for your sins in full, a man will come to you and will tell you the story of your life. Then you will know that you have been forgiven and that your past has been wiped away.'

"That is why I have listened with such eagerness to the tales of travelers and visitors to my house. That is why I was filled with longing to hear your story and disappointed when you could not remember. But now, beloved Rabbi Simeon, you have restored my peace of mind. God has forgiven me at last. Half my fortune is yours, as the bearer of good tidings!"

—— 61 ——

A Loyal Daughter of Israel

Anshel was a pious Jew. His inn near Rovno was miles away from the nearest Jewish community. He engaged an elderly Jew, Getzel, to teach his five sons and one daughter. No one knew Getzel's background. He was very learned but kept to himself. He was a man of few words. All day long he would teach the children; after that he continued his own private studies until late at night, and he was never seen at the inn.

Anshel was happy that the children were diligent and were making good progress in their studies. Sarah, who was sixteen years old, often joined in the lessons. She loved to hear the stories from the Bible. She admired the heroes and heroines of ancient Israel. She was fond of listening to stories of Rachel and Miriam. The story of Hannah and her seven sons held great fascination for her. She enjoyed hearing about the exploits of the Prophetess Deborah, who encouraged the Children of Israel in their fight against Jabin, the king of Canaan, the oppressor of Israel.

The inn was popular with the peasants. Many passing travelers stayed there. Occasionally, Sarah would help her mother serve the customers. One day, Stephan, the squire's only son, visited the inn. He saw Sarah and fell in love with her at first sight. She was tall and slender with long, black hair. Stephan spoke to her and complimented her on her looks. Sarah rebuked him modestly: "I am only a simple Jewish girl, an innkeeper's daughter. You are the son of a great squire, our landlord. We are worlds apart with nothing in common. Please leave me alone!"

Stephan was not easily put off. He visited the inn every day in the hope of seeing Sarah. Her parents became worried. Stephan's attention to their daughter could only bring them trouble, so they stopped her doing any work at the inn. The more Stephan was rejected, the greater his ardor grew. He hung about the inn in the hope that he would catch a glimpse of his beloved. Being confined to the house all day made life very difficult for Sarah.

Some weeks later Anshel was summoned to the squire's lodge. It did not take him too much by surprise when the squire told him, "As you probably already know, my son Stephan is madly in love with your daughter. He says he cannot live without her. I have no doubt that she has cast an evil spell on him. I have tried my best to dissuade him from marrying a Jewish girl, one who is not of his own class. But what can I do? He is my only son and heir to my estate. He is very obstinate, and once he has made up his mind, nothing will change it. As he is determined to marry your daughter, I will give my consent, providing she converts to our religion."

Anshel felt as if he had been struck by lightning. In vain did he plead with the squire: "My daughter is only a simple Jewish girl. She is barely sixteen, and she is a very devout Jewess. She will never agree to forsake our faith. She would rather die. Please, take pity on me! How can I bring shame upon my family and my people?"

The squire now became very angry. "How dare you speak to me like this? You should regard it an honor and a privilege that I have given my consent to this marriage. Your daughter should be proud and happy to marry my son. She will eventually become the mistress of this estate. How dare you oppose my will and cause unnecessary grief to my only son? Tomorrow I expect you to bring your daughter to our priest Paul, with whom she will lodge and who will instruct her in our faith. The marriage will take place in the cathedral next month on St. Patrick's day. Go now and tell your daughter the good news."

The "good news" caused great misery in Anshel's home. The squire's guards were already stationed around the inn, and escape was out of the question. Anshel and his wife were in tears. It was to them a day of sorrow, like the fast of the ninth day in the month of *Av*, which commemorates the destruction of the Temple in Jerusalem.

When Sarah heard why her parents were so distressed, she said, "I have a solution to this problem. To escape this terrible ordeal, I am willing to marry my teacher, Getzel, tonight. It is true that he is very old. But he is kind and considerate and very learned. By marrying him, I will escape the clutches of Stephan. You can tell the squire that in a fit of insanity I married an old man. I am sure that the squire will feel relieved."

That night, Sarah and Getzel were married. On the following day,

Anshel went to see the squire, whom he told, "My daughter has become deranged. Last night she married our old teacher, Getzel. You should be pleased that your son did not marry an unstable girl."

Sarah gave birth to a son, Aryeh Leib, who became known as Rabbi Leib Sarah. It was believed that his soul was that of the famous mystic Rabbi Hayim Ibn Attar, the author of *Or Ha-Hayim*.

After Rabbi Israel died, his followers took up his message, carrying it to the far corners of the world. The Elijah of the hasidic rabbis was Rabbi Leib, the son of Sarah. He was the guardian angel of Israel, and his mission was to help people in trouble. To fulfill this sacred task, he spent his whole life journeying from place to place. No distance was too great for him and no problem too difficult. As soon as he heard of a fellow Jew in need, the aged rabbi would hasten to him as swiftly as an eagle. He always brought hope and comfort, relief and succor. His adventures could fill many books.

——— **62** ———

The Rabbi and the Gypsy

Before he became famous, Rabbi Leib Sarah would wander from place to place, redeeming Jewish prisoners and helping anyone in trouble. One day, on reaching a village near Pultava, he was invited to spend the Sabbath in one of the Jewish homes. His host, Meshullam, made it a habit to invite strangers and people passing through the town to stay with him for the Sabbath. On that occasion there was another guest named Yidel. Both guests were made to feel very much at home.

Meshullam owned a beautiful antique silver *Kiddush* cup and two silver spoons, wedding presents from his parents. In the night Yidel, who made a living out of burglarizing people's homes, quietly removed the cup and the spoons and hid them in his bag.

On Sunday morning, Leib Sarah departed in the company of Yidel. They were both on the way to Pultava on foot. Leib Sarah noticed that his companion was behaving very strangely. He was agitated and nervous. Every few minutes he looked back to see if anyone was following them. Suddenly, they heard the galloping of horses. His companion immediately ran off to the nearby forest, leaving his bag behind. It was Meshullam pursuing them. He addressed himself to Leib Sarah: "You have taken my silver cup and my spoons. Is this how you reward me for my hospitality?"

He thoroughly searched Leib Sarah's bag but could find nothing other than his prayer shawl, phylacteries, and a few Hebrew books. He then noticed the bag left behind by Yidel, in which the missing items were soon discovered.

Leib Sarah vainly protested that this was not his bag. No one believed him. He was arrested, taken to prison in Pultava, and put in a cell with thieves, robbers, and cutthroats.

The other prisoners, on seeing Leib Sarah, his long beard, sidelocks, and kaftan, informed him, "It is customary for a new prisoner to pay an 'initiation' fee. Give us some money and we shall all drink your health!"

When Leib Sarah told them that he was penniless and had nothing to give them, the self-elected chief of the prisoners, a man with a broken nose and a mutilated face, told him, "Then we shall whip you!"

They undressed the rabbi and placed him on a bench. The chief took up a strap and was about to strike the Rabbi when blood began to pour from the chief's nose. Another prisoner took over, and blood began pouring from his nose, too. The prisoners became very frightened.

They thought Leib Sarah was a magician or a sorcerer, and they left him alone.

One of the inmates, a man dressed in gypsy fashion, approached the rabbi. He confided to him that he was a Jew. His parents had died when he was very young, and he had been found and brought up by Gypsies. He had become a horse thief. He had been caught at the Pultava fair and was now awaiting trial. He would probably be sentenced to many years' exile in Siberia. His dead parents had appeared to him in a dream and had urged him to repent and mend his ways. "Rabbi, please help me," he pleaded.

Leib Sarah now spent his time teaching the Jewish Gypsy Hebrew. He shared with him his prayer book, his prayer shawl, and his phylacteries. They were always together, and their fellow prisoners named them "the rabbi and his Gypsy thief."

After languishing in prison for nearly six weeks, Rabbi Leib Sarah dreamed that the Prophet Elijah came to see him and told him to leave the prison. He woke his Gypsy friend. Together they made for the door, which they found unlocked. All the guards were sleeping off their drunken stupor. The two reached the main gate and found the keys in the lock. They unlocked the gate and gained their freedom.

They walked all night until they reached Zlatipola, where Rabbi Leib was well known and where his Gypsy friend was given shelter. The Gypsy Jew eventually became a coachman, and Rabbi Leib Sarah was pleased to watch him repenting of his sins and settling down to a useful and honest way of life.

—— *63* ——

The Missing Servant

One day Rabbi Leib arrived in Kossov and lodged with the innkeeper Baruch. The landlord was highly flattered. There were larger inns in Kossov, and Baruch knew that it was a great honor to have the famous scholar under his roof. Baruch took great pains to make the rabbi as comfortable as possible. He gave him the finest room and took great care that the distinguished guest should not be disturbed while he studied, prayed, or meditated. Though the anxious landlord prepared elaborate meals, the rabbi ate little. From dawn until late at night he studied the holy books. On his third day at the inn, Rabbi Leib summoned Baruch. "Go to the squire of Kossov and give him this message: 'Rabbi Leib, the son of Sarah, is here. He is staying at my inn. He wants to see you urgently.'"

Baruch was dumbfounded. He grew pale and began to tremble. "Are you frightened?" asked the rabbi. "I am terrified," replied Baruch. "The squire is a hard taskmaster. He is very proud and powerful. Even the local Gentiles are afraid of him. He has a violent temper. His dungeons are always filled with prisoners. He starves them to death. His dogs, especially Titus and Vespasian, terrorize everyone. Each time I go there, I fear for my life. The squire sets his dogs at me, and my body bears the scars of these ordeals. I always give thanks to the Almighty for protecting me and letting me return home alive. Rabbi, I dare not go to him with your message!"

"Have you no trust in me?" Rabbi Leib reproached him. "Have I ever done you harm? You have been most hospitable. You have made me very comfortable. Do you think I would repay good with evil? Go, do not delay! No harm will come to you."

Though Baruch was very frightened, he could not disobey the rabbi. He bade a tearful farewell to his wife and children and set out on his dangerous mission. To his surprise, all went well. The guard at the entrance asked few questions, and the dogs were fast asleep. The servant at the manor admitted him readily and took him to the squire. This time, the squire was very friendly and greeted him kindly. Baruch, feeling reassured, spoke up boldly and delivered the message. "Rabbi Leib, the son of Sarah, is staying at my inn. He wishes to see you." Even more strangely, the squire rose at once and without further ado followed the innkeeper.

Rabbi Leib greeted the squire warmly. He took him to his room, where they had a long discussion. Then the squire returned to the manor, and Rabbi Leib, the son of Sarah, went on his mysterious way.

Baruch had a Gentile servant, Jason, who lived with him. He was Baruch's right-hand man. He looked upon Baruch as his father. He was a carefree fellow, always humming tunes. He was very popular with the peasants and very faithful to his master. Before the festival of Passover, Jason went into the forest to gather wood but did not return. His disappearance was a great mystery. Baruch was deeply worried. He was almost helpless without faithful Jason. Search parties went out to comb the district. The police in the neighboring towns and villages were notified. But it was no use. Jason could not be traced. There was no clue as to what had become of him.

Baruch had many enemies, and certain envious people spread the rumor that Baruch had murdered his servant. "Jason knew too much. That is why his master killed him," they whispered wickedly. Baruch was arrested and thrown into the squire's dungeon. He denied all knowledge of his servant's whereabouts and solemnly protested his innocence. His jailers knew no mercy. They starved him, and they tortured him until the poor man's courage gave way. He signed a full confession admitting that he had killed Jason and that he had used his blood in the preparation of the unleavened bread he baked for the festival of Passover. Of course, this was completely untrue, but his tormentors were gleeful. The prisoner was tried and sentenced to be burned at the stake. The squire was asked to sign the death warrant and to make the arrangements for the execution.

The squire, however, was in no hurry. "Baruch is a great expert on horses," he told the judges. "Tomorrow I am going to the Lemberg fair to buy horses. I must have Baruch with me. When I return from the fair, I will sign the warrant."

The squire, accompanied by Baruch chained to one of his jailers, set off for Lemberg. They watched their prisoner day and night. Baruch, meanwhile, worked diligently. He chose fine horses, and the squire was well satisfied. Just as they concluded their deals and Baruch was leaving the stable, one of the grooms looked up and cried out in amazement. He was none other than Jason, the lost servant. Baruch nearly collapsed. It was too good to be true. "Is it really you, Jason?" he inquired incredulously. "Yes, master. I am Jason. I was overpowered by robbers as I was gathering wood in the forest. They bound me and carried me off. For almost three months I was their closely guarded slave. Only last week I managed to escape. I made my way to Lemberg and hired myself out as a stable hand in order to earn enough money to return to you."

"Jason, you have saved my life!" cried Baruch, as he took Jason to meet the squire. Baruch was freed and his troubles were at an end.

On their way home, the squire told Baruch, "I am sure you remember that four months ago, Rabbi Leib, the son of Sarah, summoned me to him and had a long conversation with me. Do you know what he said to me?"

"No, squire, I do not know," replied Baruch.

"Well, he told me, 'Soon Baruch will be accused of murder. He will be sentenced to death. Upon pain of your own death, you must not sign the warrant immediately. First take him to the Lemberg fair to buy your horses. If you disobey my command, the fury of heaven will smite you.' I faithfully promised the rabbi that I would carry out his instructions, and as he had foretold, so it came to pass."

In this manner did the holy man, Rabbi Leib, repay his host's hospitality.

64

A Good Teacher

Rabbi Aryeh Leib of Shpola, or the "grandfather," as he was lovingly called, was renowned for his hasidic dancing. This was not confined to the *mitzvah* dance, the "handkerchief" dance at weddings, but included dancing after the Friday-evening service. His dance represented the highest level of religious fervor. Hands as well as feet were caught up in the passion of his dance. It was more like a prayer, an experience that expressed love for the Creator and His work.

One day the rabbi told his followers that it was none other than the Prophet Elijah who had taught him to dance. It happened in this way, the rabbi said: "One day when I was staying for the Sabbath in a village with a man by the name of Shahor, he told me that his neighbor Tanhum had been languishing in the nearby dungeon for the past three weeks. He owed the squire several hundred rubles and was, in punishment, thrown into this deep dungeon, although he had a large family. Every day Shahor brought him some bread and water. Otherwise he would have starved to death.

" 'How could one help him?' " I asked my host.

" 'Next week is the squire's birthday. This is celebrated with a grand party to which all his friends and relatives are invited. Large amounts of alcohol are consumed. To entertain the guests, it is customary to ask the prisoner to dance, dressed in a bearskin. If the prisoner dances to the satisfaction of the squire and his friends, he is freed. If he does not perform well, he is thrown to the fierce dogs. Tanhum is ailing as well as lame, so he cannot dance at all. There is no disguising the fact that his life is in great danger.'

"When I heard this, I was anxious to help Tanhum. 'But I, too, cannot dance!' I said aloud. 'I have never danced in my life except on the day of the Rejoicing of the Law.'

"To my relief, at that juncture, the Prophet Elijah appeared to me. 'You want to save Tanhum,' he said. 'I will teach you to dance.' The prophet then gave me dancing lessons. Nightly, when everyone in the house was asleep, the prophet was guiding me through the intricate steps of the dance. On the morning of the birthday party, I lowered myself into the pit and changed clothes with Tanhum.

"On the evening of the party, the squire's manager pulled me out of the dungeon and dressed me in bearskins. The musicians began to play, and I was obliged to dance to the rhythm of the music. I performed the prophet's dance in front of the squire and his guests; my hands and feet, though covered with the fur of bears, were caught up in the passion of the dance.

"The squire and his guests were much impressed by my performance. They loudly applauded. 'He deserves to be freed for his wonderful performance!' announced the squire. I was permitted to return to the inn.

"With Shahor's help, I was able to pull Tanhum up to freedom. 'You are now free to resume your life!'

"Now you can understand that it is thanks to the teaching of Elijah the prophet that I am able to dance so well!'"

---- **65** ----

It's All for the Best

Many centuries ago there lived a sage who was known as *Nahum Ish Gamzu* because whatever happened to him, he would say, "It's all for the best" (in Hebrew, *Gamzu Le-Tovah*). So it was with the hero of this story, Rabbi Aryeh Leib of Shpola. Aryeh Leib suffered much, but he always saw the bright side of things and never gave up hope. He believed in making the best of things.

One day a friend came to him, weeping bitterly. "Rabbi, I am in terrible trouble. Enemies have borne false witness against me, and I have been sentenced to imprisonment for a month. I am innocent. Why should I languish in prison for a crime I didn't commit?"

Rabbi Aryeh Leib comforted his friend. "It's all for the best," he assured him. "Nothing is done on earth unless it is ordained in heaven. My dear friend, listen to my story. Once, I had a similar experience.

"Many, many years ago, when I was about forty years old, I wandered from place to place. I wore old garments. No one recognized me, and I did not reveal my identity. In some places the people were friendly, but in others there was nowhere to rest and nowhere to eat. A stranger had to manage as best he could on the hard benches in the synagogue.

"One day I arrived in the city of Zhitomir. The innkeeper, Amiel, was kindhearted and famed for his hospitality. He welcomed the stranger like a brother. The inn was always crowded with customers and guests.

"Amiel greeted me warmly, and I decided to spend the Sabbath with him. Late on Friday afternoon, another stranger arrived, a most unpleasant fellow.

"He boasted incessantly about his great fortune and his successful adventures. He was also very inquisitive and gave me no peace. He wanted to know what I was doing and where I was going. Instinctively I mistrusted him, and afterward I realized why.

"The stranger was a thief. Saturday night, while the whole household was fast asleep, the thief removed the valuable silver dishes and stowed them away in his bag. In the morning, I thanked Amiel warmly for his kindness and set out on my way to Brody. To my displeasure, I was soon joined by the stranger. He carried a very heavy bag and must have had a guilty conscience. Every few yards he turned back to see whether anyone was following him. Every sound startled him, and every footstep made him jump.

"His fears were well founded. Suddenly, we heard the sound of horses in rapid pursuit. Soon the wagon caught up to us, and we recognized Amiel, accompanied by policemen. My companion turned as white as a sheet. Without a word he dropped the bag and began to run as fast as he could. There was a thick forest nearby, and within a few minutes he had vanished into it. Before I had time to collect my thoughts, Amiel and the two policemen were upon me.

"Amiel was a changed man. His normally kind words gave way to bitter insults. 'Thief! Thief!' he called, grasping my arm to make sure I did not escape. 'Is this the way you repay hospitality?' I began to protest my innocence. Meanwhile the police had opened the bag, and the stolen articles were revealed for all to see. 'Not only are you a thief, you are a liar as well!' cried the angry innkeeper. 'You are a danger to society. Your place is in prison.' Without further discussion, he handed me over to the police.

"They threw me into prison. The jail was a disused old castle, overcrowded with prisoners. Many of them were serving life sentences for murder or highway robbery. They were overjoyed at my arrival.

Life in prison is monotonous, and the sight of a man with a long black beard and long sidelocks excited their curiosity. They teased and taunted me.

" 'Tell us whom you have robbed. How were you caught? Are you hiding the money behind your beard?' In vain did I protest my innocence. 'You innocent lamb,' they sneered. They even physically assaulted me. I suffered in silence and no longer protested. My attitude infuriated them, and they decided to beat me. First, they bound me to a table. Their self-appointed leader took a whip and was about to strike me. But as he lifted up the whip, he let out a cry of agony. He could not move his hand either to the left or to the right. It was completely paralyzed. The prisoners regarded this as an act of God. From then on, I was left alone and was no longer molested. In time, I even won their respect. They confided in me. They sought my advice, and I often settled their quarrels.

"Among them was a swarthy fellow serving a long sentence for horse stealing. At first I paid no attention to him. But one night, while everyone in the cell was fast asleep, he came to me. 'Rabbi,' he said, 'I know you will be surprised to hear that I am of your faith. My parents were murdered by a gang of robbers when I was very young. My aunt took me in. She was a cruel woman with a heart of stone. She begrudged me food. She made me work from early morning until late at night. Life was worse than hell. I was very unhappy, and I ran away.

" 'I fell in with a band of robbers, and I did not know the difference between right and wrong. To eat, I had to steal; to live, I had to rob. For more than thirty years I roamed the country, living by my wits and by my wickedness. I knew no better. Rabbi, your behavior here has made me think. I want to turn over a new leaf. I want to repent and to live an honest life. Teach me the Torah. I know nothing and there is so much to learn.'

"I was happy to help the repentant sinner. He became a new man, and I knew I had gained a soul for Israel.

"One night the Prophet Elijah appeared to me in a dream. 'Arise and leave the prison,' he said. I opened my eyes and wakened my new disciple. We found the door of the prison unlocked and the guard fast asleep. Without much difficulty, we made our escape. My sufferings in prison had been well worthwhile. I knew that they were part of a great Godly plan to rescue a lost soul. I realized all the more the truth of the saying, 'It's all for the best.' "

—— 66 ——

The Miller and the Miracle

In one of the villages on the great estate of Count Radziwill lived for many years a Jewish miller, Berish. He was hardworking and conscientious, and farmers brought their wheat to him, even from afar. They trusted the honest miller. He was a charitable man, and those who knocked on his door for help were never turned away empty-handed. Berish was contented with his life. His only regret was that there were not enough Jews in the village to establish a synagogue. Only on the high festivals was he able to hold services in his own home for fellow Jews who would walk to his temporary synagogue from miles around.

Berish's nearest Jewish neighbor was Jacob Reiff, the owner of the local inn, a mean and miserly man. Jacob was a complete contrast to Berish. He spent his days and nights serving liquor, and he drank as much liquor as he served, so that he was rarely sober. Berish felt sorry for his drunken neighbor. He begged Jacob to control his drinking, but it was of no use. Jacob could not resist the temptation, and when he was drunk he was without human feelings.

The miller had a son. Jakir was a fine, intelligent lad. He was a childhood friend of Dinah, Jacob's eldest daughter. Their friendship ripened into love, and the young lovers were eager to become betrothed. But the course of true love did not run smoothly. Berish objected to the match. It was true that he was fond of Dinah, but he disapproved strongly of her father. "I will never allow my son to marry a drunkard's daughter," declared the miller.

Dinah was heartbroken, and Jacob was furious. And so a bitter feud raged between the two families. The two neighbors became enemies. Jacob was determined to avenge his daughter's rejection. He began to cast envious eyes on Berish's mill and spacious home. "If only I could get his mill and his house," he mused enviously, "then my happiness would be complete." So Jacob plotted and waited patiently for the chance to put his wicked plan into action.

One of Jacob's regular customers was Peter, the manager of the count's estates. Peter spent many hours at the inn, drinking and making merry with his friends. The scheming innkeeper plied the manager with drink, treated him with great deference, and often refused to charge him for the liquor he had drunk and the food he had eaten. Gradually, Jacob won his confidence, and Peter became his friend.

Then one day Jacob was bold enough to unfold the evil scheme he had devised many months ago. "I will give you two hundred rubles and twenty bottles of whiskey if you will arrange for the mill to be handed over to me." Drunk though he was, Peter protested indignantly. "How dare you ask such a shameful thing? Berish has run the mill for more than thirty years. He is a fine man, an ideal tenant. He pays promptly. He satisfies all his customers. I would never have the heart to deprive him of his livelihood."

Jacob was not abashed. He continued to urge his friend. Day after day, he brought up the subject. And what reason and persuasion could not achieve, liquor and bribes finally accomplished. Peter at last agreed to persuade the count not to renew the tenancy of the mill.

The news came as a shock to the miller. He had been so secure, so well established. He felt as if the whole world had become dark. He swallowed his pride and went to his enemy. On bended knee, Berish implored Jacob to forgive and forget. "Do not ruin me," he wept. Jacob, however, hardened his heart. Berish's insult, "My son will never marry a drunkard's daughter," still rang in his ears. He would not listen to the pleas of Berish. He turned him away from his door. Berish was desperate. He did not know where to turn. His only hope was Rabbi Aryeh Leib of Shpola, for he had often heard wondrous tales of the miracles the rabbi had performed.

So Berish hastened to Shpola, and there he unburdened his heavy heart. The rabbi listened sympathetically to his story. He felt pity for the miller and wanted to help him. "I have heard with dismay and horror," he wrote in a letter to Jacob, "that you are planning to take over Berish's home. It is absolutely forbidden to supplant a neighbor. Please do not continue with your evil designs. Repent before it is too late." Berish himself handed the letter to Jacob. The innkeeper read the note and burst out laughing.

"How will the Rabbi of Shpola stop me from moving?" he scoffed. "Will he send angels to prevent me? No one can hinder me! I fear neither angels nor devils." Berish realized that he had to accept his misfortune. There was nothing he could do. He moved to a neighboring village and hired himself out as a laborer. Jacob became the new miller and the proud owner of the home of Berish.

The new home made a great difference to Feige, Jacob's wife. She had always hated the inn—the liquor, the drunken customers, the late nights, the noise, and the smoke. She hoped that the new surroundings would bring a change of heart in her husband. She loved the mill, the house, and the garden, with its glorious view of the river. How she loved the river! Whenever she had a moment to spare, Feige would sit by the riverbank and gaze at the crystal-clear water as it rippled and flowed in never-ending waves. She and her daughter loved to swim there. It was so cool, so refreshing, especially in the hot summer weather. Feige liked to watch Dinah splashing and playing in the water.

One evening Feige and Dinah went swimming as usual. It was during the rainy season and the river was high, the tide fast and strong. Suddenly, Feige felt faint. Powerless against the mighty currents, she was swept away by the rushing water. Dinah screamed, but there was no one to hear her. The heavens were overcast. Rain began to come down in torrents, accompanied by thunder and lightning. Dinah tried to reach her mother, but it was no use. More dead than alive, she staggered home to tell the tragic tale.

Her mother's disappearance and apparent death were a terrible shock to Dinah. Bitterly, she blamed herself for the calamity. "If only I had tried harder," she reproached herself day and night. "I could have saved my mother!" The beautiful girl languished. She seemed to fade before her father's eyes. She lost her gaiety. She lost all interest in life. She shut herself up in her room and refused food and drink. The doctors were helpless. "It is difficult to keep alive a person who does not want to live," they said.

Jacob's arrogance vanished. He had been devoted to his wife, and he dearly loved his daughter. Now Feige had disappeared, and Dinah's life was in the balance. The possession of the mill and the fine house was a doubtful pleasure. The house was empty, and the river was the source of all his grief. Jacob searched his heart, and it dawned on him that the rabbi of Shpola was the only one who could help him. He had not only injured his neighbor, he had also mocked the saintly rabbi.

Jacob made the pilgrimage to Shpola. "Rabbi, I am a sinner!" he cried. "I have taken away the home and the livelihood of Berish. I have been envious and greedy. Please, Rabbi, help me! Without my wife and my daughter, my life is not worth living!"

"Jacob," the rabbi replied gently, "you have indeed sinned grievously. Great, however, is the power of repentance. It cancels out punishment and sorrow. As it is written, 'Penitence and good deeds shield against retribution.' Give back the mill and the house to Berish, to whom they belong, and may the Lord return that which belongs to you!" Jacob quickly carried out the rabbi's orders. He moved back to the inn, and Berish returned to the mill.

The very next day, Feige miraculously reappeared. She had much to tell her relieved husband and daughter. "For some time," she related, "I was tossed about by the stormy waves until I was thrown onto the bank of the river, some distance upstream. There, I lost consciousness for what seemed a very long time. I awoke weak, cold, and hungry. My clothes were wet and torn in shreds. I looked around for food and found that I was in a swamp. There was no trace of human life. But in my search for food I had wandered into a forest and soon lost my way. Out of fear of wild animals, I climbed a tree at nightfall and slept in the highest branches. Every noise filled my heart with fear. But one day, I heard the barking of dogs. I found that the count and his retinue were out hunting. I rushed toward them. At first the hunters were terrified of me, a strange, wild woman. I told them my story, and they brought me home."

The villagers could hardly recognize the innkeeper. He was a changed man, sober and quiet, kindly and charitable. As soon as Dinah was better (and she recovered very quickly under her mother's loving care), Berish happily agreed to the betrothal of the two faithful lovers. The whole village was invited to the wedding, and all rejoiced at the sight of the devoted young couple and the onetime enemies who remained loyal friends ever after.

—— 67 ——

The Power of Song

Rabbi Baruch worked hard. The whole week he worked from dawn until midnight. He returned home weary and exhausted. All week long he looked forward to the Sabbath, a day of bliss and beauty, a taste of paradise. On Friday, all his workday chores were completed. Everything was made ready before the setting of the sun. Baruch dressed in his best Sabbath garments. His table was covered with a cloth as white as snow. The candles filled his home with a dancing light. His Sabbath meal was special. Every dish was seasoned with a specific Sabbath spice. He sang his favorite table songs, tuneful songs of joy and praise. He particularly loved to hear the melodies sung by his eight-year-old grandson, Saul. Saul had a beautiful voice. His tuneful rendering of the hymns touched everyone's heart.

One Friday evening, just as Baruch was reciting the "Grace after Meals," thanking God for the lovely food he had just eaten, a neighbor rushed in. He told Baruch that Beril, the shopkeeper, had been arrested. It was the governor's birthday, which the governor was celebrating with a riotous party in his mansion. There were many guests. They drank heavily, with the result that they ran out of drink. The governor sent his servants to purchase more vodka and gin. The only liquor store in the village was Beril's. But it was Friday night, and Beril told them, "Tonight is the beginning of the Sabbath. My shop is closed. I do not trade on this holy day."

"How dare you refuse to serve the governor?" shouted the servants. They beat him up and threw him into the town's dungeon.

"Please, Rabbi, go to the governor. He respects you. You are the only one who can help Beril," begged the neighbor.

Rabbi Baruch was at first very reluctant to leave his Sabbath table. The governor's residence was outside the town. It was the middle of winter. The roads were icy and dangerous. But he realized that Beril's life was in danger. He took his grandson with him. It was nearly midnight when he arrived at the manor. The party was still going on. The sounds of riotous merriment and revelry could be heard. Baruch and his grandson were ordered to wait in an antechamber. He asked the boy, "Saul, please sing the Sabbath melody again!"

Saul's beautiful voice filled the house. Even the guards stopped to listen. The guests stopped eating and drinking and listened attentively to the angelic voice. The governor, too, stopped his merrymaking and listened spellbound. He was a heartless and cruel man. He was a bitter and implacable foe of the Jews. But on hearing this beautiful melody sung by the child, his stony heart melted and he addressed Rabbi Baruch: "Thank you for bringing your grandson. His singing has been the highlight of my party. Is there anything I can do for you?"

Rabbi Baruch pleaded for Beril. "Please let him go. He is a God-fearing man. He is very hardworking. He does not trade on the Sabbath, for it was on the seventh day that God rested and He blessed that day. No disrespect to you was meant by Beril's refusal to sell you liquor."

"Say no more," interrupted the governor. "Beril is free to go home. It is thanks to your grandson's singing that I grant him a pardon."

68

A Contented Man

Rabbi Pinhas of Korets employed ten scholars (*batlanim*) who spent their entire day in his House of Study. Each one received a regular stipend of two rubles per week. Rabbi Jacob was in charge of the scholars. Every Thursday Rabbi Pinhas would hand him twenty rubles to distribute to his fellows. Jacob was known for his unworldliness. He was always satisfied with his lot. He never complained. His greatest joy was to study all day long and to be near Rabbi Pinhas, for whom he had great admiration. He enjoyed listening to Rabbi Pinhas' discourses. His colleagues treated the rabbi like a father, and he in turn would help them any way he could.

Jacob's wife, Malka, was, however, of a different temperament. She always complained, and her moans gave Jacob no rest. "How long will you continue staying in the House of Study all week? Our children are going about barefooted. They have very few clothes. Our daughter, Rebecca, is almost fourteen. Who will marry her? She is dressed in rags. How can I manage on two rubles per week? The house is unheated. I cannot afford to buy even a few logs for the stove. We owe the butcher and the baker and the fishmonger. They are refusing to continue giving me credit."

Jacob listened patiently to her daily complaints but never replied. He was too absorbed in his studies. These were his main delights.

One Thursday, Rabbi Pinhas gave Jacob only eighteen rubles, two rubles short. Jacob promptly distributed the money to his colleagues, but there was nothing left for him. His two rubles were missing. He was terrified to go home empty-handed. He just could not face Malka's

reproaches. He took his silver snuffbox and his Sabbath spice box to
Nehesh, the pawnbroker, who gave him four rubles for them.

The following Thursday, Rabbi Pinhas once again gave only eighteen rubles to Jacob. This time Jacob had nothing left to pawn. The
pawnbroker asked him, "Why don't you engage in business? It is not
fair for you to allow your family to starve."

"What can I do?" replied the anxious Jacob. "All my life I have spent
in the House of Study. I have no understanding of worldly pursuits."

"I will give you a number of articles that were never redeemed,"
suggested Nehesh. "Take them to the marketplace and sell them."

At first Jacob hesitated. He had never sold anything in his life. He had
no idea how to go about it. Yet, with his wife's complaints echoing in
his ears and with the faces of his starving children before him, he took
the articles to the marketplace. Jacob's appearance there created a
sensation. He was known as "the perpetual student," the "unworldly
scholar." People crowded around him. Within minutes, all his articles
were sold. Nehesh gave him five rubles' commission. Malka was
overjoyed. For the first time in her married life she bought *hallot*, the
soft, white, braided Sabbath loaves. She even bought a new dress for
Rebecca and shoes for all the children.

His initial business transactions gave Jacob confidence. Helped by
Nehesh, he took a stall in the market. There he sold some of the
unredeemed items that had been left at the pawnbroker's for a long
time. After a time he opened a small shop where he sold watches, rings,
and silver and gold articles.

Even the local squire bought his jewelry from Jacob. One day, he
called on Jacob and inquired, "Could you buy on my behalf a rare
collection of snuffboxes in India? I will give you one thousand rubles
for your trouble." The idea of leaving his family and his rabbi and
traveling so far afield did not appeal to Jacob. He had never left his
native town before, not even for a single day. He went to consult Rabbi
Pinhas, but the rabbi was not available. He tried the following day,

again without success. Finally, he wrote a letter to the rabbi and enclosed two hundred rubles.

Jacob then left Korets. He traveled on land for some time, and later he took a ship. After a week at sea, the boat stopped at an island on which there was a small Jewish community. Jacob went to the synagogue, but on his return, the ship had gone. All his money and possessions were on it. Once again, he was penniless and had to beg for a piece of bread. More than a year had passed before he returned home again.

Things had changed in Jacob's absence. The squire had died. The pawnbroker had moved away. Jacob's wife, Malka, who could not maintain the shop, had closed it. She owed money everywhere. In distress, Jacob went to see Rabbi Pinhas.

"Here are the two hundred rubles you sent me. Go and start another business. The Almighty will surely help you. Remember what the rabbis say: 'Who is rich? He who is content with his portion!' "

----- **69** -----

The Wedding Present

At a guest house near Lyzhansk worked two orphans, a young man, Motke, and Peshe, the maid. Both of them were hardworking and conscientious. Motke looked after the guests. He was always on his feet. He brought in logs from the forest. He lit the fires in the rooms. He cleaned the rooms and made the beds. He looked after the bar and did his best to make the guests as comfortable as possible. He loved looking after the animals. The tired and weary horses had a great friend in him. He unharnessed them. He gave them their fodder and water.

Peshe, too, was very industrious and helpful. She spent the whole day in the kitchen, cooking and baking and serving the guests.

The landlord, Solomon, and his wife, Mindel, were pleased with the orphans' work and treated them like members of the family.

Motke and Peshe, who had grown up together, eventually decided to get married. They had saved every penny they earned. They were hoping to buy a cottage and to set up a small general store.

Solomon and Mindel had four sons and five daughters. The children were sickly, suffering from all kinds of childhood diseases. Mindel was busy day and night nursing them. Doctors were frequent visitors to the house. All Solomon's earnings were spent on medicines.

When the time arrived for Solomon to pay the annual rent of one hundred rubles on his home, there was no money available. Solomon was faced with instant eviction and imprisonment. He and his wife spent many sleepless nights worrying about how they could face their landlord empty-handed. What worried them even more was the thought of their ailing children, who were in constant need of care and attention, being made homeless. Motke shared his master's worries. He spoke about it to Peshe. "Our dear master and his wife have been very good to us. They brought us up and have always treated us well. They now urgently need one hundred rubles. Let us give them our savings and repay them for all their goodness."

Peshe readily agreed. They handed over to Solomon their entire savings. Despite the fact that the orphans now no longer had any money, Solomon insisted that their marriage should take place. He invited the whole village, including Rabbi Elimelech of Lyzhansk and his disciples, to the wedding festivities. Rabbi Elimelech was impressed when he heard of Motke and Peshe's readiness to help Solomon. He was moved by the sacrifice they had made in handing their savings to their master.

At the wedding feast, Rabbi Elimelech announced, "As a wedding present I give Motke and Peshe the inn of Lyzhansk, together with the rights to distill liquor in perpetuity, and one hundred rubles." The rabbi's words were taken as a joke by the assembled guests. The idea of Motke and Peshe receiving such riches seemed totally unrealistic.

"How can the rabbi give them the inn of Lyzhansk and the right to distill liquor? These are the property of the Count Urlow!" remarked Mindel.

When the Seven Days of the *Sheva Berachot* (the seven days following the wedding, when seven blessings are repeated after each festive meal) came to an end, Motke and Peshe left the guest house where they had spent practically all their lives. They set out to start their new life. Solomon lent them a small cart and a horse in which to transport their few possessions.

As they were going through the forest that borders Lyzhansk, the couple heard faint human cries for help. Motke realized that the cries came from the marshy part of the forest. He was very familiar with the forest, where he had regularly gathered wood, and he knew of the danger lurking in its dark corners. He carefully made his way to the spot from where the cries were coming. He spotted the arms and the head of a person, the body having already become submerged in the marsh. He realized that there was not a moment to lose.

Motke rushed back to the cart, took a heavy rope, and threw it to the unfortunate victim. With the help of the horse and Peshe, Motke, after much effort, succeeded in rescuing the almost suffocating man. They gently laid him on the ground and covered him with blankets. They lit a fire and revived him with hot drinks. After he had rested awhile, the young man fully recovered from his ordeal. He thanked them for their help and told them that he was Ignacy, the only son and heir of the squire of Lyzhansk, Count Urlow.

He told them, "I went out riding this morning and lost my way. I stumbled into the swamp. My horse sank first, and I was about to follow. Had you not come to my rescue, I would have been dead by now."

There was great joy at the castle of Count Urlow when Motke and Peshe brought Ignacy home. The count had already given up hope of ever seeing him alive. A search party with dogs had combed the forest but had found no trace of Ignacy. The count was overcome by joy and gratitude. "Ignacy tells me that you are newly married. I would like to give you a wedding gift," he said to them. "I make you a present of the local inn. You may live there free of rent for the rest of your lives."

"I, too, want to give you a wedding present," joined in the countess. "I give you the rights to distill liquor and the fishing rights to the river."

Ignacy, too, expressed his gratitude to his saviors: "I give you one hundred rubles as a wedding gift."

Thus, the words of Rabbi Elimelech were fulfilled. Motke and Peshe lived happily for many, many years.

—— *70* ——

The Lost Coat

On the outskirts of the town of Lyzhansk lived a man by the name of Yehiel. He was a mysterious person. It was believed that he possessed an "evil eye," which could cause people harm. It was rumored that he practiced magic and witchcraft and that he studied the mystical "Book of Creation." He was seen outside the town drawing magical circles on the ground, while reciting Psalm 51. He maintained that the entire world is populated by invisible demons who can change the fate and fortune of every human being. He consorted with weird and frightful spirits.

No one was ever permitted to enter Yehiel's house. It was always in darkness. It was full of animals—cats, dogs, and birds. He spent the black hours of the night in the cemetery. It was rumored that he practiced the ancient art of calling up the spirits of the dead. Nobody knew how he made a living. People avoided him. Parents warned their children not to walk past his house. The peasants, too, believed that he could cast a spell on anyone against whom he bore a grudge. He was nicknamed "Yehiel the Magician."

In the synagogue, Yehiel sat near the door, and no one spoke to him. One day, Rabbi Elimelech invited him to a Sabbath meal. Yehiel felt very flattered to be invited. He had never before been offered hospitality by anyone. He lived on his own and did everything himself.

For the visit, Yehiel dressed himself in his best clothes. It was midsummer. It was very warm. The rabbi's house was full of people. The windows were, however, firmly closed. Yehiel felt he was suffocating. He took off his overcoat. He untied his tie and undid his collar. The heat was still too much for him. He began to sweat. The rabbi noticed how uncomfortable Yehiel was and suggested that he go outside for a breath of fresh air.

Once outside the rabbi's house, Yehiel fell into a trance. He was in dreamland. The rabbi's house, the street, the entire town of Lyzhansk had vanished. He found himself in a forest. He was violently attacked by a band of armed robbers. They took his money and stripped him of his clothes. He eventually recovered and made his way through the forest. He was hungry and thirsty but could see no sign of human habitation. After two days of aimlessly wandering in the forest, he came to a small hut. He went in and found it uninhabited. In a cupboard, he found food and drink and some clothes. He dressed himself. He ate and drank and felt revived. He returned to town, where he was conscripted into the Russian army and sent to the front in Podolia. There he joined in fighting the Turks.

Yehiel was brave and courageous. Single-handedly, he caught many Turkish prisoners. He was promoted first to corporal, then to captain. He was put in command of a battalion of soldiers. He decided to take revenge on the rabbi. He marched his troops to Lyzhansk. Just as he reached the rabbi's house, he awoke from his trance. He well remembered his dream.

Yehiel reentered the house of the rabbi, who greeted him. "I am glad you have returned to us, Yehiel. You left your overcoat here."

Yehiel realized the folly of his ways. He had been stupid to engage in magic, which is prohibited by the Bible as "an abomination unto the Lord." He begged the rabbi to show him how to repent. He became a devout follower of the rabbi.

—— **71** ——

Elijah's Cure

Everyone has problems. Abba, though wealthy and well known, was no exception. He lived in a large house, surrounded by orchards and vineyards. He was lucky in business. Whatever he undertook prospered. He never took a wrong step. But Abba's prosperity and happiness were marred. He had an only son, Pinny, who was barely seventeen years old. Pinny was tall and handsome and very intelligent. He was a diligent student, and his teachers predicted a bright future for him. His father was looking forward to sending him to a *yeshivah*.

Suddenly, out of the blue, Pinny seemed to lose his reason. He began to see visions and to hear voices. His memory was impaired, and he suffered from sleeplessness. He felt that everyone, even his parents, was conspiring against him. One day he claimed to be King David, another day King Saul. Some days he would revert to childhood: he would suck his thumb, pick his nose, and bite his nails. He could not cope with the normal tasks of life. He went about half-dressed, would not eat his meals, was insulting to people, and broke things. Abba employed two people to look after him day and night. Pinny could not be left alone for one minute, in case he harmed himself or others.

The doctors of Vilna and Warsaw were of no help. Their advice to the unhappy parents was to consign their son to an insane asylum. Instead, Abba decided to take his son to see Rabbi Elimelech of Lyzhansk, of whose success in healing the sick, the lame, and even the blind he had heard.

On their way to Lyzhansk, they stopped at a water trough to allow the horses to rest awhile. A man dressed in a sheepskin with a rope tied around his waist and worn boots approached them. Pinny with his two guards had remained in the carriage, seemingly asleep. Suddenly, he called out, "Father, look at this poor, unfortunate man! He looks half-starved. Give him some money!"

Abba was surprised to hear Pinny speak so clearly. He had not done so for a long time. Happily, he gave the man a large silver coin. "Where are you going?" the stranger asked him. "We are traveling to see Rabbi Elimelech. We hope the rabbi will be able to cure my son of his insanity."

"There is nothing wrong with your son," replied the stranger.

"There is no need to trouble the rabbi unnecessarily." He then turned and disappeared from sight, and the travelers continued on their way.

When he met the rabbi, Abba gave him a donation of eighteen silver coins, eighteen in Hebrew being the equivalent to the word *hai*, which means "life." Rabbi Elimelech looked at the eighteen silver coins curiously. "Strange," he mused. "Very strange. To Elijah the prophet, you gave only one silver coin and to me you give eighteen, when it was Elijah who cured your boy."

Abba was overjoyed to be told the good news, and it was decided that Pinny would remain there in the *yeshivah* and study under Rabbi Elimelech.

—— 72 ——

The Impostor

The squire of Lyzhansk, Count Plevne, was a pleasure-loving individual. He spent his time drinking, gambling, hunting, and playing cards. He left the management of his estate to his stepbrother, Gregory, who was in appearance very much like him. Gregory was greatly influenced in his dealings with the Jews by the priest Paulus, who hated them. Every Sunday the priest would incite his ignorant congregation against the killers of their Lord who, he told them, robbed and cheated them. The priest particularly disliked Rabbi Elimelech of Lyzhansk. He was filled with jealousy and hatred of the rabbi, who was loved by both Jews and Gentiles. Wagons full of the rabbi's followers regularly passed the priest's house. "More and more people are visiting the rabbi," he groaned. "Surely, he has cast a spell over those who follow him!"

On Paulus's advice, Gregory ordered Rabbi Elimelech to leave Lyzhansk within thirty days. After giving this vile order, he joined the squire for a day's boar hunting. After a long day's chase through the woods in the heat of summer, Count Plevne grew tired. When they reached the banks of a river, the count cast off his clothes and plunged into the cool waters. Being an excellent swimmer, he soon reached the opposite bank and, feeling exhausted, fell asleep. It was already dark when he awoke. He returned to the other side of the river, but there was no trace of his stepbrother or of his other companions. They had all gone. Nor could he find his clothes or his horse.

Naked, he waited until dawn to return to Lyzhansk, where he was greeted with derision by the villagers, who thought he was a madman. In vain did he tell them he was their squire. One poor peasant took pity on him and gave him some old rags to cover himself. He made his way to his residence, but the guards drove him away. No one recognized him.

On the following Sunday, the squire went to church. There, in his seat and wearing his clothes, sat his stepbrother, Gregory, passing himself off as the squire.

Finding no one in his own circle to believe he was Count Plevne, he approached Rabbi Elimelech and told him his sad story. The rabbi gave him a sum of money and advised him to have a tailor make him suitable clothes. On the following Sunday, the now correctly dressed squire once again went to the church. His chariot was in its usual place. "Take me home," he ordered the coachman. On his return home, he summoned a few loyal guards, with whom he returned to the church.

When stepbrother Gregory emerged from the church, he was seized

by the guards and put in chains. After a short trial, he was condemned
to exile in Siberia for his treachery. The priest Paulus, too, was removed
from his post for conspiring with Gregory.

Count Plevne remained a grateful follower of the Rabbi of Lyzhansk
and, unlike his brother, was proud to have him as his neighbor.

—— **73** ——

Rabbi Zusya's Faith

In Annopol, where Rabbi Zusya lived, resided a Polish nobleman,
Stefan Skewutz. He lived in an old castle and employed many
servants. One day the nobleman discovered that the sum of one
thousand rubles was missing from his safe. Stefan disliked Jews and
always blamed them for everything. If it rained hard, he blamed the
Jews. If there was a drought, he blamed them. If there was a cholera
epidemic, the Jews were responsible. If his sheep failed to lamb, the
Jews had cast a spell on his animals. Now that one thousand rubles were
missing, it was surely the Jews who had taken the money!

The squire announced that unless the money was returned to him, he
would expel all the Jews from Annopol. The Jewish community was
very worried. Jews had lived there for many generations. It was there
that the bones of their fathers were buried. Where could they go? They
turned to Rabbi Zusya for guidance. "What shall we do to avert the evil
decree of Stefan?"

Rabbi Zusya was not worried. He told Asher, a Jew who had many business dealings with the squire, "Go to him and tell him that within a year the thousand rubles will be returned to him. Not one ruble will be missing."

As instructed, Asher went to the squire and conveyed to him Rabbi Zusya's message.

"How can I trust him?" asked Stefan. "I do not know him. I have never met him. I have never had any dealings with him."

"Rabbi Zusya is a saintly man, a man of God, a miracle-worker. He spends his entire day studying and praying. He has never failed to keep a promise," Asher informed him.

"I will agree," acknowledged the squire, "only if you, Asher, whom I have known for many years, will undertake to pay back the money, should your rabbi not keep his promise."

To this Asher replied, "I have great faith in Rabbi Zusya. Should he not be able to pay you the money, I pledge to give it to you in full, despite the fact that no Jew took your money."

Weeks and months passed, and Asher was getting concerned. One thousand rubles was a lot of money. The Jews of Annopol were very poor. Asher thought that Rabbi Zusya would begin a collection, traveling from town to town. Few people would have refused to make a contribution. Rabbi Zusya, however, made no efforts in this direction. He never left Annopol. He appeared to be completely unconcerned.

Eleven months had passed, and Asher could no longer keep silent. He gently reminded Rabbi Zusya that within four weeks the money had to be found. "Have you no faith?" the rabbi reprimanded him. "I am fully aware of the promise you made to Stefan."

The month soon passed, and once again Asher reminded Rabbi Zusya that on the next day he would have to face the squire. "I am pleased that you reminded me," Rabbi Zusya said to him. "Go to the squire and tell him I will come to him at midday tomorrow to settle the matter. Tell him to assemble his entire staff in the courtyard. Everyone employed in the castle should be there. There should not be anyone missing!"

The following day the squire and his staff were assembled in the courtyard. Even the priest was there. "Have you brought the thousand rubles?" asked the squire.

"Are all your employees here? Is anyone missing?" inquired Rabbi Zusya. All names were called, and it was discovered that the stable lad Pollock was missing. When he was brought into the courtyard, he looked around at the assembled servants, the priest, and the rabbi. He began to tremble and threw himself at the feet of the squire. "I am the thief," he confessed. "Last year when I was cleaning the grate, I noticed that the door of the safe was wide open. Then I saw all that money. I do not know what came over me. I just could not resist the impulse to take the money. I still have all of it in the stable. I often wanted to return it, but I had no courage. I have been living in terror all year. Have pity on me!"

The money was retrieved, and Pollock was thrown into the dungeon. A grateful squire expressed his satisfaction to Asher: "I now realize why you put your trust in your rabbi. He is a true man of God."

—— **74** ——

The Miser

Mr. Kamzan was very wealthy. He owned a mill to which the peasants brought their grain. He owned forests and employed many to cut down the trees and to transport them on large barges down the Vistula to Danzig. Most of the property in the town belonged to him. He was, however, very mean. He made a point of avoiding the poor like the plague. His largest donation was five kopecks (cents).

Most of Mr. Kamzan's Jewish compatriots were always short of money. Cash was needed for the poor, the orphans, and the sick. He was deaf to pleas from the local rabbi. It was not worthwhile to approach Kamzan.

The town was busy celebrating the marriage of two orphans, Noah and Zelda. Their parents had been murdered by the cossacks, and the community had looked after them since. Noah helped the beadle. He fetched firewood, stocked the large stove, and cleaned the synagogue. Every morning he went around the town, knocking on the shutters of the Jewish homes, calling the men to the morning service. "Arise, Jews" he would cry, "to serve the Lord!" Zelda worked as domestic help in several households.

The whole community was involved in the preparations for the wedding. The women were baking cakes. The butcher supplied the meat free of charge. The grocer and the greengrocer donated all the other ingredients. The musicians volunteered their services. Enough money had been collected to rent a small hut near the cemetery in which Noah and Zelda would live after they were married.

On the morning of the wedding, the chief of the town, Vobrov, caught Noah as he was walking to the synagogue and drafted him as a soldier for the army of Czar Nicholas, to be sent with a military escort to the Kiev barracks. The leaders of the community pleaded with Vobrov to release the young bridegroom on his wedding day. Being a greedy and unscrupulous individual, Vobrov demanded a ransom of one thousand rubles. This presented an impossible target for the impecunious community.

By sheer coincidence, Rabbi Shneur Zalman of Lyady happened to be in the town just at that time. The synagogue elders approached him: "Rabbi, what shall we do? How can we collect such a vast sum in one day? We are all poor here!"

"Is there not one rich man among you?" asked the rabbi. "Yes, we have a very wealthy man here, Kamzan, but he is a terrible miser. He has a heart of stone. All he ever gives is five kopecks."

"I will go to him," said the rabbi.

When Rabbi Shneur Zalman asked Kamzan for a donation, Kamzan gave him the customary five kopecks. The rabbi took the coin and blessed him: "May you be able to perform many more good deeds for many years to come!" The rabbi's attitude was a revelation to Kamzan. Everyone in the town usually ignored him, some even cursed him, others threw the coin back in his face. He was never given any honor in the synagogue.

"You are the first person to bless me. I am now willing to do anything you ask!" he exclaimed.

"If you wish to inherit the World to Come," said the rabbi, "now is your chance. Give me one thousand rubles to ransom Noah, so that he and Zelda can get married today." Without hesitation, Kamzan paid the ransom, and Noah was led to the wedding canopy with great joy.

A week later, Noah, walking by the bank of the river, found a bag containing one thousand rubles. It had belonged to Vobrov, who had been thrown from his horse and killed the night before. Noah returned the thousand rubles to Kamzan. Much to his surprise, Kamzan refused to take the money and said, "This is my wedding present to you and Zelda. May you live many years together in joy and in happiness!"

— 75 —

The Teacher and the Minister

Rabbi Moses, the son of Rabbi Phinehas of Korets, wanted to establish a printing press in his own town of Slavuta in order to publish Bibles, the Talmud, and other religious books. In those days, no printing press could be set up without a special permit from the Russian minister of education in St. Petersburg.

Before setting out on his journey to St. Petersburg, Rabbi Moses, who was a devoted follower of Rabbi Shneur Zalman of Lyady, went to see the rabbi to obtain his blessing.

Rabbi Shneur Zalman wholeheartedly approved of his plan but advised him to first visit the town of Mohilev to find the Hebrew teacher Shepsil, and to ask Shepsil to accompany him to Vilna. Moses could not understand why the rabbi wished him to first go to Mohilev and then to Vilna. How could a Hebrew teacher in Mohilev help him to obtain a permit to set up a printing press in Slavuta?

However, as Moses had great faith in his rabbi, he traveled to Mohilev and found Shepsil, who was a pious and God-fearing man. He was an unworldly man who had no contact whatsoever with any Russian official. He had to work hard to earn his living and was at first unwilling to accompany Moses to Vilna. "What use will I be to you? I do not know anyone in Vilna. Besides, who is going to look after my pupils?"

To this Moses replied, "I do not know the reason I am troubling you. But it was the rabbi who advised me to approach you. I have complete faith in him. I am sure he knows what is for the best. I will pay for another teacher to take your place."

Shepsil finally agreed to this arrangement. When they arrived in Vilna, they were at a loss as to what to do. They visited the synagogues and the Houses of Study, of which there were many, as Vilna was known as the "Jerusalem of Lithuania." It was there that Elijah, the Gaon of Vilna, had lived and died. It was a town full of scholars and students, and the voice of the Torah could be heard by day and by night. It also had a very flourishing Jewish printing press.

One day Moses and Shepsil, on their way back to their lodging house from morning service, were passing through a park. A tall man dressed in Russian garments stood staring at them. Eventually, he approached Shepsil and asked, "Are you Shepsil, the Hebrew teacher from Mohilev? Don't you recognize me?"

Shepsil looked at the man in bewilderment. He could not place this tall stranger who did not fit into his Mohilev existence. Without waiting for an answer, the stranger continued. "Let me remind you who I am. I am Rivlin. My parents died when I was a baby. As I had no relatives, you and your wife looked after me. You gave me a home and treated me as one of your children. One morning, just as I was returning home from synagogue, two *snatchers* ("soldiers") kidnapped me. They took me to the nearest army barracks, where I was conscripted as a boy soldier. I spent twenty-five years in the army. I fought against the Turks and, under General Kutzov, against the French. I was promoted and eventually became an officer. After my time in the army, I worked for the ministry of education, and last week I was appointed minister. I stopped in Vilna for a day on my way to Warsaw. What a coincidence to meet you here after all these years! I owe you and your wife a great debt of gratitude. Here is a sum of money. Please take it!"

"Thank you very much," replied Shepsil. "I cannot accept your gift. I am earning enough for our needs teaching the young. I have no need of money."

"Is there anything else I can do for you?" asked the minister.

"You can do something for my companion, Moses. He is anxious to establish a printing press in Slavuta. For this he requires your permission."

"Is this all you want? I readily give your friend my permission."

Rabbi Shneur Zalman's strange advice for Moses to go first to Mohilev and to take Shepsil, the Hebrew teacher, with him to Vilna, was now clear for all to understand. Rabbi Moses returned to Slavuta, and his printing press became famous throughout the Jewish world for its fine and painstaking work. It used to be the custom for a man to present his new son-in-law with a set of Rabbi Moses' edition of the Talmud. This edition of the Talmud is highly esteemed to this day.

—— 76 ——

Sparkling Coins

Kalonymus was a devoted follower of Rabbi Shneur Zalman of Lyady, who was lovingly called *Der Alter Rebbe* ("the old rebbe"). Kalonymus owned a general store in Lyady and was very prosperous. He was also very charitable and would give the rabbi a sum of money for the needy every month.

The outbreak of the Franco-Russian war affected the livelihood of Kalonymus. His store was looted and vandalized by the retreating Russians, who set his house on fire. He was in debt and had to struggle hard to make ends meet. He was especially sad that he was no longer able to donate to the rabbi's fund. Though he visited the rabbi frequently, he never complained about his poverty.

One day, the rabbi asked Kalonymus for two hundred rubles he urgently needed to send to the poor *hasidim* in the Holy Land. There had been an earthquake in Safed. Many homes had been destroyed, and his followers there were in great need.

This request unnerved Kalonymus. Surely, the rabbi knew how poor he had become, as he had stopped making his usual contributions. He now owed money to everyone, and the best he could do was to provide dry bread for his family. Where could he obtain such a sum of money? His wife, Gitel, shared his worries. She knew well her husband's position and wanted to help him.

One day, on Kalonymus's return home, Gitel handed him two hundred rubles. "Where did you get all this money?" Kalonymus asked. "This morning you did not possess a single coin!" "I pawned my jewelry, the silver candlesticks, our *Kiddush* cup, and the spice box. For these I was given the money. Take it to the *rebbe*!"

Much relieved and with tears in his eyes, Kalonymus took the bag of coins. When the coins were placed on the table, the *rebbe* could not help but admire them: "Look how each one of them is sparkling and shiny, just as if they had been freshly minted in St. Petersburg! I know of your financial plight. The shiny coins are a pointer to me. Give up your store and become a jeweler! Deal in watches and rings, and the Almighty will bless you!"

When Kalonymus returned home, he asked Gitel, "How come the coins were so shiny?"

"When the pawnbroker gave me the coins, they were dirty and worn," she told him. "I spent the whole morning polishing them. I wanted to share in the great *mitzvah* of helping the poor in the Holy Land."

Kalonymus did as the rabbi had advised him and began dealing in precious stones. His honesty and integrity attracted many customers. Once again he became wealthy. His greatest joy in life was to resume his monthly charitable donations to the rabbi.

——— 77 ———

Sound Advice

Amram, the merchant, found himself bankrupt. He was owed large sums of money by many and thus could not pay his creditors. They gave him no peace. He felt that the solution would be for him to leave home and to hire himself out as a Hebrew teacher. He left his wife and children with her parents and found himself a position as tutor on an estate near Berdichev. He worked very hard, and after three years he had saved three hundred rubles. With this sum of money, he decided to return home and to repay his creditors.

On the return journey, Amram stopped in Berdichev, where he met Rabbi Levi Yitzhak. Amram was very impressed with the gentle sage, who loved every human being. His words struck fire in the heart of Amram. His warm spirit touched Amram. He felt that this legendary rabbi lived in the presence of God. After a week spent in Berdichev, Amram went to bid farewell to the rabbi.

"I would like to give you advice on three matters, though each piece of advice will cost you one hundred rubles. I urgently need this money to distribute to the needy for the Festival of Passover."

Amram found himself in a difficult position. He had worked hard to acquire the three hundred rubles. It had taken him three years of sweat and toil. How could he return home empty-handed? What would his wife say? He could hear her reproaches: "How could you give away your hard-earned money for charity? Charity surely begins at home. Have you no feelings for your own starving family? How long can my father maintain us?"

Rabbi Levi Yitzhak had, however, made too great an impact on him, and he could not refuse him. He handed over the three hundred rubles to the rabbi, who said to him, "Remember these three things: If someone asks you whether to take the road to the right or to the left, tell him the right. If you see an old man with a young woman, suspect murder, and only believe what you see with your own eyes."

Amram listened carefully, and with a heavy heart and empty pockets he departed from Berdichev. He was in no hurry. He was terrified to face his family after three years' absence. A few miles outside Berdichev, Amram heard the sound of horses. Guards were pursuing a thief who had stolen a large sum of money from the local pawnbroker. "Tell us," they asked Amram, "which road did the thief take? Was it to the right or to the left?" "To the right," replied Amram, according to the rabbi's instructions.

The guards soon caught the thief and handed Amram a reward of two hundred rubles. Amram felt relieved. Now he could once again face the homeward journey without worry. He decided to rest awhile at the nearest inn. On entering, he noticed that the landlord was a very old man who was helped by a young woman. The old man welcomed him, but the woman threatened him: "We do not want beggars here! Get out or I will call the guards! We are closed today."

In vain did the old landlord try to restrain her. She threw Amram out. He then lay down to rest under a tree near the inn. In the middle of the night, he observed four armed men in a wagon stopping at the inn. The young woman opened the door and let them in. He heard the old man struggle and protest. Amram rushed to the door of the inn and knocked hard and loud. The noise frightened the robbers and they, with the woman, escaped through the back door. Amram forced his way into the inn and found the old man lying on the floor, gagged and bound. Amram untied him and when the old man had recovered, he told Amram they had intended to kill him, but Amram's knocking had disturbed them and had thus saved his life. As a reward, he gave Amram two hundred rubles.

When Amram at long last arrived in his hometown, he did not straightaway go to his family but stopped at an inn. No one recognized him. When he asked about his family, he was told that every night his wife and daughters were visited by a tall, un-Jewish-looking man. Once again, he recalled the advice of the rabbi of Berdichev: "Believe only what you see with your own eyes!"

He went home and was pleased to find his wife and daughters well. "Where is our son, Gronem?" he asked. "Gronem was taken by the squire as a surety for the debts you owe. In spite of living among Gentiles, he is still a devout Jew. Every night he steals away from his quarters and comes here to say his prayers and to study. The squire has promised to release him for two hundred rubles."

The very next day, Amram paid his debt to the squire, who released Gronem. The family was once again united and, thanks to the good advice of Rabbi Levi Yitzhak, was able to resume its old life again.

———— 78 ————

A Place in Paradise

Who ever heard of celebrating the Festival of Tabernacles without an *etrog*, a citron, one of the four species used in the synagogue service? Yet, this nearly came to pass in Berdichev. Once, Rabbi Levi Yitzhak was unable to obtain an *etrog*. The Russo-Franco War had restricted the import of this fruit. It was scarce and costly. The rabbi tried very hard to locate one, but a week before the festival he was still without it.

The Jews of Berdichev were worried. Messengers were sent to other Jewish communities in Poland and Russia, to Warsaw to Brody to Minsk, with the object of buying at least one *etrog* at any price. Just before the Day of Atonement, all the messengers returned empty-handed. There was no *etrog* to be found. There were now only five days left to the beginning of the Festival. Only a miracle could supply Berdichev with the much-desired citron. The rabbi was sad. The *mitzvah* of "reciting the special blessing over the *etrog*" was very important to him. Often, on the eve of the festival, he would sit up all night, impatient for daybreak, in order to recite this blessing at the earliest possible moment. And now, for the first time in his life, the aged saint would be unable to fulfill this commandment. The whole community grieved with him, but no one could help.

By the eve of the festival, everyone had given up hope. That afternoon, a merchant, hurrying home for the festival, stopped for a while at Berdichev. When eating his lunch at the inn, the merchant, Pesah, remarked that he had been lucky to get hold of an *etrog*, a real beauty. The innkeeper was filled with excitement. At once, he took Pesah to the rabbi to tell him the good news. An *etrog* had at long last found its way to Berdichev! But there was one snag. Pesah refused to part with his treasure. He was offered twice the price he had paid. He was entreated to remain in Berdichev and to enjoy the hospitality of the town. But he stood firm and refused to be tempted. He wanted to spend the festival with his family, and no amount of money would persuade him to part with his *etrog*. It soon became clear that the stranger's mind was made up and that nothing could change it.

The rabbi was silent and sorrowful. He had offered every argument and every possible inducement. There was nothing else he could do. The faces around him reflected disappointment and dismay. Then, when all argument had been exhausted, Pesah himself made a startling offer.

"Rabbi," declared the merchant, "on one condition, and on one condition only, am I willing to share the *etrog* with you and remain here away from my dear ones on this happy festival. You must promise me faithfully that in return for my letting you have my *etrog*, you will grant me the privilege of being your neighbor in paradise. I do not desire money or power or fame. All I want is to sit next to you in the World of Eternity."

A hush fell on the people. This was no small request. To sit for all eternity at the side of this great and beloved saint! How could the rabbi agree to have a worldly, unlearned merchant as his neighbor for time without end!

But the rabbi rejoiced at the idea of having an *etrog*. No price was too high to pay for this privilege. Solemnly, he gave the merchant his word of honor that he would sit at his side in the Life Everlasting. The beautiful *etrog* now rested in the loving hands of the rabbi, and the merchant was invited to spend the Holy Days with the people of Berdichev.

Just before the beginning of the festival, when all were putting the finishing touches to their *sukkot*, the rabbi issued an order: "Let Pesah be entertained royally. Let everything be provided for him at the expense of the community. Give him the best accommodation, meet his every request. But on no account permit him to eat in a *sukkah*!" This strange command was, of course, obeyed without question.

Pesah was surprised when he returned from the synagogue on the first night of the festival to find that his meal was served to him in the house. The host and his family ate in the *sukkah* but would not allow him to join them. He left the house in anger and went elsewhere. Again, he was warmly received. He was offered all the food he could eat but refused the right to eat it in the *sukkah*. Finally, Pesah was told that this was at the express command of the rabbi. The merchant rushed to Rabbi

Levi Yitzhak. "Is this my reward?" he questioned with tears of anguish in his eyes. "I have given you my *etrog*. Why do you prevent me from eating in the *sukkah*?"

"You put me in a difficult position this morning," replied the rabbi. "You presented me with an ultimatum. I had to choose between not having an *etrog* and having you as my neighbor in paradise. I had no choice. I could not imagine the festival without an *etrog*. So I promised you a place next to me in the World to Come, and I will keep my promise. But now you must make your choice: if you wish to sit by my side in the next world, you must forgo the pleasure of sitting in the *sukkah* this year."

Without a moment's hesitation, the merchant made his decision. "Rabbi, I release you from your promise," he said joyfully. "I wish to fulfill the *mitzvah* of eating in the *sukkah* like every Jew." Straightaway the rabbi issued new instructions, and Pesah was an honored and welcome guest in every *sukkah* in the town.

Pesah tried to enjoy the festival, but none of the ceremonials were able to raise his spirits. He felt very sad. He felt cheated. He had lost a once-in-a-lifetime chance. He could have been for all time the companion and neighbor of the saintly Rabbi Levi Yitzhak of Berdichev and could have basked in the reflection of his glory.

When the festival ended, Pesah went to take his leave of the rabbi. The rabbi embraced him like a brother and to Pesah's inexpressible joy told him smilingly, "My dear Pesah, I promise you faithfully that you will indeed be my neighbor in Paradise. I merely wanted to test you. I had to find out whether you would be a worthy companion. But you, who had sacrificed your heart's desire for the privilege of fulfilling the *mitzvah* of eating in the *sukkah*, are indeed a worthy neighbor. I shall be happy to have you at my side when we meet in the hereafter."

—— 79 ——

The Rabbi and the Baby

Throughout the world, wherever there are Jews, *Kol Nidre*, the service that ushers in the Day of Atonement, is a solemn and sacred occasion. For the pious people of Berdichev and their great rabbi, the saintly Rabbi Levi Yitzhak, this was a sublime and soul-stirring occasion.

On the great Day of Atonement, the entire city of Berdichev was deserted. All Jews—men, women, and children—crowded into the synagogue. The men, wrapped in their prayer shawls, and the women, white-robed, bent over their High Holy Day prayer books. The children were hushed and awed. The reader stood at the head of the congregation, ready to begin the moving chant of the *Kol Nidre* service. Only one worshiper was missing. All eyes were fixed on his empty pew. Where was the rabbi?

This was especially strange, because Rabbi Levi Yitzhak was always the first to enter the House of God. Yet, tonight of all nights, he was not there. Several people, when passing his house, had seen the rabbi leave his home for the synagogue. What could have delayed him? The reader waited and waited until he could wait no longer. Then, with a heavy heart, he began the service. What could have happened to the rabbi? What had kept him from the House of God on this sacred night?

When Rabbi Levi Yitzhak was making his way to the House of Prayer, he walked slowly, absorbed in pious meditation. Every single service was a battle in which he fought for the House of Israel. His prayers were as fervent as his character was gentle. He was always carried away in his prayers, and he carried the congregation with him.

Every word of his prayers was purposeful and meaningful, and listening to him praying was a most remarkable experience. He prayed earnestly for his people. He was their staunch defender who could never see evil in any Jew. They were all God's children, all precious jewels in the crown of the Almighty. The Day of Atonement was his Day of Days. He had to gather all his strength in order to fight and to conquer the accusers and enemies of Israel.

As he walked through the streets of Berdichev, he thought aloud, "Ah, what a great people are Your people, the Children of Israel! See, the streets of Berdichev are deserted! Mothers and fathers are already in the synagogue, fearful lest they miss one moment of the solemn service." This thought strengthened the rabbi, and the frail leader became lionlike in his pleadings and prayers for his people.

Suddenly the rabbi heard a cry. He stopped. He listened. The sound came from a little cottage nearby. The door was unlocked. He lifted the latch and walked in. By the light of the festival candles he saw a baby. The baby was weeping bitterly for his mother. The rabbi bent over the cradle, soothing and comforting the little one. There in the dark cottage the rabbi spent the evening—the entire evening—of the most solemn day in the Jewish calendar. And there he remained guarding the infant until the surprised and grateful parents returned from the synagogue.

"How could I go to the House of God and pray to the Almighty," the rabbi told his congregation the next day, "while a Jewish baby wept and needed comfort?"

80

Good for Evil

Rabbi Nahman of Horodenka was a real father to the poor and needy. Though poor himself, he always looked after those who were in need. He would go around daily collecting money, which he immediately distributed to the poor. He was so loved by all that he was never turned away empty-handed.

One day, when he needed a large sum of money, Rabbi Nahman went to see a Jewish lawyer, Sonderman, who had a large practice and often traveled to St. Petersburg and Moscow on behalf of his clients.

Sonderman came from a religious family. His father was a scholarly and saintly man, but the son had gradually abandoned many Jewish customs and observances. He had little contact with the Jewish community and attended the synagogue only on the New Year and on the Day of Atonement. He professed not to understand Yiddish and spoke only Russian. He moved from a mainly Jewish area to live among the non-Jews.

"How dare you disturb me in the evening," was his greeting to Rabbi Nahman. "I work hard all day, and I deserve some peace and quiet in the evening. I am sick of beggars knocking at my door. They are parasites! They should work for a living!" The gentle rabbi did not reply, and Sonderman shut the door in his face.

Rabbi Nahman, however, was not despondent. He recalled the talmudic saying that abuse should not be answered by more abuse.

Three months later, the lawyer was arrested on a charge of high treason. It was alleged that he was in contact with revolutionaries who had assassinated the governor of the province. Sonderman found himself in Sparlierno prison in St. Petersburg, abandoned by all of his friends. He spent his accumulated fortune on his defense, but still his sentence was three years' exile in Siberia and a fine of ten thousand rubles. His wife had to sell all their possessions, including their large home, to pay the fine. She moved to cramped accommodations in the Jewish quarter. With no money left, she faced starvation.

When Rabbi Nahman heard of her plight, he visited her and promised to look after her and her children by giving her a weekly allowance. For the following three years, the rabbi kept his promise.

Sonderman eventually returned home after his three years' exile. He was delighted to find that his wife and children were well cared for and had survived the ordeal. "How did you manage to carry on?" he asked his wife.

To his surprise she told him, "It was Rabbi Nahman, the rabbi you refused a donation years ago, who cared for us. He was our guardian angel."

A grateful Sonderman rushed to see Rabbi Nahman. "Tell me, rabbi, what I can do to repay you for all you have done for my family."

"I do not want any repayment. I would be fully rewarded if you were to repent and to return to the ways of your late father, and above all if you were to be charitable and share the Almighty's blessing with those who need it!"

—— 81 ——

The Rabbi's Gift

Rabbi Moses Leib of Sasov studied under Rabbi Shmelke Horowitz in Nikolsburg, Moravia. After seven years, Rabbi Shmelke said to him, "You have been a very diligent student. The time has now come for you to return home and become a rabbi." He then gave his pupil three gifts: one large silver coin, a loaf of bread, and his own shirt, which he wore only on special solemn occasions.

Moses Leib bid his master farewell and started his journey home. He could not afford to pay for a place in a wagon. He would not use this silver coin, which he wanted to retain as a memento of his great teacher. He walked by day and slept in synagogue hostels by night.

At one point on his journey, Moses Leib heard faint sounds of the groaning of a human being. He followed the sound and reached a deep pit that had been used as a dungeon. He looked down and saw a Jew in there. When questioned, the man said he had been cast into the dungeon by his landlord because he owed him money. He had already spent three days in the pit without food or drink. Moses Leib did not waste any time. He took a knife and cut his own loaf into small pieces and lowered them gently into the pit. He found a brook nearby and lowered down a bottle of water to the prisoner. "Don't worry," he told the starving prisoner, "I will get you out!"

Moses Leib made his way to the landlord. "I have just passed the dungeon where you keep a fellow Jew. Release him! He is old and will not survive the ordeal."

"He owes me two hundred rubles," replied the landlord. "As soon as I receive the money, he will be freed."

"I am sorry, I do not have two hundred rubles," replied Moses Leib. "But I do have a silver coin. Take it and release him. Of what advantage will it be to you if he dies of starvation? If you free him, he may eventually repay the debt."

The landlord became very angry. "How dare you offer me a mere silver coin! He owes me two hundred rubles. You are impudent, and I will teach you a lesson!"

He owned three large dogs, which were the terror of the neighborhood. Their master needed only to nod to them and they would swiftly attack and often tear the victim to pieces. On this occasion, he ordered the dogs to be released from their kennel and nodded to them to teach Moses Leib a lesson.

While this was taking place, Moses Leib took the opportunity to put on Rabbi Shmelke's shirt. When the fierce dogs reached him, they became completely transformed. They became docile, and instead of attacking him, they ringed themselves around him and licked him.

"Attack him! Tear him to pieces!" shouted the landlord. To his surprise and amazement, the dogs ignored their master's orders. He and his servants were stunned. This had never happened before. The landlord realized that Moses Leib was no ordinary man. He ordered the prisoner to be released and even offered Moses Leib a seat in a wagon to take him home.

Moses Leib now realized that with the help of Rabbi Shmelke's three gifts, he had performed his first good deed of saving a human life.

—— 82 ——

The Power of Language

It was Friday evening, and Rabbi Moses Leib was in the synagogue. The afternoon service had been read, and the rabbi was reciting King Solomon's Song of Songs, which expresses Israel's love of God. Just as he was preparing to welcome Queen Sabbath, his beadle, Mordecai, whispered to him that the count had tied one of his followers, Yehudah, to his carriage, which was dragging him through the town. Rabbi Moses Leib could not carry on with the service while a

Jewish life was in danger. He decided to ask the congregation to interrupt their prayers and wait for his return. He made his way to the marketplace to try to save Yehudah.

As soon as the count saw the rabbi standing in middle of the square, he ordered his coachman to stop. "Why are we stopping?" asked his wife in surprise. "I am stopping to speak to Rabbi Moses Leib, whom I have known all my life."

The count had married a Hungarian woman some years ago. She could speak neither Polish nor Russian, and as she had made no attempt to learn the local language, she had no friends in the area. After some years of childlessness, she eventually gave birth to a son. He was a lovely boy, the apple of her eye, but he was not able to speak, nor could he hear what was said to him. She consulted many doctors, but no cure could be found. The priest regularly recited prayers, but there was no improvement.

To the countess's amazement, Rabbi Moses Leib now addressed her in Hungarian. "I spent seven years in Nikolsburg, where I learned the language."

"I was born in Nikolsburg," replied the astonished woman.

"What can I do for you?" the count asked Rabbi Moses Leib. "I know that your Sabbath is about to commence, and it must be something urgent."

"Yes it is a question of life and death. Release Yehudah! You are endangering his life. He is already bleeding. He has a large family. He is very trustworthy. It is not his fault that he is in debt. Armed bandits recently attacked his home and robbed him of all he had. They wounded him, and he has been ill ever since."

"But he owes me a large sum of money," the count said.

"If you free him, your child and heir will be able to speak," Rabbi Moses Leib assured him.

"We have been to so many doctors and were told that there was no hope," said the countess.

"Mommy, Mommy," the little boy suddenly cried out. These were the first words they had ever heard the child say. Yehudah was immediately released and his debt canceled.

"How can I reward you?" the countess asked the rabbi.

"You have already given me all I want. I can now return to the synagogue and welcome Queen Sabbath."

The rabbi reentered the synagogue, chanting, "Come my beloved, with chorus of praise; welcome Bride Sabbath, the Queen of the days."

—— *83* ——

Time Is Money

Alter was a farmer who lived near Krasni. He was a great admirer of Rabbi Hayim. He regularly visited him once a month and always left a sum of money to be distributed to the poor. He would give readily and willingly whenever money was required to redeem a captive or a debtor. Rabbi Hayim valued Alter's generosity.

One year, the country experienced a bad drought. The river near Krasni could be crossed dry-shod. The harvest failed. This led to famine and disease. Alter was unable to pay his rent. Nor did he have enough money to buy fresh seeds. For the first time in his life, he missed his monthly visits to the rabbi. He was ashamed to face him empty-handed.

Alter's wife, Beitshe, urged him to continue the visits. "You have been a faithful follower of the *rebbe* all your life. You never failed to be generous when you visited him. Go and see the rabbi now. He is learned and wise. He may give you some good advice."

Alter was reluctant to do so. He knew Rabbi Hayim depended upon his donations, especially at a time of hardship. Eventually, after much urging on Beitshe's part, he found the courage to go. On Alter's arrival, Rabbi Hayim barely gave him time to exchange a few words. The rabbi said, "Return home immediately! You have not a minute to lose!" He then went to his study and would not speak to Alter, who felt very disappointed. He had looked forward to unburdening his heart to the *rebbe*. He had hoped for a blessing. He could not comprehend Rabbi Hayim's lack of interest and abruptness. He returned home with a heavy heart.

As he neared his home, Alter saw Beitshe running to meet him. "I am so glad you have come back. There is a Russian general waiting to see you. He has been waiting impatiently for you for some time!"

After exchanging greetings, his important visitor informed Alter, "My parents died when I was very young. I was brought up in an orphanage. I have never married, and I have no known relatives. I have now been ordered by the czar to fight the Turks in Podolia. I have heard that you are a trustworthy person. I have in my possession two thousand rubles. Take the money and keep it safe for me. If I survive the war, you will return half the money to me. Should I be killed in battle or taken prisoner, all the money is yours." After handing Alter the money, the general left the house hurriedly.

Alter rushed after him. He wanted to know more about his benefactor, but all he could see was the general riding away. It now became clear to him why the *rebbe* had urged him to return home without delay.

—— 84 ——

The Man Who Slept through the Seder

Rabbi Jacob Yitzhak Horowitz of Lublin was known as the "Seer." He possessed strange and wonderful prophetic powers. He knew what was happening hundreds of miles away. He communed with the angels and was as much at home in heaven as on earth. His teacher had once said, "When Rabbi Jacob Yitzhak recites the Benedictions, the entire heavenly court thunders 'Amen.'"

Rabbi Jacob Yitzhak loved the holy festivals; Passover was his favorite. The whole year he looked forward to the first two days of Passover, to the *seder* nights with all their picturesque symbols: the three *matzot*, the roasted egg, the four cups of wine, the roasted shank bone, the salt water, the container of *haroset*, the bitter herbs, the sprig of parsley, and the cup of Elijah. The rabbi felt a great awe and affection for Elijah, the savior of persecuted Israel and the forerunner of the Messiah. So Rabbi Jacob Yitzhak of Lublin waited eagerly for the great moment when the large silver goblet was filled, the door opened, and the Prophet Elijah solemnly invited to enter while the rabbi repeated the traditional prayer: "Pour out Your wrath upon the heathens that know You not, and upon the kingdoms that call not on Your name, for they have devoured Jacob and laid waste his habitation."

One *seder* night, the rabbi sat among his family and followers in the largest room of his house. The *seder* table was beautifully laid. The rabbi's wife had supervised every detail and had gone to great trouble and expense to get everything exactly right. Nothing was too precious for this night of nights. The best linen decked the table, and upon it stood costly silver goblets and rich dishes. The rabbi was in high spirits.

Slowly and carefully he recited the *Haggadah*, the story of his ancestors in Egypt, and how Moses had led them as free men out of bondage. He sang the traditional melodies, and the house echoed with notes of joy and faith. He dwelt on many passages in the *Haggadah*, explaining their meaning at length. It was not until dawn that the *seder* finally came to an end. With a contented mind and with peace in his heart, the rabbi soon fell asleep.

Then he dreamed a strange dream. In his dream, he stood in heaven in the presence of the Prophet Elijah. The prophet was giving an account of the *seder* in Jewish homes. He told how eagerly the children looked forward to his visit. He described how the little ones discussed it earnestly among themselves. "Will the prophet really come in?" "Will he taste the wine?" "How can he be everywhere at once?" "How long will he stay?" Anxious eyes heavy with sleep were glued to the mystical cup. How disappointing for the young people when they could see no actual sign of the visit, no apparent diminution of the wine.

"Which *seder* was the most important?" someone asked the prophet. "Was it not the *seder* of Rabbi Jacob Yitzhak of Lublin?"

"The service of Rabbi Jacob Yitzhak was indeed moving," replied Elijah the Tishbite. "But it cannot compare with the *seder* of Hayim of Lublin. Never have I seen a *seder* more impressive."

The rabbi awoke at once and rose from his bed, anxious and troubled. He summoned his faithful beadle, Tzvi Hirsh, and said, "Go fetch me Hayim!" The beadle was perplexed. Lublin had a large Jewish community. There were many men called Hayim. The rabbi had given him no address and no details about the man he wished to see. However, Tzvi Hirsh was well trained. He knew that the rabbi resented unnecessary questions. He had been given an order, and he would obey. Now, the leader of the community was called Hayim. Tzvi Hirsh made his way to him and told him that the rabbi wished to see him. Naturally Hayim felt highly flattered to be singled out in this way, and he immediately went to the rabbi's house.

"This is not the man I want," said the rabbi. So the beadle tried again. He went to another man called Hayim, a learned judge, the president of the rabbinical court, and brought him to the rabbi. Once again, the man was dismissed. Then the beadle brought Hayim the cantor before his master, and for the third time that day the rabbi told him, "This is not the man!"

Weary and dispirited, the beadle turned into a shabby, narrow little street, and there he met the town's water carrier, also named Hayim. Instinctively, Tzvi Hirsh knew that he had found the man he was looking for. "The rabbi wants to see you," he said without thinking. Hayim did not look surprised at this honor.

"I was expecting this summons," he said with a sigh. "I knew the rabbi would seek me out. I am a sinner. I deserve to be punished. Let us go to him. I am ready to atone for my sins."

This time the rabbi was pleased with the beadle, and he welcomed the water carrier with open arms. "Tell me, my good Hayim, what happened last night? Tell me everything!"

"Rabbi, you know I am a water carrier," began Hayim. "Every day after the early-morning service, I carry buckets of water to Jewish homes. I am over seventy years old and the work is not easy. The well is outside the town, some distance away. The pay is very small. Still, I don't complain. Every day I thank and praise the Almighty for His mercy and kindness. He has given me the health and strength that enables me to earn my bread by the sweat of my brow and saves me from asking for charity. Yesterday, the day before the festival, was a very hard day. All the houses were being cleaned, and all the vessels were being washed. Water was in great demand. No sooner did I fetch one pail than they demanded another. All day long, from dawn until dusk, I slaved away without a moment's rest. Backward and forward I trudged with my load. My feet grew heavy, my back ached, but I did not dare slacken. At last the long day came to an end, and I wearily made my way home. I arrived at my cottage more dead than alive, just as my wife was lighting the festival candles. I could hardly move.

" 'Let me rest awhile', I said to my wife. 'Soon I will prepare myself for the *seder*.' My wife, too, was exhausted. All day she had been busy cleaning houses for the rich in the neighborhood to earn the extra money required for the Passover. I closed my eyes and soon I was fast asleep. When I awoke it was nearly dawn.

"I looked at the table. Nothing had been touched. The *matzot* were unbroken and the wine untasted. I wept. 'O God, why should I be punished?' I demanded. 'Is it not enough that I work like a donkey all the year round? Must my festival be turned into sadness? Am I such a sinner that I am not privileged to observe the *seder*?'

"There was no time now to recite the whole *Haggadah*. But I drank the four cups of wine and ate a piece of *matzah*. I lifted up my eyes to heaven and said, 'Almighty God, I, Hayim, the water carrier, am not much of a scholar. The great rabbi of Lublin is wise and learned. He knows divine mysteries. All I know is that You, O God, are our Redeemer. You have delivered us in the past from the cruel Egyptian yoke and have performed wonders and miracles for our forefathers. Break today the yoke of our exile. Put an end to the troubles of the House of Israel.' "

Hayim looked at the rabbi, who was deep in thought. "Oh, Rabbi," Hayim continued, "I am a sinner. I did not conduct the *seder* as it should be done. Punish me for my transgression!"

"Hayim, Hayim," replied the rabbi, his face shining with joy. "You are no sinner. Would that we had many like you in Israel. Your *seder* was the most pleasing to the Prophet Elijah, the wandering prophet of a wandering people. Your *seder* was more important than mine or any other of the House of Israel."

——— *85* ———

Brother and Sister

Once there stood an inn at the crossroads near Brody, and the innkeeper was named Reuben. It was a busy place, constantly crowded with guests. Only on the holy Sabbath did the doors of the inn remain closed. Peasants and passersby found it a pleasant place to rest and have refreshments. Reuben, always obliging and eager to satisfy, created a friendly atmosphere. He was a popular host, known and liked for miles around. He was particularly known for his kindness to those in need. Rarely was a poor man refused a meal.

The inn belonged to Count Sokoloff, a harsh landlord who lived on a large estate and spent his days and nights drinking and feasting with his friends. He had been a soldier in his youth, and he often refought his battles with his companions. Reuben paid his rent regularly, and the wicked count could find no fault with him, however hard he tried.

Then a terrible drought struck the countryside for two terrible years. The crops were ruined, the cattle died. The peasants almost starved to death. There was no money to buy bread, let alone liquor. Traveling was dangerous because of attacks by bands of robbers, and few travelers came to the inn. It remained deserted, and life was hard for Reuben. When the New Year approached, Reuben did not have enough money to pay the rent. This was the first time he had ever fallen behind with his payments. Reuben went trembling to the landlord and told him of his plight. But the count showed no pity. He ordered Reuben and his family to be evicted from the inn and thrown into the castle dungeon. "Let them rot," snarled the count, "until they pay their debts."

In the dark, dark cavern, the wretched family languished. The prisoners were closely guarded by two watchmen. Ivan watched over them by night. He was a drunkard and as vicious and cruel as his master. He enjoyed seeing people suffer and took delight in torturing his helpless victims. Although a frequent visitor at the inn, he had never paid for his drinks. Reuben even suspected Ivan of having stolen money from the till when no one was watching.

Ludwig, their daytime guard, was honest and kindhearted. He was very fond of Reuben and his family. Reuben's eldest child, Avner, was four years old, the same age as Ludwig's son, Peter. The two children had played together, and when Peter was ill, Reuben had lent Ludwig money and had given him clothes and toys for the little boy. Now Ludwig could not bear to see his good friend suffer. He did his best to help in every possible way. While he was on guard, he brought them extra food and cheered them up. The unhappy prisoners were comforted in the knowledge that they had at least one friend left.

For three months, Reuben and his family lived this miserable existence. Their cell was cold and damp, the food scant, and their health suffered. Little Avner fell ill. His condition grew worse and worse. Soon the child was so weak that he could not even lift his little head. All day and all night the boy tossed feverishly on his straw pallet, moaning. Ludwig could no longer bear to witness the suffering of his friends. Avner's life was in danger, and he made up his mind to save the child and his family.

The next day, when Ludwig was on duty, he quietly unfolded his scheme to the prisoners. "Here is a large bottle of vodka," he told them. "Tonight, as soon as Ivan takes over from me, give him the bottle. He loves vodka so much that he will not bother to ask questions. He will drink it all up and will soon be fast asleep. Then, at midnight, I will steal his key and unlock the door of the dungeon."

Reuben was excited at the idea of escape. He did exactly as he was told. Ivan, just as Ludwig had predicted, seized the bottle greedily and drank it up fast. Soon he fell senseless and sodden to the floor. The trick had worked. At the stroke of twelve, the loyal Ludwig arrived. He unlocked the gate and released the prisoners. It was a bitterly cold night as they crept out. Snow was falling heavily. Little Avner was seriously ill, and his parents were filled with anxiety.

"He will not survive the long journey," said Ludwig sadly. "If you take the child with you, he will die on the way. The frontier is more than a hundred miles away. You have not a moment to lose. You must hurry on your way. Leave Avner with me, and Stephina, my good wife, will look after him most tenderly." The parents were torn at the heart-rending decision they had to make quickly. They hated to leave their young son behind, but they knew full well that Ludwig was right. So they left Avner with him, and with their three other children, they began the long, weary trek to safety.

Ludwig took Avner home, and Stephina tended him with loving care. For many weeks the frail little boy hovered between life and death. The doctor shook his head and sighed, but Stephina refused to give up hope. By some miracle, the boy recovered. He grew into a happy and healthy little boy. He was too young to remember the terrible ordeal he had experienced. Ludwig and Stephina brought him up as a member of the family. He knew no father except Ludwig and no mother except Stephina, and Peter was his dearly loved brother.

Six years passed, and Avner had reached his tenth birthday. He was dressed like a peasant boy, but somehow he did not look or act like one. He was a dreamy, sensitive lad, a contrast to his "brother," Peter. He was quiet and shy. He liked to be on his own and avoided other children as much as possible. It was not surprising, therefore, that they disliked him. They resented the boy who was always deep in thought and seemed to hold himself aloof. One day he quarreled with one of his schoolmates. "You are a Jew!" taunted the boy. Avner was stunned. He rushed home to his father and begged him to explain the reason for this strange accusation.

At first, Ludwig tried with soft words to soothe the troubled little boy. "Why, Avner, you are our dear son. We love you dearly, as much as we love your brother, Peter." But Avner was too intelligent to be deceived. He insisted on being told the truth, and Ludwig eventually related the whole sad story of his parents' misfortune.

Then Avner became restless and unhappy. Ludwig and Stephina did their best to comfort him. "You are our son," they repeated over and over again. "It is no use brooding over your real parents. You will never see them again. No doubt they perished on the journey. Or they may have settled in some distant land." But such reassurance could not calm the lad. Stronger and stronger grew the urge to find his family and to rejoin his people. So Avner lovingly took leave of his kind foster parents and his brother and courageously set out to find his parents. He crossed frontiers and traveled on the same road his parents had taken six years before him. He made his way to Zloczow, the home of the saint and scholar, Rabbi Yehiel Meir. He poured his tragic tale into the ears of the aged rabbi and piteously sought his assistance. "Help me!" pleaded Avner. "I want to find my parents. I want to be a Jew!"

Rabbi Yehiel Meir was moved. He took the child and supervised his education. He taught him Hebrew, marveling at the speed with which Avner mastered the unfamiliar tongue. He renamed him Meir. Meir was a very good student. He grew to love the Torah and spent days and nights studying the holy books. At the end of four years, he became an accomplished talmudic scholar. The rabbi was proud of his remarkable disciple. "You will be a light to Israel," he predicted.

Yet knowledge brought neither happiness nor peace of mind to the young scholar. Once again he became moody and restless. He still thought with longing of his parents, his brothers and his sister, wondering whether they were still alive. At length, he could bear the uncertainty no longer. He decided to go and find them. Rabbi Yehiel was heartbroken. He loved Meir deeply and was very reluctant to let him go. But when he saw that Meir's mind was made up and that nothing could sway him, the rabbi blessed him.

"Go in peace, and may the Almighty prosper you on your journey," said the venerable teacher. "Here is a small parchment scroll. I am going to sew it into your prayer shawl. I want you to carry this little scroll with you wherever you go. Keep it with you always but do not open it until the day of your wedding. Before you step beneath the wedding canopy, unroll the piece of parchment and read it."

Taking his walking stick and few belongings, Meir set out on his journey. He went from town to town, from village to village. He suffered hunger and thirst, cold and solitude. One day, he stopped at an inn in a village four miles from the city of Sosnowiec. The innkeeper, a Jew, was impressed with the young traveler and confided in him. "I have two young sons," said the innkeeper. "Joseph is eleven and Pinhas twelve. We live many miles from the nearest Jewish community. I have no one to teach the children. They are growing up in ignorance. From the way you prayed this morning, I can see that you are a student, learned in the law. Will you please stay with us for a while and teach my little sons how to pray in our holy language?"

Meir could not refuse the father's request. He stayed at the inn for six months, devoting all his time and energy to Joseph and Pinhas. They were bright children and made good progress in their studies. The innkeeper was well contented, and he and his wife became greatly attached to the earnest and upright young teacher. The whole family loved Meir. Especially fond of him was the daughter of the house, Zipporah. From her corner she followed his lessons intently, occasionally casting shy glances at the tutor.

Meir felt very happy at the inn. In no other place had he ever felt so much at home. In due course, he became betrothed to Zipporah and the wedding date was fixed. The rabbi of Sosnowiec, Rabbi Shalom, arrived in time for the wedding. He talked to Meir and was astounded at his profound knowledge of the Talmud. "He is fit to be the principal of a rabbinical college," the rabbi told the wedding guests. "You are indeed fortunate," he said to the innkeeper, "to gain so great a scholar as your son-in-law. I pray to God that my own daughter Rachel may find so worthy a husband."

The musicians took their places. The wedding canopy stood ready. The scribe was busy writing the marriage contract. The tables were laid. The guests had assembled. It was time for the wedding ceremony to commence. Then Meir took the rabbi aside. "Before the ceremony takes place," he explained, "I have to read a mysterious message given me by my saintly master, Rabbi Yehiel Meir of Zloczow."

Together they opened the prayer shawl and extracted the little parchment scroll. On it they read the words, "Is it right for a brother to marry his own sister?"

The bridegroom and the rabbi were startled by this message. The innkeeper and his wife were hurriedly summoned and closely questioned. It was soon learned that the innkeeper was none other than Reuben and that Meir was indeed his long-lost son.

Reuben and his wife were overjoyed. Instead of a son-in-law they had found their son, and Zipporah had found a brother. The wedding feast became a thanksgiving party, and the guests rejoiced at this unusual and exciting turn of events. The rabbi of Sosnowiec was particularly happy, for Meir would soon marry his own daughter, the beautiful Rachel.

—— 86 ——

A Broken Promise

Shemariah and his wife, Kreindel, lived near Kozienice in Poland. Shemariah dealt in grain and spices. They had been married for nearly fifteen years but had no children. Kreindel longed for a baby. She consulted doctors in Lublin and even traveled to Danzig, but no one could help her. She loved Shemariah. He was a good man, respected by all. If only they had a child, their happiness would be complete.

The fame of Rabbi Israel Hofstein, the preacher of Kozienice, was spreading. Many people came to consult him. Even the childless Countess Potoczki came to ask for his blessing and subsequently produced an heir.

Kreindel urged her husband to visit Rabbi Israel. "We have traveled as far as Danzig. The rabbi lives only a short distance from here. Could we not approach this holy man?" Shemariah gave in to her entreaties and visited the rabbi, asking for his blessing.

The rabbi asked him, "How much are you worth?" to which Shemariah replied, "If I were to sell my warehouse and my home, and counting the cash I have, I could raise a total of seven hundred rubles."

"You have a choice," the rabbi told him. "If you are willing to hand over to me your entire wealth, which would mean that you would be very poor, you would then be blessed with a child."

Shemariah decided to consult his wife. Kreindel had no hesitation. "A child means more to me than all the money in the world. Surely, God will not forsake us!"

Shemariah sold his warehouse and his home and moved with Kreindel to a small cottage. He then handed over all his money to Rabbi Israel.

Rabbi Israel returned the money and revealed to him, "When you were very young, barely fifteen years old, you were betrothed to Yette, a girl from Ozarow. Her father lost all his money and could not honor his obligations. He could not give a dowry to his daughter. Your late father then broke off the engagement. Yette was shamed in the process. It broke her heart. You must go and find her and ask her forgiveness. Only then will you be blessed with a child."

"So many years have passed since then. How will I ever find Yette?" asked Shemariah.

"You will find her at the trade fair in Yaroslav," replied the rabbi.

Shemariah immediately left for Yaroslav. The town was teeming with people, buyers and sellers, Jews and Gentiles. Shemariah was no stranger there. He knew the town well and was well known to dealers and merchants. But this time he was neither buying nor selling.

The fair lasted three days. Shemariah inquired at every boarding-house and at every inn, but no one had heard of Yette. She was just not there. On the last day of the fair, when the traders were loading their wagons for the homeward journey, Shemariah noticed a woman standing near a coach that was getting ready to depart. Some sixth sense told him that this was Yette. He approached her and said, "If you are Yette, please forgive me for the grief I caused you. I was very young then, and it was my father who broke off the betrothal. I was not consulted. My father thought it was for the best. Do forgive me!"

Yette was very surprised to be addressed by a stranger. It was only after he had finished speaking that she realized he was none other than her former betrothed, Shemariah. When she had sufficiently recovered, she replied "Yes. You did cause me shame, humiliation, and grief, but so many years have passed since then! I am now happily married, and I am willing to forgive you on one condition. I have a brother, Gavriel, who lives in Bilgoray, near Lublin. He is very poor. He has seven daughters. His eldest daughter is betrothed, and he needs seven hundred rubles for the marriage to go ahead. Unless he has the money within the next seven days, the betrothal will be broken, and my niece Peninah will suffer the same fate I did many years ago."

Shemariah did not delay. He traveled to Bilgoray and handed the money to Gavriel. The marriage of Peninah was celebrated with great joy. Shemariah stayed on to participate in the festivities.

To Shemariah's great delight, Kreindel bore him a son within a year.

—— 87 ——

It's a Small World

When a young boy, Nissim enjoyed playing with his friends. They played the games all children play, such as hide-and-seek, and often amused themselves by throwing pebbles into the fast-flowing river.

On one occasion Nissim's stone accidentally hit the chief of police, who was slowly riding by with a number of companions. The stone hit him on his forehead. He lost his balance and fell off his horse. The bleeding had to be stopped by the local barber-surgeon. The chief's friends seized Nissim and accused him of deliberately seeking to injure the chief of police. The boy was taken to Smolensk, where he was conscripted to serve as a "soldier of Nicholas" in the czarist army for a period of twenty-five years. His training would take place in far-off Siberia.

Nissim was handed over to a military guard, who was to deliver him to the nearest barracks, some fifty miles away. Nissim and his guard set out on their journey. They stopped at a Jewish inn for refreshments and rest. The innkeeper, Shragai, felt great pity for Nissim, who was barely twelve years old. He had the long sidelocks and wore the hat and kaftan of the *yeshivah* student. Shragai plied the guard with free drinks and food.

"Why do you wish to take this boy to the barracks?" Shragai asked the guard. "You know he is a good lad. What happened was an accident. He never intended to hurt the chief of police. He is not the type to make a good soldier. He will be no asset to the army. He will get sick and die there. Why don't you leave him here with me and tell the police chief he died on the way. As a reward, I will give you one hundred rubles."

The guard could not resist such temptation. One hundred rubles was a fortune to him. With such a sum, he could acquire a farm. He took the money and left Nissim with Shragai, who treated Nissim like a son. He was brought up with Shragai's only daughter, Breinah.

Nissim was a diligent student. He had a phenomenal memory. He could remember many pages of the Talmud by heart. Shragai sent him to a talmudical college in Lublin, where he remained for many years. Eventually, he became the rabbi of Poznan.

Years passed. Shragai became very poor. He had to leave the inn, and he and his family moved to Poznan. There were many Jews who owed money to the collector of taxes. To make sure of getting the money, he took hostages. One of these was Breinah, Shragai's only daughter.

Breinah was held prisoner in a first-floor room. The door was securely bolted, but she noticed that one of the windows was partially open. Being a resourceful girl, she tore up a sheet and made it into a rope. She disguised herself by dressing in the tax collector's uniform, which she found in a wardrobe in the room.

In the middle of the night, Breinah made her escape. She was afraid to return to her parents' home, so she decided to take shelter in Rabbi Nissim's house. Nissim recognized her and sent for her parents. He told them that if they were to tear open the lining of the tax collector's coat, they would find hidden there one hundred rubles, the identical sum Shragai had paid to bribe the guard to release young Nissim from the clutches of the czar's army. The former guard was now the tax collector of Poznan.

"Take the money. The tax collector is bound to search for your daughter. She is not safe here. With the hundred rubles you can settle in Stettin. And with the help of the Almighty you will succeed in business. You saved me once. Now your daughter has to be saved!"

—— 88 ——

The Professor of Miropol

Herzka came to Rabbi Mordecai of Neschitz. "I am very ill. I have spent a fortune on doctors and medicines. I spent weeks taking the waters at different spas, but I am still very ill. No one has helped me so far. You are my only hope. Please help me! I have a wife and nine young children. I want to live to see them married."

"Herzka, why are you so worried? Why do you not consult the professor of Miropol? He will surely help you," the rabbi advised him.

Herzka did not delay. He ordered a coach and set out for Miropol. After a long and tiring journey on bumpy roads, he arrived at this small town of about two hundred Jewish inhabitants. When he had settled at an inn, he asked the innkeeper, "Where can I find the professor?"

"Professor?" queried the innkeeper in amazement. "What professor? We have no professor here." Herzka could not believe his ears. He went to the synagogue and asked the beadle, "Where does the professor live?"

The townspeople thought he was mad. "What professor? There are no professors here!"

"Have you a doctor in the town?" inquired Herzka.

"No. We are a very tiny and poor community. We have no doctor here. We do not even have a *feldger* (barber-surgeon)."

"So what do you do when someone is ill?" asked Herzka. "We pray to God, the great and faithful Healer," replied the beadle.

Herzka returned to Neschitz and reported to Rabbi Mordecai his unsuccessful search for the nonexistent professor of Miropol. "Your journey was not in vain," the rabbi said to him. "You have learned that it is God who is the only true and faithful Healer."

— *89* —

Marriages Are Made in Heaven

Melech was an orphan. His parents, his brothers, and his sisters had been murdered by the cossacks. As he had no close relatives, Rabbi Tzvi Hirsch of Rymanov took him into his house. Melech loved the rabbi and would accompany him to the ritual bath every morning. He would light the fire in the rabbi's study and act as his beadle. He would stand guard outside the rabbi's room and stop anyone from disturbing the rabbi in his devotions and study. He would also help Zissa, the rabbi's wife, in the kitchen. He would run errands and make himself generally useful. Rabbi Tzvi Hirsch was a man of great compassion. He never lost his temper. Melech became part of his household and made himself indispensable.

One night, Rabbi Tzvi Hirsch lost his temper and shouted at Melech, "Get out of the house. I do not want you here anymore. I have had enough of you. Leave my house immediately!"

The rabbi's uncharacteristic outburst came to Melech as a bolt from the blue. The rabbi always spoke softly. He never raised his voice. He loved Melech as if he were his own son. His behavior was very hard to explain. In vain did his wife, Zissa, plead with her husband. "What has come over you? What has Melech done to deserve such harsh treatment? He is always so helpful and considerate. Why do you drive him out in the middle of the night? Where will he go? He has lived with us all his life. It is freezing outside. He will catch the death of a cold!"

Rabbi Tzvi Hirsch was not to be moved. Melech, with tears in his eyes, collected his meager belongings and left the only home he had ever known. He was in a daze. He could not understand what he had done to deserve to be cast out without any explanation.

When Melech left the rabbi's house, it was snowing heavily. He had to find shelter. He stopped at the nearest inn. The landlord, Lapidus, was out of town. He was away at a fair buying provisions. His wife, Geilah, and her daughter, Gitah, were looking after the inn. Geilah knew Melech. He was a frequent caller. When she saw him with his bundle, covered in snow, she welcomed him and allowed him to spend the night with them. Melech, who felt exhausted and aged by his experience, lay down next to the large stove and fell asleep.

At that time, two merchants were staying at the inn. They were celebrating the successful conclusion of a business deal. They had secured a contract to cut down the timber of the local forest. They were being served by Geilah and Gitah. They ordered wine and drank much. They were almost drunk. They saw Melech lying on the bench fast asleep. They woke him up and asked him to join them. In jest, one merchant said to the other, "We have here a nice young man and a presentable young woman. An ideal match. Why not marry them off here and now?"

One of the merchants took a ring out of his pocket and handed it to Melech, saying, "Place this ring on the forefinger of the right hand of Gitah and say the traditional words: 'Behold, you are consecrated unto me with this ring, according to the law of Moses and of Israel.'" Melech was too tired to know what he was doing. He regarded the whole thing as a joke. After all, the following week would be Purim, the season of jollity! He placed the ring on the girl's right index finger and said the required words. He then returned to his place near the stove and resumed his sleep.

Early the next morning, the merchants departed, and Lapidus returned from the fair. His wife told him of the incident that had taken place the night before. She explained to him how the merchants had arranged a mock wedding between Melech and their daughter, Gitah.

Lapidus was very angry. "Why did you allow such a wedding to take place? Gitah is our only daughter, and Melech is just a poor orphan. He is not learned. He is merely the rabbi's beadle. The marriage is valid and cannot now be dissolved except by divorce."

He decided to take the young couple to the rabbi. On entering the house, Rabbi Tzvi Hirsch exclaimed, "*Mazel Tov*, congratulations! I am so happy to see you. This marriage was arranged in heaven where, according to the Talmud, forty days prior to the birth of a child its marriage partner is ordained. The rich and proud Lapidus would never have consented to a marriage between Melech and his only daughter. I love Melech very dearly. I deliberately drove him out of the house last night because I knew that he was destined to marry Gitah. Lapidus, you go home now and arrange the wedding feast. The two young people are meant for each other. They are indeed an ideal couple."

90

Be Careful of What You Say

Rabbi David of Lelov was a devoted follower of Rabbi Elimelech of Lyzhansk. As he could not always afford the coach fare, he often walked all the way to Lyzhansk. One day, when he was on the way to the rabbi, a carriage drawn by four horses stopped beside him. It belonged to the wealthy Gedaliah, who was a contractor to the Russian army. Whenever Gedaliah concluded a deal, he would travel to the rabbi for his blessing.

Gedaliah was pleased to hear that the man to whom he had offered a free ride in his coach was also on his way to the rabbi. When he discovered that his traveling companion spent all his day in the House of Study, he reprimanded him: "It is wrong not to earn one's living. If you are not capable of working, why not become a Hebrew teacher?"

Rabbi David listened carefully but said nothing. After their arrival in Lyzhansk, Gedaliah did not stay long. He had pressing business to attend to in Warsaw and Danzig, so he left on the following day. He bade farewell to his fellow traveler, who told him in parting, "If you hear someone crying out for help on your return journey, do not ignore it!"

Gedaliah could not understand these instructions. He was too pre-occupied with his own affairs to query them. Without delay, he departed in the waiting carriage. After some hours' travel, he heard in the stillness of the night a cry for help. He asked the coachman to stop. With the help of a lantern, they discovered a man in military uniform lying on the ground, groaning in pain. They moved him to the coach. They covered him with blankets and gave him a hot drink. It became evident that one of his legs was broken. Gedaliah asked the coach driver to take him to the nearest town, where the man's leg was set.

They had rescued a general in the Austrian army on a special trip to Russia to attend army maneuvers. The general was not familiar with the roads. He had fallen off his horse and had been lying bruised and injured by the side of the road without food or drink for the last twenty-four hours. He told Gedaliah, "You have saved my life. I would like to give you a reward of one thousand rubles."

Gedaliah refused to accept this offer, saying, "I am not short of money. I was only too happy to help you. Doing a good deed is a reward in itself!" He then returned home and forgot all about the incident.

Gedaliah's prosperity did not last. His extensive warehouse, full of timber and army supplies, burned down. He was accused of starting the fire. He was released on bail, pending trial. He was facing a long prison sentence, as he could not prove his innocence. His Polish manager, Tavinsky, who had been in his employ for many years, had long been plotting Gedaliah's downfall. He wanted to take over the business and swore falsely that Gedaliah had caused the fire.

Gedaliah had no desire to spend many years innocently confined to prison and decided to escape to neighboring Austria. He collected what ready cash he could and engaged a guide to smuggle him across the frontier. On arrival in Austria, he discovered that his wallet containing his money and valuables was gone. It had probably been stolen by his guide during the night. He was now penniless. He did not possess even enough money to pay for lodging.

He became a beggar. He slept at night, free of charge, in the *hekdesh*, a small communal room next to the synagogue, together with other beggars.

After many miles of walking, Gedaliah arrived in Cracow. The town was in an uproar. The streets were lined with troops. Bands were playing martial music. He was told that the town was welcoming the new governor general of the city. Gedaliah took his place near Wavel Castle. The trumpets were sounded as a state carriage arrived. The troops presented arms, and the new governor stepped out of the carriage to take the salute. He was dressed in the uniform of a field marshal, bedecked with medals. Suddenly, he recognized Gedaliah, who was standing behind the soldiers. He called him over. "You are the man who saved my life four years ago! Why are you now dressed in rags?"

Gedaliah told him his story. The governor was so concerned to hear what had befallen Gedaliah that he lent him a large sum of money. Once again, Gedaliah started trading and was soon able to bring his family to Cracow.

By that time, Rabbi Elimelech was no longer alive. The fame of Rabbi David of Lelov was, however, spreading through the land. Gedaliah once again made the journey to receive a blessing. On his arrival, the rabbi reminded him, "I was the young man to whom you once gave a ride in your carriage on your way to Lyzhansk. I recall how you embarrassed me with your remarks. For this you were punished. But now your sins have been forgiven. From now on, remember the rabbinic saying: 'Wise men, be heedful of what you say!' "

—— 91 ——

An Old Debt

Rabbi Hayim Halberstam of Sanz once spent a few days in Budapest. Many people came to see the rabbi, who was known for his great scholarship and wisdom. Among the visitors who sought his guidance was the well-known banker Polikoff. He was not an observant Jew. He rarely attended the synagogue. His only son was very ill. He had consulted many physicians. They had done all they could but could do no more for the young man. Polikoff had heard of the wonder-working *rebbe*, so he turned to him in desperation.

Rabbi Hayim, in wishing the son a very speedy recovery, assured the anxious father that the young man would fully recover. The banker, in gratitude, offered the rabbi four hundred rubles, which he refused to accept.

Twenty years passed. Wolf, a devoted follower of the rabbi, came to see him. His daughter was to be married to a scholarly young man. He urgently needed four hundred rubles to pay for the dowry, the trousseau, and the wedding celebrations. Rabbi Hayim told him not to worry. "Take this letter to the banker Polikoff in Budapest. Do not accept less than four hundred rubles."

Wolf traveled to Budapest and found the offices of the banker. He was at first refused admittance, then he was offered a few rubles. Wolf declined. He would not leave. "I have a letter to Polikoff that I must hand to him personally."

Eventually, he was allowed to see the banker and handed him the letter. It contained only a brief note: "Please give Wolf four hundred rubles."

Polikoff lost his temper. "Who is this rabbi who demands such a large sum? I do not mind giving you a donation of ten or even fifteen rubles. But four hundred rubles is a lot of money. I may be a banker, but I do not print money!"

The banker was becoming more and more agitated, when his wife entered the office. He showed her the note, saying, "What an impertinence to demand such a large sum from a stranger!"

"My dear husband," replied his wife, "you really owe him the money. Try to remember! It was Rabbi Hayim who, twenty years ago, saved our son. You offered him four hundred rubles, which he declined."

Shamefacedly, the banker gave Wolf the money. Wolf and his family were overjoyed to be able to go ahead with the preparation for the marriage, which was celebrated with great joy and happiness.

—— 92 ——

No Beggar

Nahum was known for his hospitality. He built a house where the needy and homeless would find food and shelter. One night an unkempt old man, dressed in tattered garments and torn boots, stayed with him. Nahum offered him a donation, but the man declined. Nahum increased the amount of money, but once againthe man refused to take it. Nahum was surprised. This was the first time anyone had refused to accept a donation. The stranger soon explained. "My name is Aryeh. I am not really a beggar. In fact, I am very wealthy. I live in a large house near Budapest. I own an extensive orchard and a vineyard. My wine is sold throughout the country. I also deal in wheat. I have an office in Budapest where I employ many people.

"One day I found that four hundred rubles were missing from the till. A thorough search was made, but no trace of the money was found. An orphan girl, Abigail, who was working for me as a servant, was the most likely suspect. The police arrested her, and in spite of her protestations of innocence, she was sentenced to three years' imprisonment. She was frail and could not bear the rigors of prison life. After a short while, she died of consumption.

"Some time later, another large sum of money was found to be missing. It had been noticed that Tobias, the bookkeeper, was living above his means. He was wearing expensive clothes and had acquired a valuable Swiss watch and a diamond ring for his wife. When confronted, he confessed that he had been stealing for many years.

"I began suffering from bad headaches, unexplained dizziness, unusual tiredness, insomnia, and depression. None of the doctors in Budapest or Vienna could find a cure for my problems. They applied leeches to purify my blood. The sent me to the spa town of Marienbad, but to no avail. I then went to see Rabbi Meir of Premishlany. He said to me, 'Nahum, you have committed a terrible sin. You accused a poor orphan of having committed a theft. She was innocent. She had served you faithfully for many years. God is the Father of the orphans, and her blood is crying out for revenge.'

" 'Rabbi!' I cried. 'Help me! I will do anything to atone for my sin.' Rabbi Meir then told me that I would have to suffer before I could find full atonement. 'You must leave your home and business. Dress in beggar's clothes. Wander from town to town for three years. Do not stay in any one place longer than a day. Accept only food and lodging.

After three years, your sin will be forgiven, and you will then be allowed to return to your home and business.'

"The three years are just coming to an end. I am grateful to you for your hospitality. Thank you, too, for offering me a donation. This I cannot accept, as it is part of my penance for putting to shame an innocent orphan."

——— 93 ———

The Rabbi Came Late

Everyone loved the aged Rabbi Yitzhak of Nemirov. The whole community looked up to him with the greatest affection and respect. Never in all his life had Rabbi Yitzhak refused help to anyone in trouble or need. When a shivering beggar once told him that he had no coat for the winter, the gentle rabbi took off his own coat and handed it to the stranger. He never returned home without bringing several hungry guests with whom he was happy to share his frugal meal. He was happiest when he helped the poor and the needy. He felt that however much he did, he did not do enough, and whatever he gave, he was still not giving enough. He could not bear to see anyone suffer.

Before every festival, especially before the Festival of Passover, he would go around to all the members of the community and collect money for the poor. Few could refuse him on his errand of mercy. The poor looked upon him as a loving father and a merciful protector. They knew that the rabbi of Nemirov was a friend on whom they could rely.

It happened that one Sabbath eve, the rabbi was not seen in his usual place in the synagogue. The House of Worship was crowded, and the reader had already begun the afternoon service. Naturally, he waited patiently for the rabbi's appearance before beginning the evening prayers. The rabbi of Nemirov was usually the first to arrive at the synagogue. He would take his seat at the eastern wall and lose himself in meditation and prayer. He would recite with great fervor the mystical hymn, "Come My Beloved to Welcome the Bride Sabbath, the Queen of the Days." Every word was weighed and every letter had some special meaning. The congregation enjoyed his singing of the beautiful Friday-evening melodies. His presence gave them new courage, new hope. He had been guiding the community for nearly forty years, and the whole town had experienced Rabbi Yitzhak's loving care. Even the elders could not recall a time when the rabbi had not led them and looked after them. Now, for the first time in memory, he had not appeared in the synagogue. The venerable scholar, frail and with his strength waning, had left his home early that afternoon without telling anyone where he was going.

It was an anxious night for the community, especially for the rabbi's family. Great was their relief when, at last, they heard the rabbi's familiar footsteps. Rabbi Yitzhak at once recited the evening prayers with great devotion and sanctified the holy Sabbath. "Where have you been these last six hours?" asked his frantic wife. "Father, we were so worried!" exclaimed his children. "The whole congregation was alarmed."

The rabbi then explained. "As you know, I went out early this afternoon. I went to visit the widow Brachah. Her late husband, Moses, was a great scholar. She is now a very, very old lady with no friends or relatives. She is poor and blind. When the beadle told me that she was sick, I thought I would go to see her.

"She lives in a wretched little hut. When I arrived she was lying in her bed, covered with old rags and shivering. The room was dark and cold.

There was no fire to warm her, no candle to light the darkness. When she heard my footsteps she called out weakly, 'Who's there?'

"In order to reassure her I replied, 'I am Ivan the woodcutter.' Had she known who I really was, she would have been embarrassed and ashamed."

" 'What do you want?' she asked fearfully.

" 'I want to help you,' I replied.

" 'You want to help me?' she questioned. 'How can that be? I am all alone. No one cares about me. Even my neighbors don't bother to look in.'

" 'God has not deserted you,' I assured her. 'I have brought you some wood.'

" 'Wood!' she exclaimed. 'I have no money to buy wood!'

" 'Forget about the money,' I comforted her.

" 'So what's the use of wood!' she further inquired. 'I am too weak to light a fire!'

" 'Do not worry,' I told her, 'I will do it for you willingly.'

"I cleared out the grate and lit the fire, which soon filled the hut with warmth and light. Then I went to the neighboring houses and borrowed some food. I took it back to the hut and cooked her a meal. She was too weak to hold a spoon, so I fed her. The nourishing broth brought new life to the poor woman. She smiled with pleasure, finished her meal, and fell sound asleep. I was then able to return home. By that time, it was very late and I had missed the service in the synagogue. But I felt I had been of service to a sick old woman. May the Lord forgive me, and may He preserve her!"

—— 94 ——

My Help Cometh from the Lord

Sender was a follower of the rabbi of Lubavitch. He was a very wealthy man. He had businesses in many different towns. This involved long journeys, and he was often away from home. He relied on his Polish manager, Sobiesky, to deal with his affairs in his absence. He even trusted Sobiesky with the keys to his safe.

Sender soon discovered that sums of money were missing. After a thorough investigation, it transpired that Sobiesky was the thief. He had taken advantage of his master's frequent absences to rob him. Sender dismissed Sobiesky but did not notify the police. In revenge, Sobiesky informed the authorities that Sender was evading taxation by keeping two sets of account books. Sender was arrested but released on bail pending his trial.

He went to consult the rabbi of Lubavitch. "I have been falsely accused. Unfortunately, it is my word against Sobiesky's. If I am convicted I shall be imprisoned for many years. Whence will my help come?"

The rabbi listened carefully and replied, "You have just used the words of the Psalmist, 'Whence will my help come?' Remember, should you ever meet a Jew who uses the identical phrase, help him as much as you can."

Sender returned home. He was told that in his absence his neighbor, Gad, had lost all his possessions in a fire that destroyed his timber yard and his home. Sender was grieved to hear the bad news. He had known Gad almost all his life. They were not only neighbors but also close friends. They often made business deals. He rushed to offer his help and sympathy to Gad.

"How can you help me? I need at least one thousand rubles. You are in trouble yourself. Whence will my help come?"

As soon as Sender heard Gad quoting this verse from the Psalms, he recalled the rabbi's words and immediately gave Gad the one thousand rubles.

After a lapse of several months, the trial of Sender took place. In vain did he protest his innocence. Sobiesky persisted in his allegations that Sender was a cheat and had been in the habit of evading taxation. The outcome of the trial now depended on the judge.

"Many years ago," the judge told the court, "I was a penniless student from a poor family. I was studying law in Moscow. After returning to Moscow, from a holiday with my parents, I found that I did not possess a single coin. I slept on a bench in the railway station. I almost froze to death, when snow covered me like a blanket. I suddenly woke to see a man standing over me, saying, 'You are blue with the cold. Here is some money. Buy yourself a hot drink and something to eat.' I did as the stranger had instructed me. He even gave me money to buy myself a railway ticket. This stranger now stands before me accused of tax fraud. It is his word against that of Sobiesky. I have no hesitation in deciding whom to believe. Sobiesky is nothing but a thief. Where did he get the money to start his own timber business and wear expensive clothes? He is lucky I do not send him to prison for leveling false charges against an innocent man."

Sender returned home a free man. He realized how right the rabbi had been when he had told him to remember the phrase, "Whence will my help come?"

95

Washing One's Hands

An American-born Jewish soldier, Mark Stein, was drafted to fight in the Korean war in 1954. Prior to his departure for Korea, he went to Rabbi Menachem Mendel Schneerson, the Lubavitcher *rebbe* in Brooklyn, for a blessing. The rabbi impressed upon him that he should do his utmost to observe as many commandments as possible, and above all he should not eat before washing his hands and reciting the customary blessing: "Blessed are You, O Lord, our God, King of the universe, who has sanctified us with His commandments and has commanded us concerning the washing of the hands."

Mark Stein spent a whole year with the army in Korea. One day, after a deadly skirmish with the elusive, deceptive, and dangerous enemy, his battalion found a disused and dilapidated hut to rest in and sat down by a half-broken table to consume some of their army rations. Before eating, Mark recalled the rabbi's advice, but there were no washing facilities there. He left the hut in search of water. The whole area had been devastated, homes destroyed, trees uprooted, and animals killed. He walked for several hundred yards before he found a small brook, where he washed his hands and made the benediction.

While he was reciting the blessing, enemy planes flew overhead and dropped many high explosives and incendiary bombs. Mark ducked under an old truck for safety, as debris was flying everywhere.

After a while Mark returned to his battalion. The hut was no longer there. It had received a direct hit, and the entire company had perished. He was the only survivor, thanks to following the advice of the *rebbe* of Lubavitch.

96

The Grass Is Greener

In the old town of Cracow, the ancient capital of Poland, there lived a poor Hebrew teacher named Rabbi Yitzhak. His home was a one-room cottage that served as bedroom, dining room, kitchen, and classroom. From early morning until late in the afternoon, the little room would be crowded with children, thirty or more, studying Hebrew. Some sat around the table on wooden stools, others on benches arranged against the wall.

Rabbi Yitzhak was a most learned man. From his earliest childhood he had devoted his life to the study of the Torah. The words of God's law never departed from him by day or by night. He loved to teach as much as he loved to study. It was a labor of love for him to teach the little ones the way of our faith. He taught them the Hebrew alphabet. He introduced them to the prayer book, the Five Books of Moses, and the great commentary of Rabbi Shlomoh ben Yitzhak.

The highlight of every day was the story hour. The children looked forward eagerly to Rabbi Yitzhak's tales. Rabbi Yitzhak was a wonderful storyteller. He told stories from the Bible, the Talmud, the Midrash, stories of the famous rabbis and the saints, legends of Hasidism and its great rabbis.

Rabbi Yitzhak brought alive for his children these legends of the past. He had a vivid imagination. If the story was a joyous one, like the victory of David over Goliath, the building of the Temple, or the triumph of the Maccabees, his face shone with enthusiasm and radiated happiness. If the story was a sad one, like that of the destruction of the

Temple or the tale of the Ten Martyrs, Rabbi Yitzhak's eyes were moist with tears. The children always listened with rapt attention. Rabbi Yitzhak lifted them up on a magic carpet and took them from Cracow to distant lands, to Roman Palestine, to Moslem Spain, to lands peopled with giants, heroes, warriors, scholars.

Rabbi Yitzhak was completely unworldly. He never demanded fees. He was content to take whatever the parents of his pupils would give him. Most of them came from very poor homes and could simply not afford to pay anything for tuition, but this made no difference to their devoted teacher. All were children of God, and all were equal. Everyone was entitled to learn and to be taught. Rabbi Yitzhak had no interest in money. He had no desire for honor or for power. His aim in life was to teach his pupils to be honest, good, and kind.

Rabbi Yitzhak's wife, Zlata, looked at matters differently. Their poverty irked her, and every single day she complained bitterly and reproached her husband: "You spend your whole life teaching others, but what do you do for yourself? You never ask for money, so how am I to pay the butcher, the baker, and the grocer? Our children are growing up. Hanah is nearly fourteen years old, almost old enough to become betrothed. She has not even one decent dress. Sarah, the younger one, goes about barefoot. She has never had a decent pair of shoes. And what about me? Ever since I married you, we have not had one good meal. We live a life of hardship and poverty. Is this the reward for your piety and godliness?"

Rabbi Yitzhak listened patiently, making no reply. Zlata's continual grumblings did not destroy his spirit, and her tears did not embitter him. "Who is rich?" ask the rabbis. "He who is content with his portion." Rabbi Yitzhak was rich in faith.

One Friday night, the rabbi dreamed a strange dream. "Go to Prague," he was told. "Dig beneath the royal palace, and you will discover a great treasure." Rabbi Yitzhak awoke and felt amused. He recalled the talmudic saying, "Dreams are of no consequence. No wheat without chaff. No dreams without nonsense." He told no one of his dream, not even his wife, and dismissed it from his mind.

On Saturday night, he dreamed the same dream. Once again, he heard a voice telling him, "Go to Prague, dig beneath the royal palace, and you will find a treasure." Rabbi Yitzhak felt that he could no longer ignore the dream or its message and decided to make his way to Prague. It was not very easy for Rabbi Yitzhak to undertake this journey. He had been born in Cracow and not once in all his life had he left his hometown. It took courage to make such a journey. He had many problems to overcome. He could not bear to leave his pupils. And he had to find some money. He could scarcely find five rubles to buy a seat on the coach. With his staff in one hand and a book in the other, Rabbi Yitzhak set out on his long journey to the strange and distant capital of Bohemia.

On the rabbi's long journey, charitable Jews provided him with food, and he slept many a weary night on a hard bench in a synagogue. His resolution and courage often wavered, and he frequently wanted to turn back. He was frightened of the unknown, the strange language, and the strange people.

At long last, after many days of travel, Rabbi Yitzhak arrived in Prague, a picturesque town with many beautiful buildings, with palaces and towers and handsome bridges spanning the river Moldau, which separates the old town from the new.

Rabbi Yitzhak, however, had no eye for the beauty of the city. His mind was obsessed with his dream and its messages. After resting awhile in the *Judenstadt*, the Jewish quarter, he made his way to the fourteenth-century royal palace. Here his courage forsook him. He was overawed by the grandeur of the palace, an imposing building, closely guarded by soldiers and imperial guardsmen. He walked round and round the imperial grounds and wondered what to do. "How is it possible to dig beneath the royal palace? They will either shoot me, imprison me, or put me in an asylum. What foolishness has made me forsake my family and my pupils to come on this futile errand?"

On the following day, Rabbi Yitzhak, as if drawn by a magnet, once again walked around the palace, deep in thought. On the third day, one of the guards approached him. "Tell me, stranger, is there anything I can do for you? I have been watching you these three days, going round the palace aimlessly. Have you lost something?"

At first, Rabbi Yitzhak was terrified. He had always been afraid of soldiers, but somehow this soldier was different. Rabbi Yitzhak, gaining confidence, unburdened his heart to the friendly guardsman. "I have had a remarkable dream," he confessed. "In my dream, I was told that if I dug beneath the royal palace I would discover a great treasure. But now that I am here, I do not know what to do."

The soldier smiled. "I thought you Jews were intelligent people guided by reason as well as emotion. And yet you believe in dreams! Why, look at me! I, Dimitri Massarek, one of His Majesty's guards, have dreamed the same dream on two consecutive nights: 'Go to Cracow,' said a voice to me. 'Dig in the yard of Rabbi Yitzhak, the Hebrew teacher, and you will discover a treasure.' But I take no heed of such foolishness. I would not waste my time or money journeying to Cracow. I don't believe in dreams!"

Then Rabbi Yitzhak realized his dream had brought him to Prague in order to hear the soldier's story. At once, he set out on his homeward journey. His family and pupils were disappointed to see him return empty-handed. They had hoped so much to see him return loaded with riches.

"Well, my millionaire, where is your gold and silver?" taunted Zlata. "A pauper you were born and a pauper you will die!" Rabbi Yitzhak was silent. He took a spade and made his way to his garden.

The neighbors were astonished to see the teacher turn gardener. Rabbi Yitzhak began to dig with great energy. With superhuman strength and unflagging zeal, he dug deeper and deeper. The neighbors now mocked him and made fun of him. "He has gone out of his mind," they whispered. Rabbi Yitzhak took no notice but went on working. He was soon rewarded. Beneath the stones and the infertile soil lay a casket containing diamonds and rubies. He had uncovered a priceless treasure.

But wealth did not spoil Rabbi Yitzhak or change his values. He built a large stone synagogue and a big schoolhouse, and he continued to teach the Torah to little children. "The moral of my dream," he would tell them, "is clear to all who wish to understand. Every man has a treasure in his own garden. It is vain and foolish to search for happiness elsewhere. All that we want we have inside ourselves."

The burned-out shell of the synagogue, despite repeated Nazi attempts to destroy it, is to this day standing in Cracow on a street bearing the name of the Hebrew teacher.

—— 97 ——

The Lost Princess

After Rabbi Nahman of Bratslav

Once upon a time there was a king who had six sons and one daughter. He loved all his children, but his favorite was the little princess. Every day, the king found time away from the affairs of state to play with his small daughter. But one day the royal father was in a bad mood. In a fit of temper he snapped at the child. "May the evil powers take you," he growled thoughtlessly.

The next day the princess vanished from the palace. The grounds were searched, but there was no trace of the missing child. The king shut himself up in his room and mourned his darling daughter. The chief minister could not bear to witness the anguish of the king and decided to go and seek her himself. The bereaved father gratefully agreed, and the minister set out on his journey.

He traveled for many days, until he came to a strongly guarded fortress. At the gates he hesitated, but to his amazement the soldiers moved aside and permitted him to enter unhindered. Unharmed, he walked through the long passageways until he reached the royal apartments. On the throne sat a king with a crown on his head and a scepter in his hands. In a corner of the chamber stood a small forlorn figure, and behold! It was the little lost princess.

The minister rushed to her side and a hurried conversation took place. "Tell me," whispered the minister, "how can you get out of here?"

"There is but one way," she replied. "You have to wait one year for me. Think of me always, every moment of every day. On the last day of the year, fast and stay awake the whole time."

The minister carried out these instructions to the letter. Throughout the year, his thoughts were centered on the princess. On the last day, he fasted and did not sleep and eagerly set out to rescue her. As he approached the fortress, he noticed a tree with beautiful apples. The temptation proved too great. He stretched out his hand and plucked an apple and ate the luscious fruit. At once, he fell sound asleep. He slept for a long time.

Then, with many apologies, the minister sought out the princess. Once more, the royal maiden gave him the same detailed instructions. Another year had to pass in the same manner, and on the last day the minister was permitted to eat but strictly forbidden to drink. The minister swore solemnly to do exactly as she had commanded.

The year passed. He had obeyed in every detail. On the last day, he again set out for the fortress. On the way he crossed a little brook, and again the temptation was too great. He drank of the water and fell fast asleep. The princess passed by him with her retinue and wept bitterly when she saw him asleep. Hope of rescue was now very remote. But she dropped her glove as she passed, and in it was a mysterious message: "They are taking me to the Castle of Pearls on the Mountain of Gold. Find me!"

The minister awoke and found the message. He was full of remorse. Frantically, he searched but could find no clue as to the whereabouts of the Castle of Pearls. Then he met a giant and begged for help.

"I am in charge of all the animals," the giant told him proudly. He called together his charges and questioned them. But no one had ever heard of the castle. The giant then advised the minister to travel farther to find the giant's brother, who was in charge of the birds. "Perhaps the creatures of the air know of the place you seek."

So the minister traveled on until he found the master of the birds. The birds were assembled and questioned but they, too, could not help him. However, the master directed him to pursue his search: "I have a brother who is the keeper of the winds. Perchance the winds can help you."

The minister refused to be discouraged. He sought out the keeper of the winds. All the winds were summoned, and not one of them could help. But just as the keeper was about to dismiss them, a soft breeze arrived breathlessly at the gathering. The keeper was angry. "Why are you so late?" he asked crossly. "Did I not command all of you to appear before me? Why did you not obey?"

"I was delayed," apologized the soft breeze. "I have only just now finished my work. I bore a princess to the Castle of Pearls on the Mountain of Gold."

The keeper then turned to the minister. "You will need a great deal of money to make this journey to rescue your princess. But do not despair. I will help you."

He gave the minister a magic purse filled with coins, and no matter how much the minister spent, the purse was always full. So he was able to find the Castle of Pearls on the Mountain of Gold. And in it he found the most precious pearl of all, the little princess. He brought her safely home and restored her to the arms of her loving father. Never again was a harsh word heard in the palace, and everyone lived happily ever after.

——— 98 ———

The Obstacles

There was once a rabbi named Joseph who was very learned and pious. He did not approve of the new sect of the *hasidim*. He could not understand their ways. He hated the hasidic rabbis and did not believe the marvelous tales of the miracles these wonder-workers performed.

Rabbi Joseph had one son who was the light of his eyes. The father spent his days and nights instructing his son in the Torah. The boy, however, was restless. He was unhappy and felt himself imprisoned. He longed for the open spaces, for the meadows and the fields. He confided in his companions, and they told him of the famous hasidic rabbi and of the new doctrines he was teaching. The young student became very interested. He wanted to go to see the rabbi. He begged permission, but his father could not be persuaded. It was hard for him to refuse his son anything, but this was one wish he could not grant. He did not want his only son to come under the influence of the *hasidim*. The boy pined and fell ill. His father was finally moved. He could not bear to see his son so ill and so sad, and at last he consented to the journey.

On the way they met with an accident. Their carriage overturned. The rabbi took this as a divine sign that his journey was unnecessary, and he persuaded his son to return home. Again the boy became ill. Again he grew sad and gloomy. Again he begged his father to take him to the rabbi. So, once again, father and son set out. And this time, as before, the travelers were unlucky. Their horses became lame, and they were forced to turn back.

The boy's condition again deteriorated. He became weaker and weaker. Doctors were called in, but they could find no cure. Rabbi Joseph, unable to bear seeing his son suffer, consented for the third time to the journey to see the rabbi.

This time, everything went well, and the two travelers arrived safely in the town where the great rabbi lived. They stopped at the inn, and there they fell into conversation with a merchant.

"I have just visited the rabbi," the merchant confided to them, "and he is godless and fears not the Almighty." Rabbi Joseph had heard enough, and he promptly took his son home. The son became ill again and died soon afterward.

The father was heartbroken and could find no comfort. He saw strange visions and dreamed disturbing dreams. In one of his dreams, his son came to him and urged him to go to the rabbi. Rabbi Joseph yielded, and for the fourth time he set out on the familiar road. Once again, he met the merchant.

"Are you not the same man who told us of the rabbi's godlessness?" asked the bereaved father.

"Yes, I am," the man replied. "It was always I who prevented your seeing the rabbi. It was I who overturned your carriage, maimed your horses, and told you lies about the rabbi. I am not really a merchant. I am Satan. I could not leave any stone unturned. I had to prevent your son from meeting the great rabbi, for had the two met, their power could have moved heaven and earth. They could even have forced the Messiah to descend at once and bring peace to all mankind."

99

The Prince and the Servant

There was once a kingdom where the queen and her personal maid were both expecting babies around the same time. The queen loved the faithful maid and engaged a midwife to attend them both at the birth of their children. It came to pass that both women gave birth to boys the same night. The midwife deliberately exchanged the newborn babies. She dressed the queen's child in cheap linen garments and the maid's child in costly clothes befitting a royal prince. The queen was very happy and took care of the child she thought was her own.

The children grew up. The false prince, Aladdin, had been educated in the manner of an heir to the throne, and the real prince, Alexander, was living on a farm, receiving little in the way of education, completely unaware of his great origin.

The midwife was getting old and felt that she would soon die. She had kept her secret for many years, and it had become a mental strain on her. She felt that she had to tell it to someone, but to whom? So she decided to whisper it to the wind. The wind swiftly carried it to every corner of the land. Soon many people were whispering to one another that it was not Aladdin but Alexander, the son of the servant girl, who was the true prince.

Meanwhile, the king had died and Aladdin succeeded him. The truth about his lowly birth was now so widely known that it reached even the ears of the newly crowned king. He began persecuting the "father" of Alexander by disturbing his freshly sown field. The farmer quickly realized that Alexander was in great danger and that Aladdin would before long try to kill him. So he advised Alexander to flee to a neighboring country.

Alexander took this advice and left his home to escape the clutches of the cruel King Aladdin. He spent his days in idleness, and to "eat, drink and be merry" became his way of life. Several nights running he dreamed that he should leave his present abode and travel to a fair in a faraway country.

Alexander eventually decided to make his way to the fair. He was by then destitute. All his money was gone. To survive, he hired himself out to a farmer who had a large herd of cattle. He had to watch that no animal strayed from the herd. The farmer turned out to be a heartless and hard taskmaster. If Alexander's work was not to his satisfaction, he punished him with a severe beating.

One day, when Alexander was left in charge of the cattle, two animals strayed from the herd. He pursued them but could not catch them. He was afraid to return to his master without them. He decided to continue the search. By now he was in the middle of a forest, a long way from his herd. He was frightened by the roaring of the wild animals roaming the forest. He was afraid for his life. He climbed a high tree and spent the night on one of the branches.

In the morning, Alexander saw the two lost animals standing at the bottom of the tree. He climbed down, but before he reached them they had wandered off and had disappeared from sight. He kept up his search all day and once again found shelter for the night in the branches of a tall tree. There, he encountered another human being, Aladdin, who told him that he, too, could not find his way out of the forest. He had been searching for his lost horse. The two wanderers decided to stay together and to help each other.

When they heard weird laughter reverberating through the forest, they realized that they must be in the kingdom of evil spirits. They gazed down and saw the two missing animals and the horse standing below. By the time they reached the ground, the animals had once again disappeared. They continued searching for their missing animals and, in doing so, lost sight of each other.

During his search, Alexander found a bag of freshly baked loaves of bread. He was delighted with this treasure. He then encountered the "man of the forest," whose clothes were made of lizard skins. This was surely an evil spirit in disguise. Alexander followed him and in doing so found his companion, who was still looking for his horse. When Aladdin saw Alexander's sackful of bread, he asked for some, but Alexander was unwilling to part with any. Aladdin was so famished that he volunteered to become Alexander's slave for life.

The "man of the forest" now took them to a house that was located in midair. There they found shelter, food, and drink. Aladdin then revealed to Alexander that he really was a king, but when rumors casting doubt on his true identity reached him, he had been greatly disturbed and troubled. He had begun to harass the reputed true prince and forced him to flee his native country. He regretted his persecution of the true prince and had decided to forsake his kingdom in order to search out Alexander, the son of the servant girl, and to make amends for his behavior. Alexander listened to this confession in silence.

The "man of the forest" now looked after them and gave Alexander an instrument made of special wood. It had the magical power to produce beautiful melodies when it came in contact with birds and animals. He advised them to visit a country that was known at that particular time as "the foolish country with a wise king."

They eventually reached that country. One could enter its capital city only through one gate. They were told that the country had acquired its name because the former king had been a wise and learned man who ruled the country with compassion and understanding. When he was succeeded by his son, who was not very wise, the country's name changed to "the wise land with a foolish king." Its counselors were now very anxious to restore the image of their country to its former glory. The new king was quite willing to give way to anyone who could prove himself to be of the caliber to restore the country to its previous status.

Alexander was anxious to try, but he did not know how to go about it. Just then a man dressed in black on a black horse passed by them. Alexander touched the horse with his magic instrument, and it began playing a wonderful melody. The man was so impressed that he suggested that Alexander give him his magic instrument in exchange for being taught the powers of logical deduction, which would enable Alexander to solve any problem. Alexander agreed to this proposition and acquired the mastery of solving the most intricate problems.

Being thus equipped, Alexander now had no qualms about approaching the city fathers with the assurance that he could restore the country to its former glory. He was told that he would first have to pass two difficult tests. He would first of all have to prove his ability to enter and remain for some time in a haunted garden. Usually, anyone entering the garden would quickly be chased away by evil spirits. They would not give the intruder a moment's peace until he left. Alexander undertook to do this. He carefully observed the circumstances. He noticed that the garden was surrounded by a high wall but that the gate was wide open and that there were no guards there. To one side there was a statue of a man who wore a golden crown and was dressed in a mantle of ivory. Above the statue was a tablet on which was written that this man had reigned over the kingdom many years before, when the country had enjoyed total peace. When the spirits began to molest Alexander, he moved near the statue, and the spirits left him alone. From this, he deduced that the statue had power over the spirits, and he moved it to the middle of the garden. It provided him with complete protection. The spirits had lost their power to harm him.

When the city authorities saw that he had passed the first test, they made him undergo the second, a more demanding and rigorous test.

In a prominent place in the kingdom stood a large and elaborate throne, which was surrounded by many ornate carvings of animals and birds. Near the throne stood a bed and a table. A lamp rested on the table. Anyone sitting on the throne could see the entire country, from end to end. To get to the throne it was possible to choose one of several paths. One would lead to a lion, who would devour whomever he met, another to a fierce leopard, who would also attack any contestant.

Alexander, with his keen powers of observation, noticed that a rose was missing from the top of the throne and that it was lying on the floor at the foot of the throne. He observed that the rose was made of the same material as his musical instrument. He took up the rose and replaced it in its original position. He then rearranged the bed, the table, and the lamp. He sat down on the throne and was able to survey the whole kingdom. With the rose back in its place, harmony prevailed, and all the carved animals surrounding the throne burst forth in a delightful melody.

When the city fathers saw what Alexander had achieved, they were happy to crown him their king. Alexander then turned to his traveling companion, Aladdin, and told him, "I am the true king. You, Aladdin, are the son of my mother's serving maid."

100

The Prince Who Turned into a Rooster

Once upon a time there was a king and a queen who had an only son, whom they loved dearly. The king engaged the wisest teachers to instruct his son in laws and customs. He was taught several languages. The prince was also an athlete. Few could equal his riding and fencing. He played the violin and loved music. He was encouraged to travel and see the world. He was a very cultured and accomplished young man with whom it was a pleasure to converse and who was loved by all.

The king would consult the prince on matters of state. He knew he could rely on his sound common sense. He was happy to think that his son would one day be a worthy successor and that he would rule the kingdom after him with justice and with mercy.

The prince commanded his father's armies and won many victories. After one lengthy campaign, however, he returned home and complained of feeling unwell. He acted very irrationally. He was not violent, but he behaved as if he were a rooster. He stopped speaking. Instead he crowed, "Cock-a-doodle-doo." He refused to dress or sit at the table but lay on the floor and ate only corn.

The king summoned all the physicians in the land, but they could not help. Healers were brought in from other countries, but they, too, could find no cure. Even soothsayers and magicians were invited. They cast spells, prescribed amulets, and uttered incantations, but they were of no use.

The royal parents were desperate. The prince had to be kept in a heavily guarded room, and his parents had almost given up hope of seeing their son take his rightful place.

One day an old man approached the king and said, "I may be able to cure your son."

"What are your remedies, your medicines?" asked the king.

"I have none with me," replied the old man. "But let me stay with your son for seven days, and I will cure him!"

When the old man was let into the room, he found the prince almost naked, crawling on the floor. The old man then took off his own clothes. "Who are you?" whispered the prince. "Why are you lying on the floor?"

"I, too, am a rooster," the old man assured him. "I have come to join you. Roosters should keep together."

"I am so glad you have come," said the prince. "I felt rather lonely, shut in one room all by myself. I am delighted to have a companion now."

The following day, having gained the prince's confidence, the old man stood up and started to walk about like a human being. The prince was pleased to follow his companion's example.

One day later, the old man dressed himself and said, "There is no harm in a rooster dressing in the style of human beings!" The prince followed suit.

On the day after that, the old man sat down at the table and ate his food from a plate, using a knife and fork. "Even a rooster can eat normally," he justified his action to the prince.

The next day, the old man lay down on a bed. "Even though I am a rooster, there is no reason I should be uncomfortable and sleep on the floor." He then started discussing with the prince matters of state and the economic and social problems facing the country. "Roosters, too, can think and talk."

On the seventh day the old man said to the prince, "You know that a rooster's life is always in danger. He is constantly exposed to the hunter, who kills him without mercy. He is so defenseless. You should, like me, pretend that you are a human being, and then you will come to no harm."

The old man then took his leave of the prince and his family. The prince was now completely cured and was able to resume his princely role. In due course, he succeeded his father and ruled the kingdom both fairly and wisely. In his heart of hearts, however, he still thought himself a rooster pretending to be a human being.

Glossary

Afikoman   The piece of *matzah* eaten at the conclusion of the meal on the first two nights of Passover.

Ahiyah of Shiloh   The prophet who lived at the time of Solomon and Jeroboam and was, according to hasidic tradition, the teacher of Rabbi Israel Baal Shem Tov.

Alef Bet   The first two letters of the Hebrew alphabet.

Baal Shem   Literally, "the Master of God's Name." A name given to a man who works wonders through his piety and the employment of the "Divine Name" in accordance with the doctrines of the *Kabbalah*.

Bar Mitzvah   Literally, "the son of the commandment." Celebration of the occasion at which, at thirteen years of age, a boy becomes personally responsible for observing the commandments of the Torah.

Beadle   (Hebrew, *Shammash*) Literally, "one who serves." The synagogue beadle fulfilled a number of extrasynagogal functions, such as calling worshipers to prayer and being an usher of the *Bet Din*.

Besht   This name is given to the Baal Shem Tov and is formed from his initials.

Bet Hamidrash   House of Study.

Book of Life   (Hebrew, *Sefer HaHayyim*) The book frequently spoken of in the Bible (Exodus 32:32; Isaiah 4:3; Psalms 69:29) in which God inscribes the names of the pious who are to be granted life.

Bridal Canopy (Hebrew, *huppah*) A canopy spread over four posts under which the wedding ceremony is performed.

Covenant of Abraham Another name for the ceremony of circumcision taken from Genesis 17:10–12, in which God says to Abraham, "This is My covenant, which you shall keep between Me and you."

Dalet The fourth letter of the Hebrew alphabet.

Day of Atonement See Yom Kippur.

Elijah The prophet who, in Jewish tradition, is the bringer of good tidings and the precursor of the Messiah. His activities are thought of as not confined to his time on earth but as continuing ever since.

Elul The sixth month of the Hebrew calendar corresponding approximately to September.

Etrog A citron. A member of the lemon family and one of the four symbolic plants ("the fruit of a goodly tree" [Leviticus 23:40]) used during the Festival of Tabernacles.

Fast Days There are five public fast days in addition to the Day of Atonement in the Jewish calendar. They all commemorate historical events: four, the destruction of the Temple; one, the saving of the Jews by Queen Esther.

Four Cups Four cups of wine are drunk at the Passover *seder*. According to some authorities, the four cups correspond to the four references to redemption in the Book of Exodus 6:6–7 to describe God's deliverance of Israel from Egypt.

Galut The dispersion of Israel.

Gan Eden Paradise. So named after the first abode of Adam. A place of comfort and pleasure.

Gehinom Hell. So named after a valley near Jerusalem where fires constantly burned on altars on which sacrifices were being offered to idols.

Gimmel The third letter of the Hebrew alphabet.

Golem An image endowed with life as a result of wonder-working words; a robot. The most famous *Golem* was created by Judah Löw of Prague (c. 1525–1609), known as the Hohe Rabbi Löw.

Grace after Meals The practice of reciting grace after a meal is based on the biblical injunction, "And you shall eat and be satisfied, and bless the Lord your God for the good land which He has given you" (Deuteronomy 8:10). It consists of four benedictions.

Haggadah Literally, "narration." The nonlegal portion of the Talmud and rabbinic literature; also the book that tells the story of the Exodus from Egypt, which is recited at the Passover *seder*.

Hallah A braided white loaf of bread, baked especially for the Sabbath.

Haman Chief minister of King Ahasuerus, who planned the extermination of the Jews throughout the Persian Empire.

Haroset A mixture of chopped apple, nuts, and cinnamon eaten during the Passover *seder*. It symbolizes the mortar used for the making of bricks by the Jewish slaves in Egypt.

Hasid (Plural, *hasidim*) Literally, "pious." A follower of the pietist movement, Hasidism.

Havdalah Literally, "distinction." The blessing, usually made over wine, by which the Sabbath or any other holy day is ushered out.

Heder Literally, "room." A private Hebrew school, so called because it met at the teacher's house.

Kabbalah Literally, "tradition." The system of Jewish mystical philosophy.

Kavanah (Plural, *kavanot*) Literally, "direction, intention." The devotion to God one feels while performing a religious act.

Kiddush Literally, "sanctification." The ceremony ushering in the Sabbath or a festival.

Kol Nidre Literally, "all vows." The opening words of the Aramaic prayer recited in the synagogue preceding the evening service on the eve of the Day of Atonement.

Maggid   (Plural, *maggidim*) Literally, "to tell" or "to narrate." A popular preacher.

Mahzor   A prayer book for solemn days and festivals.

Marriage Contract   (Hebrew, *ketubah*) Literally, "a written document." It lists the bridegroom's obligations to his bride.

Matzah   Unleavened bread eaten during the week of Passover in recollection of the Exodus from Egypt: "Seven days you shall eat unleavened bread" (Leviticus 23:6).

Mazal   Literally, "the planets or constellations in the skies at one's birth" and by extension "luck." The phrase *Mazal Tov* is a congratulatory greeting used especially on happy occasions.

Messiah   Literally, "the anointed." The Messiah was to be a divinely appointed person who would bring an end to the exile of Israel.

Midrash   (Plural, *midrashim*) Literally, "exposition." Books of the talmudic and post-talmudic times devoted to the explanation of the Scriptures.

Minyan   A quorum of ten Jewish men over the age of thirteen required for the conduct of a religious service.

Mishnah   Literally, "to repeat." The *Mishnah* consists of the halachic (traditional) teachings of the rabbis who lived between 30 B.C.E. and 219 C.E. It is divided into six orders, each consisting of a number of treatises.

Mitzvah   Literally, "commandment." A religious act, a good deed.

Ne'ilah   Literally, "closing." The last of the five services on the Day of Atonement.

Passover   The festival commemorating the liberation of the Jews from bondage in Egypt. It lasts eight days, beginning on the fifteenth of *Nisan* (March or April).

Rebbe   Rabbi, frequently applied to hasidic rabbis.

Rejoicing of the Law   (Hebrew, *Simhat Torah*) This celebration marks the completion of the reading of the Pentateuch. In the Diaspora, it takes place on the twenty-third of *Tishri*, the day after Shemini Atzeret. It is post-talmudic in origin.

Rosh Hashanah   Literally, "head of the year." The Jewish New Year, observed on the first and second day of *Tishri* (September or October).

Sandek   The one who holds the baby during circumcision.

Satan   Satan's functions are clearly described. He descends to earth and leads men astray. Then he ascends and induces God's wrath by reporting man's sins. Hasidic rabbis avoided the name of Satan by using the terms "accuser" or "opponent."

Seder   Literally, "order." The order of service held in the home on the first and second nights of Passover when the *Haggadah* is recited.

Shavuot   Literally, "weeks." The festival celebrated on the sixth and seventh days of *Sivan*. It is the festival of the wheat harvest, the day of the firstfruits, and the season of the giving of the Torah. It takes place seven weeks after Passover.

Shofar   The horn of a ram, which is blown on Rosh Hashanah and daily during the month of *Elul* and at the close of the Day of Atonement.

Siddur   The authorized daily prayer book of the Jews.

Sukkot   Literally, "booths." The Feast of Tabernacles, which begins on the fifteenth of *Tishri*. Originally a harvest festival (the Festival of the Ingathering), it has come to commemorate the divine protection given to the Israelites during their wanderings through the wilderness. The *sukkah* (plural, *sukkot*) is the festive booth.

Tallit   A rectangular fringed prayer shawl.

Tallit Katan   Literally, "a small *tallit*." Worn throughout the day, usually under the shirt, by men. It has fringes at its four corners.

Tefillin   Phylacteries—two small black boxes containing passages from the Scriptures, which are affixed to the forehead and left forearm during the recital of the weekday morning prayers in accordance with Deuteronomy 6:8.

Ten Days of Penitence   The period between Rosh Hashanah and Yom Kippur.

Third Meal   (Hebrew, *seudat shelishit*) The third meal on the Sabbath, eaten after the afternoon service. It became a major feature of hasidic life.

Tishri   The seventh month of the Jewish calendar.

Torah   Literally, "teaching, doctrine, or law." Both the Pentateuch (the Five Books of Moses) and the whole body of Jewish law and teaching as embodied in rabbinic literature.

Tzaddik   Literally, "a righteous man." A religious leader of the *hasidim*.

Wailing Wall   (Hebrew, *Kotel Hamaravi*) The Western Wall of the Temple in Jerusalem, the principal Jewish place of pilgrimage.

Yeshivah   Higher Jewish Teaching Academy.

Yom Kippur   Day of Atonement, the climax of the Ten Days of Penitence. It takes place on the tenth of *Tishri*. On that day, one is prohibited from eating, drinking, bathing, and wearing shoes.

Zemirot   Hymns that are sung on Friday evening and on the Sabbath during meals.

Zohar   Literally, "splendor." A mystical commentary on the Pentateuch, attributed to Rabbi Simon bar Yohai, a Palestinian *tanna* of the second century. The book was discovered by Moses de Leon at the end of the thirteenth century.

About the Author

Rabbi Tzvi Rabinowicz, a descendant of famous hasidic and rabbinic families in Poland, was the regional rabbi of Cricklewood, Willesden, and Brondesbury synagogues in London. A noted historian and writer, Dr. Rabinowicz obtained his rabbinical diploma from Jews' College of London and received his Ph.D. in 1948 from the University of London. He is the author of many books, including *A Guide to Life: Jewish Laws and Customs of Mourning, Treasures of Judaica, Hasidism and the State of Israel,* and *Hasidism: The Movement and Its Masters.*